Waiting For Our Rainbow

Victoria Cornwall

Choc Lit

Where heroes are like chocolate – irrestible!

Published 2023 by Choc Lit Limited
Penrose House, Crawley Drive, Camberley, Surrey GU15 2AB, UK

www.choc-lit.com

EPUB: 978-1-78189-520-7
PRINT: 978-1-78189-526-9

PRINTED AND BOUND BY AMAZON

Freedom – so easily taken for granted. Only when it is threatened or taken away is its true worth valued and cherished, hitherto igniting a hidden strength and resilience in the humblest of beings in order to regain it.

I would like to dedicate this novel to all the brave men and women who endured WW2, their resilience and bravery was for their today and our tomorrow.

Acknowledgements

Although *Waiting For Our Rainbow* is a work of fiction, it was important to me to use my best efforts to depict the historical backdrop to the story accurately and sensitively. I would like to thank the following people, who have helped me with my research. Their knowledge is extensive. Any historical inaccuracies will be mine.

I would also like to state that the topic of racial segregation in the army is not easy to hear, but much of what is included was experienced or witnessed at some point during that era and does not reflect my own beliefs or those who have helped me in my research.

Joseph Balkoski
Historian
29th Infantry Division, U.S. Army.

Alexander A. Falbo-Wild
Historian
Maryland National Guard History Office

Richard T. Bass
Author Historian

BBC WW2 People's War
An archive of World War 2 memories

Instructions for American Servicemen in Britain 1942
War Department, Washington D.C.

and

the viewing of numerous online interviews where African American veteran soldiers recalled their experiences of being in the army during WW2

I would also like to acknowledge the many friends, relatives, readers and writers who have supported me in my writing journey by offering encouraging words or advice.

Finally, but by no means least, I would like to acknowledge and thank my publisher, Choc Lit Publishing, and their Tasting Panel readers, especially: Barbara Wickham, Honor Gilbert, Linda Middleton, Sara Griffin, Lisa Vasil, Brigette Hughes, Shona Nicolson, Janet Avery, Liana Vera Saez, Hilary Brown, Dimitra Evangelou, Joanne Elliott, Jo Osborne, Jenny Kinsman and Joanna Emmerson, who believed in this novel and felt it worthy of reaching a wider audience. I will be eternally grateful to you for your generosity of time and support.

Between 1942 and 1944, one and a half million American soldiers arrived in Britain in preparation for the largest amphibious assault in military history, Operation Neptune.
Later known as D-Day, it would mark the beginning of the liberation of Western Europe from Nazi occupation.

The Allied forces taking part in Operation Neptune consisted primarily of American, British and Canadian Armed Forces, however also included were sailors, soldiers and airmen from Australia, Belgium, Czechoslovakia, France, Greece, the Netherlands, New Zealand, Norway, Poland and others. In addition, the skills of meteorologists, scientists, inventors and the French Resistance were used during its planning and implementation.

This novel was inspired by the American soldiers billeted to Cornwall. Their time on British soil left a lasting impression upon their hosts and would be fondly remembered as The Friendly Invasion.

Chapter One

11 December, 1941

There are instances in one's life when momentous news, with all its far-reaching possibilities, is received in the most ordinary setting. Yet the mundanity of the surroundings does not lessen its impact or its power to change one's life forever. Anne had learnt this valuable lesson as a child, when her mother had told her that her father had died. The setting had been her primary school's rusty old gate – a place she'd barely noticed before but was now indelibly linked to her father's death. Today it was happening again.

Standing in the hardware store, with its dimly lit cluttered shelves, the owner eagerly shared what he had heard. He was smiling. His customers were smiling, despite the news being terrible for some. What else could you call it when it would inevitably result in yet more death and aching grief? But it was good news. Very good news. Anne found herself smiling too. She had to go home and find out if it was true.

Anne retrieved her bike from outside the shop and looked around. Dusk had fallen, effortlessly casting another war-weary day into the past. She could also smell an approaching shower in the air but, this time, didn't care. She turned on her bike's shielded light and headed for home. It wasn't long before she was peddling furiously, head bowed, through the pelting rain. She saw her brother, Billy, at the crossroads and knew from his hope-filled expression, that he had heard the news too. Despite being soaked by the rain, he grinned widely at her and pushed off on his bike to take the lead, riding carelessly through the muddy puddles as if it was a summer's day. Anne followed, forging a path through the silver darts of rain slicing through the beam of her bicycle's flashlight. The light bounced with each rut in the road to offer glimpses of her brother ahead. Anne could just make out through the rain a trail of mud forming on the back of his coat. Under normal circumstances she would feel duty-bound to warn her younger brother about the mess his back wheel was making … but not today.

Billy hunched over his handlebars, his hips rising and falling alternately as he pressed down on each peddle. Finally, he reached the brow of the hill and stopped to wait. He watched her with an excited grin on his face as she pushed her bike the last few yards. The rain ceased as Anne caught up with him.

'My legs are no match for your pumping legs,' complained Anne, as she reached him.

'Girls are just weak,' scoffed Billy as he impatiently waited for her to remount. Before she could retaliate, he straightened his legs and began his descent down the other side of the hill towards home. Anne glanced around her to ensure no one was watching. It was one thing for an eleven-year-old boy to ride recklessly, but quite another to be doing so as a young lady of twenty. Reassured, Anne stuck her heels out and followed her brother, before coming to a shuddering halt outside their house on the banks of Carrick Roads.

They pushed their bikes into the shed.

'This will change everything!' said Billy as he balanced his bike against the wall.

Anne slotted hers beside his. 'I wonder if Father's heard.' She tried to brush the wet mud off Billy's back as they headed towards the house, knowing it was a hopeless task.

He shrugged her off with a smile. 'Mother won't care about a bit of mud. Not tonight.'

The blacked-out windows, which helped make their little stone cottage disappear at night and protect it against any attack from the sky, gave the impression that no one was home. They opened the door and bustled inside, bursting with the gossip they'd heard. Her stepfather's presence, home early for tea, confirmed what they already knew.

'Is it true?' asked Anne as she slipped off her hat and coat and hung it on a hook.

Her stepfather nodded. 'Yes. America's declared war on Germany and Italy too.'

'They had little choice,' said her mother taking in the state of Billy's coat. She lifted his sodden cap from his head and put it by the fire to dry. 'Churchill will be falling on his knees in thanks tonight. I don't understand the man.'

'Who? Churchill?' asked Billy, reaching for a slice of cake.

His mother lightly slapped his hand. 'Cut it in half. That small cake must last us all week.' She saw the state of his hands. 'Wash your hands first.'

'She means Hitler for declaring war on America,' said Anne, as she helped lay the table. 'America had declared war on Japan not Germany.'

'Hitler must be up to something,' said Billy, briefly dipping his hands under the running tap.

Anne handed him the bar of soap he'd omitted to use. 'Or he has made the biggest mistake of his life. America is the richest, biggest country in the world *and* they are our friends.'

'I'm not going to waste my energy trying to understand the tyrant,' said her stepfather as he settled himself in the wooden chair at the head of the table. America has now been dragged into this war and that is the good news we needed. It's about time too.'

Anne saw a ghost of a smile play on her stepfather's lips as he surveyed the table's neatly laid cutlery and crockery. It was the first time she'd seen him smile since war had been declared. It told her more than they'd dared voice, that it might just be possible that they could win the war after all.

America had not been the only ones stunned by Japan's bombing of Pearl Harbour only four days ago. The attack shocked the world and, thought Anne, probably Germany too. Her stepfather's reaction to the bombing had been strategic, even cautious, born from his experience of the last war.

'If America retaliates against Japan, it might mean a separate war being fought,' he'd warned them. 'That would be a disaster. Great Britain needs America to help in the main conflict, not fight a separate one.' Everyone held their breath as Japan declared war on America and America declared war on Japan. It was the news that nobody wanted.

Now Hitler had stepped in and declared war on America, effectively dragging them into the main conflict.

For more than a year, Britain had been forced into the position of defending rather than attacking. The enemy had driven them out of Europe, forcing a large-scale evacuation from the pale sandy beaches of Dunkirk. Their brave soldiers were now fighting on another front in North Africa. The world was a mess and there seemed no end … but now America was involved there was at least hope.

As her parents discussed the news further and Billy escaped to his bedroom, Anne stepped outside into the fading light. She breathed in deeply, savouring the chill wind sweeping up from the English Channel. The view of the estuary below their house was still visible despite it being dusk on a cloudy day. Carrick Roads was an odd name for the expanse of water in front of her. The estuary was deep and wide, with lapping waters that harboured fish and invited birds to feed. It stretched from Truro to Falmouth and formed a powerful road of water through a steep-banked valley that required two ferries to cross. Channels and creeks lined the mass of water, with small, picturesque villages nestled along its route. Far to her right, hidden by the neighbouring hill, lay the deep natural harbour and bustling town of Falmouth. Large barrage balloons, tethered to the ground by thick cables, floated silently above it under the heavy blanket of dark cloud. Although they marked the port's location, they effectively protected it from an attack from the sky. Their bulbous, giant dark shapes were a constant visual reminder of the war, amongst the natural beauty that surrounded her.

It had been a gruelling two years since war was declared. At the time she'd just turned eighteen, the age when she was finally permitted by her parents to go to dances and to court a young man. She'd felt her adult life was about to begin. She had a job as a junior secretary to a reputable firm of solicitors, Sullivan and Sullivan. Romance, excitement and independence lay before her waiting for her to embrace them. However, unlike Miss Truscott, the senior secretary in the office, she had no plans to remain a spinster all her life and have no one to love but her cats. She hoped, as all her friends did, that eventually she would marry, have a house of her own and magazine-perfect children to love; Hitler, however, had other ideas.

The day war was declared was still clearly etched in Anne's memory. She should have seen it coming. Her stepfather had predicted war. He'd felt the rising tension between the countries before his family had, as the Great War had left its mark on him, leaving him with the gift of experience that the younger generation didn't possess or want to hear. However, Chamberlain's grave vocal tones, as they sat around the wireless, forced Anne to face up to what, until then, she had denied. 'This country is at war with Germany,' Chamberlain had said.

The seven words had brought tears to her mother's eyes and silently gave more gravity to the situation than anything else had done. Anne had watched her mother reach for her hat and coat. 'Why won't they ever learn!' she'd muttered angrily.

'Where are you going?' her husband had asked her.

'To the phone box. I want to speak to my sister to see if she's heard the news.'

Anne had remained where she sat, no longer listening to the newsreader who had followed the prime minister's announcement. She'd stared at her needle, her eyes smarting, the sock she'd been darning forgotten on her lap as she tried to absorb the news. *We are at war.*

The memory still sent shivers chasing along her spine. She realised at the time that her life was about to change. There would be no more excitement and fun, no fanciful discussions with her mother as they peeled potatoes, on what her future held in store. Her life would be on hold until the war ended. Looking back, Anne knew her thoughts had been selfish, but at the time she was young and naïve of what war truly meant. Instead the tears that eventually fell were self-pitying, for in that moment she'd felt she had lost her future. Whatever the cause, whether right or wrong, her sadness had been as real and despairing as her mother's had been.

Anne never cried for herself again. She soon realised, as the young local men were conscripted to fight, that she'd been indulgent and selfish. She now felt ashamed by her behaviour, particularly when the evacuees had arrived.

The first influx of children from the larger cities arrived suddenly, labelled like parcels and carrying one suitcase, with a gas mask slung across their body. They had stood in the town hall of the nearby village, wide-eyed and waiting to be collected by someone they didn't know. How scared they'd looked as they tried to be brave. Anne had volunteered to help them settle in. It wasn't easy. They had strange accents and ways which separated them from the local children. Fights and teasing inevitably broke out, but they gradually settled in. They had come together as everyone should in time of war. Now, a year and a half later, their pale cheeks were tanned from the warm summer sun and they'd made new friends, discovering a love for the countryside which would probably last the rest of their lives.

When the bombing raids of the main cities began in earnest, Anne was determined to do more to help with the war effort. She tried many things, like collecting metal or food scraps for the local pigs, but only felt she contributed to something tangible when she was called up by the government on reaching the age of twenty. Typing legal letters was replaced with repairing spitfire wings in a warehouse nearby, which was infinitely more satisfying. The hours were long, but the atmosphere inside was jovial and determined. The workers were made up of mainly women and overseen by Mr Boyle, who had a background in mechanics. The workforce was hardworking and efficient, repairing the battle-scarred wings as they listened to Vera Lyn sing heartfelt songs and read loving messages intended for the troops fighting abroad in Northern Africa.

The war had affected every part of their life in some way. Soon luxuries became a distant memory and the more mundane things became luxuries in themselves, but at least everyone was in it together and, for Anne, that brought a comfort of its own.

War had even changed her stepfather. Although he was a bank manager and very staid in his ways, he had quickly developed new skills to supplement their rationing and make use of their rural existence. He had taken up rabbit trapping at the weekends and used every spare part of their garden to grow vegetables. He'd joined the Home Guard and even gave his blessing to Billy and his friends to borrow their elderly neighbour's rowing boat to catch fish in Carrick Roads river. The fish caught provided a nourishing meal for the boys' families and always earned them favour in their mothers' eyes.

Yet today's announcement could mean that rationing would end soon and that normal life would return. America had joined the war. After all the setbacks, disruption and worry there was a very real chance that Britain could win. Anne inhaled the winter evening air deeply, savouring the fresh bite as it invaded her lungs. She had hope at last and, just as her stepfather had said, it was about time too.

Chapter Two

New York, 5 October, 1942

Joe looked at the British blue-grey ocean liner waiting for them at the end of the pier. It already appeared to have reached capacity, its deck tightly packed with American troops carrying their equipment and wearing the obligatory lifebelts they were ordered to wear when on board and above deck.

'Jeez. I hope the johns work,' said Frank as they edged forward in the queue to board.

Joe half-smiled at his friend's concern. When the news came that they were leaving Camp Kilmer, in New Jersey, for England, he knew that the first thing Frank would check out was the toilet facilities. He hadn't expected him to start before the journey had even begun.

'That's the least of our worries,' said Joe. 'I'm more concerned about us not sinking. It's looking pretty crowded.'

The 29th Infantry Division had been told they were going to take part in the upcoming invasion of Europe. England, no larger than the five states that made up the regiment, would be their stepping stone. Yet, despite its size, the country had successfully defeated Hitler's plan to invade the small island. They had turned the David and Goliath parable into reality in the skies, as they fought a bloody battle against Germany's Luftwaffe. Their resilience against the odds had earned America's respect. Joe, like many of the American people, had no stomach for war, but found their self in the middle of one. Now Joe was heading for a country he knew little about, while his pal talked of water closets.

'Want some?' asked Frank, offering him a stick of gum.

Joe shook his head. 'You better hide it. You know they've banned gum on board.' Rumour had it that the previous troops had made a mess with the sticky treat and the ship's captain had lost his rag and banned it. 'Have you been abroad before?'

Frank shook his head.

'Nor me,' replied Joe. He checked the colour of the card in his hand which told him which part of the ship he was to remain in. He wouldn't forget. Red, the same as Frank's – the colour of tomatoes; the colour of blood. He looked up. They'd almost reached the deck of the ship. His arm still ached from the vaccination received during his medical screening, while the evening breeze chilled his neck; a reminder of his most recent military haircut. The barber had been quick, up and over in a blink of an eye, as time was limited when you had several thousand men to do.

As the queue of troops moved forward in the dimming light, tall wieldy cranes loaded neighbouring ships with Jeeps, trucks and tanks. The anticipation in the air was almost palpable. Yes, this was historic. Hitler wouldn't know what hit him, thought Joe, as he stepped onto the ship.

Joe and Frank made their way below deck. The luxury ocean liner had been converted to carry more than double its original passenger capacity. Luxury furniture, paintings, tapestries, carpets, china, crystal and silver – everything and anything not needed for war – had been hastily removed in the quest for more room. What could not be taken, Joe noted, such as the exquisitely carved woodwork, was protected by swathes of leather. Joe found a vacant bed. It was one of hundreds; no more than canvas hammocks held secure by sturdy frames and tightly stacked against the walls of the ship. He claimed it with his rucksack as Frank grabbed the one above. A faint vibration moved beneath their boots, a silent but robust signal that the ship was already leaving.

'I'm going back on deck. Are you coming?' asked Joe, knowing he would go anyway, whether Frank wanted to or not. He had a hankering to say goodbye to America although he had no doubt he'd be returning one day. Frank nodded, hid his pack of gum under his pillow and followed in Joe's wake as they made their way through the crowded quarters to the deck above.

The soldiers around them were already settling into their various groups. Some were attempting to make their sleeping area feel more homely by sticking a photo of their sweetheart on the wall with gum, setting up card games and jostling for space. It was a relief when they finally reached the fresh air of the upper deck, despite the crowded conditions around them. Frank spotted a space to stand and began to nudge his way through the troops. Joe followed. They stood side by side, staring at the busy port gracefully receding into the distance.

'Goodbye America,' said Joe half out loud, half to himself.

'Are your folks in the crowd?' asked Frank.

Joe shook his head. He thought of his father. 'No. They're in Baltimore. I told them it was too far to travel just to wave goodbye.' It wasn't quite the truth but it would do for now. 'Yours?'

'Nah. I'm the oldest of five. Their hands are too full to chase after me. We said our goodbyes weeks ago.'

'So, it's just you and me now, pal.' Joe smiled at Frank. The irony of his comment, as they jostled shoulder to shoulder for room, was not lost on Frank.

'You, me and the rest. I swear to God, if anyone snores tonight, I'll deck them,' said Frank. He jerked his head towards a soldier to the side of them. 'Keep your cigarettes under your pillow tonight. I'm pretty sure Bolton nicked my last pack.'

Joe glanced over to the hard-faced soldier who was always surrounded by buddies, despite being loathed by most. Cowards, the lot of them, aligning themselves to someone who was the adult version of a schoolyard bully, to avoid being picked on themselves. He offered Frank a cigarette.

'That's rich coming from you,' he said as they shared a light.

'I told you, I just borrowed them!'

Joe smiled as he inhaled deeply. Frank always "borrowed" his cigarettes.

The bulk of New York City had shrunk in the distance, its scattered lights fading one by one in the grainy darkness. Silence settled among the troops on deck. There was no turning back now. It was as if the realisation that they'd left their loved ones behind had suddenly hit home and their future was no longer certain. A foreign country was waiting for them at the end of their journey and a raging war was waiting for them beyond that.

Joe knew that many of the new recruits, including himself, had never shot a gun in combat before. As with most divisions, the 29th was a melting pot of experience. Some had been together since Fort Meade, successfully absorbing an influx of draftees in the spring of the previous year. Frank was one of the arrivals, brought about by America's increasing concern at what was happening in Europe and the implementation of the first peace-time draft in the United States. Joe had joined a little later, one of a steady stream of draftees brought in to replace those who either left for the Army Air Force, couldn't handle the rigorous physical training or were simply considered too old for a combat zone. Joe had been accepted straight away, so they must have considered him fit, young and healthy enough to die. A contradiction, but only if you thought there was a risk in losing, and looking around him today, Joe felt sure there wasn't one soldier on deck, with their life jackets firmly around their necks, who had even considered that outcome.

Someone in the crowd moved, deciding to go to the lower deck. Gradually the rest of the troops followed suit. Frank left too, but Joe remained. He needed to be alone, or as alone as you could be on a ship carrying over a thousand men. Joe flicked the ash off his cigarette and looked up at the starlit sky.

He thought of his father. He was probably still working. He would have no idea that his son was on a ship heading for Europe right now. Would he even care? Joe knew that on paper he had little to be dissatisfied with. He'd been brought up in a wealthy family, with a home in the rich suburbs of Baltimore and a thriving family business to step into when he'd proved his self-worth. He was the next generation of the American dream. He was fortunate and should be grateful; it was all there on the plate just for the taking. All he had to do was grab it. He had his father to thank for that.

Joe watched the tip of his cigarette as he took another drag. It burned fierce and bright in the dark, until it suddenly faded away when there was no more oxygen to feed it. It reminded him of his desire to please his father, fierce, intense until it had suddenly died.

His father had worked his way through senior high and college, graduating from law school with top grades. He immediately secured employment in one of the most prestigious law firms in Baltimore and worked his way up through the firm one step at a time. The depression of the thirties had crippled many, but not his father. His ruthless personality and intelligence helped him take advantage of all that America had to offer. When many were seeking employment, he had become senior partner in the firm where his career had begun. His word was now law. No one matched the bar he set.

Joe had watched from the sidelines as his father's work consumed his every waking moment. Looking back, Joe suspected that suited his father, for if he looked outside the bubble he'd created, he would find everyone failing to match-up to his expectations. The life suited him, but it was to the detriment of his family. Joe had initially had his mother's undivided attention, but somehow, even from his earliest memories, Joe felt he had no one. He felt left out of the loop, unsure what he needed yet craving it somehow.

As an adult he could now see that all he wanted was a relationship with his father, in a way still did, but despite his father's extraordinary abilities and successes, he seemed to lack the fundamental skill of forming a relationship with a boy that wanted nothing more than to earn his affection, his pride … or just to be seen. All Joe wanted was his company, for him to watch him play baseball, someone to talk sport with, even go fishing. Everything he tried to do to please his father seemed to always fall short.

Thank God for his older brother, Michael. Michael had stepped in to take on the role, soften those sharp edges that were so painful at the time. However, he was not his father and had his own life to live. Eventually, he did leave. It was a decision that they would all, including Michael, come to regret.

His father's lack of acknowledgement of his efforts and his absence of praise, hurt every time Joe tried, and failed, to gain it. Then, one day, he suddenly realised he no longer wanted to keep trying and had packed his things and left. He wanted nothing from his father's world. The man had stabbed his heart with the cold steel of indifference once too often.

Now, standing on the deck of a foreign ship, with its belly full of strangers, he had never felt more part of something than he did in that moment. Whatever happened to him in the future he knew he was making his country proud; he had seen that message in the eyes of the strangers and the reporters on the quay who had come to wave them goodbye or grab a quote from "one of the brave soldiers". They didn't know it but they'd given him more in those few brief hours than his own father had done in his entire life.

A flurry of great black-backed gulls continued to rise and dip above the ship's white-water trail, their ravenous hunger compelling them to hunt long after their normal time to roost. They reminded him of the Chimney Swift he'd rescued in the fall of 1930. He had found it on the sidewalk of the city centre, huddled near an overflowing trash can only feet away from fast-walking feet. It was an odd place to find such a feeble creature considering there was no suitable habitat nearby. More fluff than feathers, it had little chance of survival, but its plight spoke to him in a way he couldn't understand back then. He'd taken it home and warmed and fed it in secret, day and night, every hour, lavishing attention upon it to ensure it survived. And the little bird had grown strong, just like he wanted it to. And it had flown away, free, just like he wanted to do. And it had taught him that if someone cared about something enough, anything was possible.

He took a final drag on his cigarette before flicking it into the churning, dark water of the sea far below. He turned to face into the wind and in the direction the ship was heading. His life was about to change in a way he couldn't yet quite imagine. The thought both excited and terrified him. America had helped to win the last war and they could do it again. There were no finer military forces than America's. They would show Hitler who was boss. They were about to make history, and he was going to play his part.

Joe soon found out that making history could be far from glamorous. The next few days were spent at sea, crammed with the smelly bodies of other men. The soldiers passed their time talking, playing cards and thinking of home. Minor disagreements, which took on a greater significance in the crowded quarters, ignited quickly, but were extinguished just as fast. To cater for the vast numbers, each meal had three sittings. The large dining room, which in the past had only served moderately rich, adventurous travellers, was now, for the most part of the journey, constantly full of hungry men glad of the break from the monotony of their day.

After one such meal, Joe returned to his hammock and lay down, cradling his head on the crook of his arm to watch Frank climb up onto the hammock above. The shape of Frank's body could be clearly seen and Joe prodded his back with his booted foot.

'Hey! Cut that out!' Frank called out.

Joe laughed. 'What? I didn't do anything.' It was childish banter, but it helped bond the men when there was no sport to play or women to impress.

Frank's head hung down over the side to look at him. His pencil fell out of his pocket as he did so and Joe leaned over and caught it before it fell to the floor. He offered it back to him, still smiling.

'It sure as hell looks like it was you,' said Frank, reluctantly taking the pencil and muttering his thanks. He disappeared, rummaged around for something above Joe's head and reappeared. 'Here, your turn to read this,' he said throwing a pamphlet at his head. Joe managed to catch it before its corner blinded him. He turned it over to look at it. It was the pamphlet they'd been given by the War Department, as they'd boarded the ship.

'"*Instructions for American Servicemen in Britain*",' he read aloud. He'd already read his own copy; it was concise, informal but detailed advice, printed and distributed to help alleviate the cultural changes they'd face. Joe wondered if it was about helping them settle or avoiding upsetting their hosts. He flicked through the pages again. The booklet indicated that the British "*were reserved, but resilient*" and explored their different customs, manners and language. He found himself reading it all over again until his concentration was disturbed by Frank's mid-Atlantic drawl.

'Teach you anything you didn't already know?'

'It's taught me that we're going to get into a whole lot of trouble,' replied Joe. 'Especially you.'

Frank's soft laughter floated down to him. 'Nothing new there then.'

Five days after leaving New York, they were given orders to collect their belongings and equipment and prepare to disembark. The troops, both energised and anxious to leave the confines of the ship, waited impatiently for their turn to be called up onto deck. As they emerged into the biting air, they realised their ship wasn't the only one stationed in the natural harbour they'd sailed into. Troop ships, ships of war and cargo ships from varying nationalities were either arriving, departing or anchored in the water, each with its own purpose and intended path. The port's activities provided cheap entertainment as the troops queued up and moved forward a step at a time.

The well-organised disembarkation took time and appeared a little chaotic to the untrained eye, but eventually Joe found himself stepping onto dry land. He turned to say a mental farewell to the camouflaged ocean liner and was surprised to see how many men remained on board waiting for their turn to leave. Seeing so many troops from different backgrounds, fighting for the same cause was not lost on Joe and brought about the seriousness of this war like nothing had before. It didn't matter where you came from or who you were, they were all in it together.

Joe was nudged from behind to move forward forcing him to drag his eyes away. By now the dockyard was bustling with troops and military vehicles, while local dock workers efficiently directed them the right way. Joe noticed an old, weathered dock worker gathering rope in his thick callused hands. He reminded him of his grandfather. He must have felt Joe watching as he straightened his bent back to watch him approach. Buoyed up by the idea that everyone was fighting for a common goal and eager to put into practice the advice he'd been given in the pamphlet, Joe called out to him.

'Hi there! It's good to be in England. Your country looks a beautiful place.'

The old man braced his shoulders. 'This is Scotland, ye bloody fool.'

Chapter Three

7 November, 1942

Ripples shuddered across the surface of their mother's afternoon cup of tea. They were back. Anne's eyes met her brother's across the table as the loud, deep drone grew louder above them. Only a few hours before the same low engine noise had interrupted their breakfast. Then they'd rushed outside, looked up to the sky and marvelled at the power and threat evoked by the Flying Fortresses as they flew overhead at the start of their mission.

'They're B17s. They're American.' Billy had picked up a wooden stick and pointed towards Germany, or at least where he thought it was. 'Go get them, Yanks. Charge!'

'They're not on horseback,' Anne had told him. Pleased it was a Saturday and they were both home to see the spectacle, she waved to the pilots to wish them good luck. The large dark planes had peppered the sky, their solid heavy bodies defying gravity and flying so low that Anne and Billy thought they could see the air crew waving back at them. The sight and show of strength boosted their confidence and was a sure sign that despite the recent bombing of Falmouth and ever-increasing strain on resources, there was still hope.

Now they were on their way back to base, their mission complete and hopefully victorious. Her mother sighed loudly as Anne and Billy noisily left the table to hurry outside. They looked up at the sky, their smiles wide in welcome. Immediately, they fell silent, their smiles slowly fading as they watched their heroes pass overhead.

How they'd spent the last few hours was clearly etched on the bodies of their planes. They were now bullet ridden and torn, some with parts missing such as a rudder or a tail turret. Others had a patch of blackened metal where a fire had temporarily been. They were battle weary, as would be their crew. The wings of the more damaged planes dipped dangerously, their tips almost meeting with the less damaged escorts guiding them home.

Anne heard her mother call them back inside. She looked at Billy to see if he'd heard and noticed tears welling up in his eyes. She attempted to comfort him, but he shook his older sister off and walked miserably towards the house. Their mother appeared at the door as he reached it and succeeded where Anne had failed. He leant heavily into her consoling embrace. Her understanding released something inside him and his body began to shudder with disappointed sobs which faded as they entered the house.

Anne remained outside to allow them some time together. Billy might be too old for his sister's hugs, but solace given by a mother was always welcome. Today, he'd given up the pretence that he was old enough to cope with the realities of war.

Anne defiantly brushed away her own tears and smiled brightly as she lifted her hand and waved slowly to welcome them back. It was the least she could do when so many had lost their lives.

Anne added her signature to the wing of the plane she'd just finished repairing. It was no more than a final secret mark hidden away and indiscernible to the untrained eye, but it was her way of sending a message and support to whoever went on to fly it. She looked across at her friend, Betty, but the table she worked at was vacant. Anne found her a few minutes later staring into the cracked mirror next to the coat stand.

'I think it's high time Mr Boyle bought a new mirror,' complained Betty. She vigorously searched her handbag for a lipstick. 'I told him about the crack during winter. It's almost summer now, for heaven's sake.'

Anne reached around her and grabbed her own coat from the hook. 'I doubt how their workers look is their priority and nor should it be.' She shrugged into her coat and watched her friend in the mirror as she painted a slash of bright red lipstick onto her lips from a worn-down stick.

'I think it matters. It would be good for morale,' said Betty as she pressed and rolled her lips together to smooth out the colour. 'I'm running out of lipstick now. Hitler has a lot to answer for.' She licked the tip of her finger and ran it along the arch of each brow, before making a face at Anne in the glass. Anne made a face back.

'Come on, Betty. If you have your way, we'll be here another ten minutes.'

Betty made another face, before reaching for her own coat. 'It takes time to look this good,' she teased.

Betty and Anne had been friends since childhood. At school, Betty was the more extrovert and flighty of the two, often being late or getting into trouble, although at her core there was a kind and loyal heart. Anne was the quiet, serious one, who was studious at school and devoted to her friends and family. On leaving school they were both prepared to follow the path expected by their families – taking a menial job as a stopgap until they married and had a home of their own to care for.

Instead, Anne and Betty found themselves being called up and given the choice of either working in a local factory repairing spitfires or joining one of the services. Both were up for the challenge and chose the factory in order to stay together. While the rest of the world was going mad, a friendship that had endured childhood, puberty and now the frustrations of war was a bond they were both not ready to break just yet … even if it meant losing out on a uniform and, perhaps, leaving Cornwall.

Betty suddenly stopped and lifted the hem of her overalls to examine her painted legs. 'Damn. The Silktona has run. I thought it would last longer than that.'

'It is hot in here.'

'I'm going to have to change back to gravy browning.'

Anne frowned at the marks on her friend's legs. 'Why are you wearing it under your overalls?'

'I put it on for Fred. We went to the pictures last night.'

'How was it?'

Betty dropped the hem of her overalls and rolled her eyes. 'Let's just say, one date with Fred was enough, but at least I got to see Humphrey Bogart.'

'You could wear ankle socks like me.' Betty looked at Anne, horrified. Anne burst out laughing, 'You would think I'd just stolen your ration book.'

'*That* I could tolerate, but ankle socks at twenty-two years old! I would rather die!'

The sound of several motor vehicles drew their attention; petrol rationing had resulted in less motorcars on the road – certainly not as many as the level of noise fast approaching from beyond the bend indicated. As they stepped outside, four Jeeps headed their way, the passengers and their drivers sat casually in their seats. It was their stance and laid-back attitude, more than their uniforms, which instantly marked them as different from their stiff British counterparts. They were American. The Jeeps led a convoy of camouflaged American trucks, with canvas backs, large rolling wheels and bright white stars painted on their sides. Betty and Anne quickly realised they were carrying seated soldiers who looked warily out from the back of the crowded trucks as people emerged from the surrounding buildings to line the street.

'I've never seen black people before,' said Betty as she watched the trucks roll by.

'All the soldiers are black.'

'Not the ones in the Jeeps.'

The last truck finally went by, followed by a gaggle of children. Encouraged by the children's laughter, the soldiers in the last truck grew less wary and began to throw something in the air for the children to catch. The children squealed with delight as they scrabbled on the floor to gather the objects. Their excitement only encouraged the troops further. They began to laugh, their wide smiles showing perfect white teeth against their ebony skin.

'Good-looking lot aren't they?' said Betty, unable to drag her eyes away.

One of the soldiers noticed them, stood up and threw a small object in their direction. They all cheered as Anne caught it in mid-air. Although her cheeks burned with embarrassment, she felt ridiculously happy that she'd not made a fool of herself.

'What is it?' asked Betty, peering into her hand.

'It's a sweet.'

Betty's eyes lit up as she looked back at the trucks. 'I wonder what else they have to give away.'

Anne and Betty watched the military convoy until they were no longer in sight. They left a trail of children in their wake, still scrambling for the sweets strewn on the ground and bartering for the ones already gathered. Anne and Betty exchanged smiles, equally excited as the children. They'd only seen the American GIs for a few minutes but, strangely, the town seemed a little less dull than only moments before. Their uniforms were rugged yet appeared well made, unlike the rough drab ill-fitting khaki of their own British army. They appeared generous, confident and friendly, a welcome change from the young men Anne and Betty had grown up with – shy, tongue-tied and with little money to spend. It felt as if, for a few precious moments, Hollywood had come to town, carried in trucks, oozing foreign glamour and smiling at them with large, dark brown eyes.

'Americans are black,' argued Billy as his father tuned in the wireless to hear the progress of the war. 'They are! I saw them today, up by Harry's farm. They're building a camp up there.'

'Only the ones that arrived today.' Anne turned to her stepfather. 'Betty and I saw them too. They were driving through town. The soldiers were black.' She turned to her brother. 'But not all Americans are, Billy. They aren't in the films in the cinema.'

Billy harrumphed and crossed his arms. 'I wouldn't know. I don't go.' He scuffed his shoe with the heel of the other until his mother gently slapped his leg to stop.

'We don't have enough coupons to get you another pair so don't ruin them. I won't have that stuck-up Mrs Wilbur looking at your shoes and saying I'm letting you grow wild.'

'They've sent the coloured soldiers first to set up the camps,' said her stepfather. The crackly plummy tones of the news presenter became clearer on the airwaves as he tuned it in. Satisfied, her stepfather sat back in his chair and crossed his hands over his belly to listen. 'There'll be more on the way.'

'You think more will follow?'

Her stepfather nodded.

'Why are they here?' The thought of more soldiers arriving both excited and horrified her. Suddenly using gravy browning to imitate stockings was a very real possibility.

'I think they're getting ready to counterattack, but don't say anything. You know what they say, "Careless talk costs lives" and we don't want Hitler to know what we've got planned.'

'And we certainly don't want him to know before we know ourselves,' replied her mother sitting down in a chair beside him.

Chapter Four

Joe's time in Scotland had been fleeting. As soon as they'd disembarked, they were relocated to a training barracks in Wiltshire. The journey had been laborious and didn't start well. The truck driver had forgotten that the British drove on the "wrong" side of the road and had swerved dangerously to avoid crashing into an irate delivery van, causing the tightly-packed soldiers on one side to lurch onto the laps of the men opposite. The swearing and manly pushing as they righted themselves didn't give a good impression to the onlookers gathered along the roads to welcome their arrival. They'd come with the intent of helping them to win the war, but were so green they couldn't even stay on their seats.

By the time they reached their new barracks, they firmly believed that the narrow, windy roads of England were built to discourage foreigners and found themselves yearning for the long straight highways that threaded the states and cities back home. Throughout the seven-month intensive training course that followed, Joe would witness several occasions when their military vehicles took the wrong turn and got stuck in yet another narrow lane. It wasn't surprising they found themselves in so much trouble in those early weeks. Narrow roads without signposts, removed to help confuse German spies and invaders, were equally effective at confusing Americans with limited knowledge of England's geography. Their frequent mistakes were received by the locals with a mixture of amusement and eye rolling, depending on how much inconvenience their mishaps had caused.

Their new training camp was made up of double-storied buildings lining the barracks, which also included quarters, storerooms, cook-houses and dining rooms, threaded together by walkways.

The training was basic, but what they needed. They'd been brought there in preparation for an allied invasion, yet many had never seen battle. The lessons were tough, sapping their strength till they trembled with fatigue, while taking them through the rollercoaster of determination, self-doubt and, finally, the discovery of new confidence in their ability. They learnt hand-to-hand combat, studied theory and dug trenches. They learnt to handle their guns and communicate silently through hand signals. They laid barbed wire and loaded explosions, dismantled the former and blew up the latter. They practised manoeuvres, playing war games in a surreal world of an open field, where no real danger lurked except for a disgruntled farmer.

Religious services and food were served in the Nissen huts. The meals were noisy affairs, around long, narrow tables crowded on both sides by hungry men. They were a welcome diversion when winter set in as it constantly rained, turning their camp to mud, preventing their clothes from drying and ensuring the chill never left their bones. Morale took a nosedive. They'd come to fight, yet the training and rain never seemed to end. Baltimore's winters were cold, but they weren't this wet. Even those who had no home to return to, began to feel homesick. Finally, they were told that their initial training was coming to an end. Were they about to see action across the channel? No, it emerged, they were being relocated … to Cornwall.

Chapter Five

July, 1943

Anne parked her bike in the shed, retrieved her gas mask and handbag from the basket, and made her way around the side of the house to the back door. She was about to open it, when she noticed Billy crouched in the garden looking as if he was up to something. He had grown taller since the spring, sprouting upwards like a young weed in the vegetable patch, but where nature had a way of ensuring everything was in proportion, it seemed to have forgotten young Billy. His limbs were long and spindly, his hands and feet overly large, and his coordination, as he learned to adapt to his growth spurt, left him clumsy and self-conscious. A few more months, maybe a year, everything would catch up, but for now he had the head of a boy, the body of a pubescent youth and a young man's restlessness for adventure. Seeing him so focused on something always raised Anne's suspicions. She approached him but it was only when her shadow fell over his body that he realised he wasn't alone.

'What are you doing?' Anne's gaze settled on a tin of fruit nestled in the grass. 'Are those peaches?' She picked up the tin and studied the label. 'They are! Where did you get them?'

'Some Yanks gave them to me.'

'Have you been hanging around their camp again? Why would they give you these? You should give them back.'

Billy snatched the tin from her. 'No! They're mine! I swapped fair and square!'

Anne tilted her head. 'What did *you* have to swap with an American soldier? They've no interest in anything a thirteen-year-old ragamuffin might have.' Unease swept through her veins as two bright spots formed on her brother's cheeks. Mimicking their mother's questioning tone, she prodded him again. 'Billy, tell me.' Realisation dawned on her. 'You didn't! Not again!'

She ran inside and to the only photo album the family possessed. She opened it to find yet another photo of her, missing. Billy had done it again! He'd swapped a photograph of her to some unknown GI for a tin of peaches.

'I'm going to tell Mother on you,' she shouted, shoving it back in the drawer. 'You can't give away my photographs. I have so few and that one was my favourite. It was taken in a studio. What if they think I'm in on your little game?'

'They don't care about that. They just want a picture of a woman. Any woman. They think you look like Ingrid Bergman.'

Anne raised her eyebrows in surprise. Ingrid Bergman was beautiful.

'That doesn't make me feel any better,' she lied. 'I don't want my photo being passed around from man to man for a tin of peaches. It's sordid.'

'Three tins.'

'Three?' Strangely she felt even more pleased; she'd only been worth a pack of gum last time.

'And they gave me something for you.'

Anne folded her arms, determined to not feel impressed by her brother's bartering skills. She scowled at him, but after four years of war, rationing and bad news, her curiosity got the better of her. 'What did they give you?'

Billy withdrew a packet of stockings from inside his shirt. Anne stared at them. She hadn't worn stockings before. Silk stockings were too expensive and besides, her mother had considered her too young before the war. During the war, stockings were in short supply until they were non-existent. Suddenly, a pair of *nylon* stockings were so tantalisingly close, that if she took a step forward, she'd be able to touch them. She'd heard about nylon stockings but had yet to feel them. Anne licked her dry lips. Billy held them out to her with a triumphant grin. Although she pretended to be reluctant, she reached out and took them.

'Alright, I won't tell Mother, but on one condition … you must share the peaches with everyone and you've to stop swapping my photographs for things. I don't have many and at the rate you're going I won't have any.

Billy sighed. 'All right.'

They gathered the tins and carried them indoors. Anne put two in the cupboard and left the third on the table for tea.

Billy thrust his hands in his pockets. 'Are you sure about your photographs? I can barter for more with one of yours than I can with Mother's.'

Anne was about to reply, when their mother walked in through the door, holding a letter in her hand.

'Your Aunt Rose has written. She says Pendarves Estate has been requisitioned for American officers and camps have been set up all around St. Ives, Penzance, Hayle and Helston. It seems that more troops are arriving again soon.' She gave the letter to Anne to read.

'I must tell Mrs Parker,' continued her mother, as Anne's eyes quickly raked over her aunt's familiar handwriting. 'She's the head of the Women's Voluntary Service in the area and will want us to do our bit to welcome them.'

'She probably already knows,' said Anne.

'Even so, our welcoming drinks went down very well when the first lot arrived.'

Anne slipped on her cardigan. 'I'll ride over and tell her.' She tied up her hair in a scarf and went to retrieve her bike. It was just a short ride of two miles to Mrs Parker's house and wouldn't take long.

'I'll be back for tea,' she called over her shoulder as she peddled away.

The thought of helping at another welcome event didn't faze Anne now. They'd already arranged several welcome dances, the first being hurriedly organised as a direct result of a single incident witnessed by Mrs Parker herself as she attended the Sunday morning service at her local church. A small group of American soldiers had gathered at the church's door. One of the men had handed the vicar a note. The vicar, according to Mrs Parker, had been visibly shaken when he read it, as the note asked for permission to attend the service. When the vicar asked why they felt it was necessary to ask such a question, the soldier quietly explained that in his country they weren't permitted to enter some buildings due to the colour of their skin.

News quickly spread about the appalling prejudice these polite young men had to endure in their own country, and a welcome dance was quickly arranged to show Cornwall's gratitude for all they were doing. From that day on, the soldiers became regular attendees to the church service, even forming a gospel choir and belting out songs far superior to the dull tunes and poorly harmonised voices of the Cornish congregation. Their officers, who were always white with deep southern drawls, didn't encourage the integration and, in some cases, actively tried to prevent it from developing further by visiting families who'd welcomed them into their homes for a meal. Even Anne had been warned not to mix with them, as she'd been seen sewing a button on a uniform for one of the soldiers. He had brought some thread in a shop to repair his uniform and Anne had offered to do it for him. They'd sat on a bench by a patch of grass, chatting amiably as she nimbly sewed his button with fast, well-practised strokes of the thread. The meeting was soon over, but an officer had seen and felt it his duty to warn her not to do it again.

'It's best you don't do any menial jobs for them,' the officer advised her as he fell into step beside her. 'We don't want to give them the wrong idea.'

Anne had stopped walking and looked at him, too horrified by his attitude to speak. The officer smiled at her and walked away, straight-backed and with a swagger to his shoulders. She returned to work, but the incident had troubled her for the rest of the day.

Now those pleasant young men had moved on to set up base camps elsewhere and new troops would be arriving to occupy the ones prepared.

Despite their best intentions to be the first to welcome the new arrivals, the American Red Cross beat the Woman's Voluntary Service to it. Betty watched the three beautiful women manning the especially converted truck as they served the first wave of new troops with freshly made doughnuts.

'They come over here with their Hollywood smiles and long peaked caps and think they own the place,' grumbled Betty. 'Don't they think we're capable of looking after their soldiers for them?'

'They do make the WVS look drab. Even Mother looks put out,' said Anne, checking the heat of the tea in the urn with a light pat of her hand as she watched her mother approach. Despite her mother being proud of her new green dress and burgundy cardigan uniform, which she'd recently bought with her housekeeping money, she had an intense frown on her face as she carried a plate of food from a nearby house. Her frown briefly disappeared as she nodded and smiled at the small ensemble of soldiers standing by their military vehicle, before throwing a defiant scowl at the doughnut truck opposite.

Her mother reached them and carefully placed the plate on the trestle table. 'If they fill themselves up on doughnuts, the sandwiches will curl and be fit for no one,' she muttered, angling the plate to best advantage. 'Every member of the WVS donated something and I'm afraid it will all go to waste.' Before Anne could reply, her mother muttered something about more water and walked briskly away, before disappearing into the adjacent house for extra supplies.

Anne's attention returned to the gathered soldiers. They appeared to be debating whether to leave their equipment and join the doughnut queue. Anne felt for them. They'd just arrived and were in that phase of assessing their new surroundings and wondering what was expected of them.

Although the sun had finally broken through the cloud, the morning had been cold and wet. The weather must have been the same where they'd started their journey from, as they were still wearing large winter coats which almost reached the ground. They also appeared ready for battle, as many wore their metal helmets, carried a large rucksack of equipment on their back and a gun slung over their shoulders. It was an unnerving sight; an army ready to fight in the middle of the town square surrounded by shops, a barber and the WVS. Every man also carried a roll of bedding, which they either lay on the ground or propped against their legs.

'They look a bit lost. Let's take the tea and sandwiches to them,' suggested Anne. Betty didn't need any persuading. They filled two trays with cups of tea and jam sandwiches, made from blackberries hand-gathered last summer, and walked over to them. Anne and Betty soon discovered that their smiles, warm greeting and British accents had an allure of their own, which the doughnut ladies didn't have. They glanced at one another, surprised at their sudden success, as the men began to gather around and reach for something to eat or drink. Anne noticed her mother beaming at their success from the nearby doorway.

'Thank you, ma'am,' they muttered politely as they took turns accepting a drink and a sandwich, before making way for the next man.

Betty and Anne made several returns to the tea urn and trestle table to restock as truck after truck arrived and spilled their troops out into the square for refreshments. Cigarettes hurriedly followed the drained mugs of tea until orders were casually re-laid to climb back onboard so they could be driven to their new base camp.

It was then Anne felt it – that strange sensation which pricks at the skin and heightens one's senses. She'd felt it before. The first time as a child when she'd been woken by a sudden sound in the night. Another time as a teenager walking home in the dark and feeling terrified that she was being followed. Yet this time it was subtly different. She wasn't afraid, not like before, but curious as to the cause. With the absence of threat, there could only be one reason; she had sensed she was being watched. She looked around her. A sea of nodding helmets, scraping boots and diesel fumes surrounded her, everyone pre-occupied and not looking her way. A truck's engine started up nearby, and troops climbed on board preparing to depart for their new base. One man was already sitting on the bench near the tailgate. She felt that feeling deep inside her even more strongly than before as their eyes met. He was the one who'd been watching her.

The soldier's eyes were in shadow, shielded from the light by his low fitting helmet. His hair was hidden, but his tanned skin and afternoon stubble hinted it was dark. His lips were firm and full, curving slightly as the seconds ticked by. The engine of his truck revved into life and began to move forward. He was already leaving. He lifted his hand and bid farewell with a tap of his fingers against the edge of his helmet. The casual salute wasn't at all necessary, but he'd done it all the same. And he'd done it just for her – as if in his eyes he thought she was worthy of it, even though he didn't know her at all.

Chapter Six

Joe rested the back of his head in the crook of his arm and stared at the ceiling above his head. The roof joist creaked in the rising wind, giving the impression it had a life of its own as if it was a resting animal waiting to take flight on a stronger current. For now, it was biding its time, thought Joe, just like all the soldiers who'd made the town hall their home.

His battalion had been stationed in the southwest of England for two weeks now, each company efficiently billeted to a variety of scattered buildings located in the villages and towns throughout Cornwall. Vacant village and town halls, hotels and church halls, their previous use didn't really matter – if it had the capacity, they were accepted and quickly transformed into temporary homes.

They'd arrived in crowded trucks to a surreal international welcoming party of free doughnuts, hot drinks and jelly sandwiches. He'd jumped down from the truck and followed the crowd, which appeared to be gathering around two focal points. As he'd waited for his fellow soldiers to take turns in collecting their refreshments, his gaze had wandered over the organised chaos of overdressed, travel-weary men, corralled into a small square of a quaint English town. Eventually it had been his turn and he'd found himself reaching for a chipped mug while staring at the most beautiful woman he had ever seen.

Primal lust had been the last thing he expected to experience as he waited to taste the bitter tannin of lukewarm English tea. Up to that moment he'd thought the idea of falling head over heels in love with someone at first sight was ridiculously corny, but love and lust weren't too far apart and he'd felt something akin to the latter if not the former. Suddenly it didn't seem quite so crazy after all. He'd always believed that one would need something more before that allusive emotion of love raised its head. Yet, after seeing *her*, he knew it could be possible to feel something without even a single word exchanged. It wasn't love, of course. He wasn't even sure if he was capable of feeling any type of love, having not experienced much since his mother's early death.

The woman had been preoccupied, attending to another soldier, when he'd taken his mug of tea and jelly sandwich from her. He didn't mind; it gave him the opportunity to watch her face at close quarters. She reminded him of Ingrid Bergman, with her honey-brown hair, soft curls and arched eyebrows. Her lips were full and curved in a shy smile, while her sweeping lashes framed soft, blue eyes. For those few short moments, he was oblivious to everyone else around him.

He had retreated away from the crowd to eat his sandwich and sup his tea. He continued to watch her, hoping she would eventually see him. She didn't. He realised that unless he spoke to her, he would remain just one of many, as her pretty smile, rather than the food she was serving, drew a horde of men around her. Her friend called out to her by name. Anne. The name suited her. Very British. Very feminine. Very classy. On any other day he would have asked her out on a date, but it was hardly the right time. She also didn't look the type of woman that would flirt with a stranger and he kind of liked that too. He would need to speak to her first and gain her trust. Now, during a short, crowded refreshment stop, before being transported to their new home, wasn't the right time to do it.

Eventually Frank had nudged him out of his thoughts to tell him it was time to leave. They'd climbed back into the truck and Joe had ensured he sat near the tailgate so he could still see her. He hoped she would look over in his direction and, finally, as if she'd heard him silently calling her, she'd lifted her gaze and their eyes met. It felt like he'd just hit a home run. The moment had been fleeting. The truck was already on the move and soon he'd be out of there. What could he do? They were too far apart to speak and from the enquiring look on her face she'd caught him staring. All he could do was say goodbye and hope that should they meet again, she would remember him favourably. So he had casually saluted as a soldier was drilled to do.

Now, looking back on it, he could kick himself for being so corny. He'd made a fool of himself and messed up her first impression of him. He hoped they'd meet again or he'd always wonder if he'd missed the greatest opportunity of his life by not speaking to her. He resettled his head in the crook of his arm and decided to not think of that. Instead, he would recall the sound of her voice. It was English and quaint, but softer and less clipped than the wireless presenters on the world service. He smiled at the memory.

As the days moved on, Joe convinced himself that perhaps the intense feeling he felt when he'd seen the woman was just born from prolonged celibacy. She was simply the first female he'd found pulse-thumpingly attractive since arriving in this green but backward country.

Their new training regime kept him busy and helped occupy his mind. He'd thought the initial training barracks were primitive, but their new billet was even more so. The hall was cold, although he had to admit, superior to the canvas tents they'd endured during some training exercises. The officers were billeted to nearby family accommodation; although they often joked that the soldiers under their command were better off as at least they had make-shift shower tents on some sites. It appeared that even the grandest houses in England didn't have the convenience of showers installed.

The training to prepare them for the allied invasion continued, brought to them on weekly training circulars, depicting the exercise, pick-up location and duration. Long marches, endless drills and varied scenarios were devised to help hone their skills, each different from the last and played out on different terrains. It was strange times – playing war games in a country that was at war yet had no enemy to see on the ground. It became the norm for their training to be interrupted by a reminder of normality – a wandering cow, a postman delivering the mail or an excitable youth riding his bike along the narrow country lane. Initially, their hosts would pause to watch their marching columns, but as the days and numbers of American soldiers increased, they became less of a novelty and largely ignored. The local inhabitants' sudden appearance, amidst their training missions, shone a stark light on their make-believe role-play, leaving Joe feeling both foolish for wearing camouflaged combat gear in a peaceful countryside setting, yet proud to be representing the United States of America. America, a country where life buzzed, fortunes could be made and land appeared to never end. Not like Cornwall, where it took less than a day to reach the coast in any direction. England was a strange place, where refrigerators were unheard of, warm beer was accepted and few buildings reached higher than four levels. Little made sense any more.

Passes to leave their base were gratefully received, offering respite and entertainment in the nearby town of St. Ives where the local older generation watched their friendly invasion with knowing, but sad eyes. The young men of the town were few and far between, which was a bonus as the soldiers, including Joe, felt starved of female company. High on excitement and with an illogical plan to visit every bar in Cornwall, Joe and Frank caught a ride into Truro on one of the army trucks. A beer, no matter how warm, thought Joe, would be a good way to forget his failure to speak to the woman he was trying, but failing, to forget.

At first Truro was a disappointment. They'd been told it was a city, but it was drab and small compared to Baltimore, with its towering skyscrapers, trams and continual noise. The soldiers climbed down from the truck, a little bewildered, but soon rallied when they spotted the first building that could pass as a bar. They piled in through the pub's door, their loud chatter invading the sombre drinkers inside.

After a while, some moved on to the next public house. Gradually, their numbers grew less, as soldiers broke away in twos and threes to scout the city on their own. Every public house appeared much the same to Joe. They were far darker than in Baltimore. Small rooms, dark panelling and old windows helped to suck the daylight into an abyss of tobacco smoke, while foul-tasting beer, served in glasses rather than bottles, seemed to be their only speciality. Nevertheless, Joe and Frank continued their quest and visited several in quick succession. By the third bar the warm beer tasted more palatable, the locals less scowling and the dark gloomy interiors had taken on a welcoming, cosy feel. After another pint, a game of darts and a new plan to find something to eat, they eventually stepped outside into the cooling night.

The fading evening light was a sure sign that dusk had arrived. Truro's streets were now well and truly taken over by service men. Some had already found female company and were accompanying them along the narrow sidewalk, while others were sweet-talking a couple of ladies waiting for the last bus home. The doors to a movie theatre opened and people spilled out onto the pavement in a loud chattering throng. A soldier, from across the street, called out loudly to someone in the crowd, before running across the road to meet them. Joe watched to see who he'd recognised. He grabbed Frank's arm as the soldier reached the woman and started talking to her. It was *her*. It was Anne.

'Hey!' said Frank looking down at his arm. 'What's up?'

'It's that girl … the one with the jelly sandwiches.'

Frank frowned and followed his gaze. 'The one you keep going on about?'

'I mentioned her once.'

'More than once, pal.'

'Twice. Three at the most.' He let go of his friend's arm at the same time as Frank shook him off.

'So? Are you going to do something about it or wait until that punk has asked her out?'

Joe didn't answer. He hadn't expected to see her again, but now she was here, and just a stone's throw away. He knew he should make the most of it, but how did he pull it off without looking like an overly keen idiot?

Frank shoved him forward. 'Don't just stand there! Get your butt over there and ask her out on a date.'

Joe rubbed the back of his neck. 'I dunno.'

Uneasily, he dragged his eyes away and looked at Frank. Surprise, confusion then annoyance passed over Frank's face before he had a chance to draw breath.

Frank cuffed the top of Joe's head with a flick of his hand. 'What's the matter with you? When did you turn chicken?' He jerked his head towards Anne. 'Her friend might be enjoying the attention, but your gal ain't.'

Frank was right, while her friend was smiling, Anne was looking decidedly uncomfortable. The soldier wasn't doing anything wrong; he was just way too familiar for Joe's liking and it seemed to Anne's too.

'She's crying out to be rescued,' encouraged Frank at his side. 'Be her knight in shining armour and haul your ass over there.' They crossed the road, Joe's mind completely blank as to what he was going to say and how best to say it. Frank came to his rescue – or rather stole his thunder as only a soldier pal could do.

'Is everything all right, ladies?'

The soldier turned as they approached. Joe recognised him immediately; it was only Mick from Company B. He was one of the good guys, perhaps a little full on drink, but no real threat, which was just as well as he didn't fancy brawling in the street to impress a girl, even if that girl was Anne.

'Hey, Joe! Look, it's her!' Mick waved a photo in his hand, jabbing at it drunkenly to emphasise his words. 'Won this pic in a craps game.' He shoved it in front of Joe's face. 'Look! It's her!'

Joe looked at the quivering photo in front of him. A woman's smiling face stared back. He glanced above it to the face on the other side. The same pretty eyes, only this pair wasn't muted in greyscale; they were vibrant blue and glinting in the rising moonlight. There was that jolt in his chest again, the one that caught him right between the ribs and knocked the breath out of him.

He swallowed. 'It sure is.'

Her friend burst out laughing. 'Look at his face, Anne! He thinks you're famous. You've become an American sweetheart pin-up!'

Anne tried to grab the photo from Mick's hand, but one twitch of his wrist and he expertly dodged her attempt.

'It's mine,' he teased. 'I won it, fair and square. You wouldn't upset a lonely soldier far from his home by taking his most precious possession, would you?'

Despite the fading light, Joe saw the sudden rise of scarlet heat at her neckline. Joe plucked it from Mick's fingers.

'She wouldn't, but I would.' He handed it to Anne and smiled.

Their gazes met as she tentatively reached out her hand as if she was half expecting him to steal it away again. He waited patiently for her, their fingers briefly touching as she gently took it from his fingers.

'Thank you,' she said as she immediately slipped it into her deep coat pocket.

'Hey! That's mine,' said Mick.

'Not any more,' said Joe smiling at Anne. His smile broadened as he noticed a slight curve of her lips too. Feeling more confident, he turned to Mick and cheerfully slapped him on the back. 'I'll find you another pic. A real Hollywood starlet this time.' He turned Mick to face the other way, pulling him close with a brotherly guiding arm. 'If you leave now,' he whispered into his ear, 'the drinks are on me the next time you're in town.'

Mick considered his offer as he swayed against him. 'How many?'

'All of them. One night only.'

Mick nodded drunkenly. 'Only for you, Joe,' he muttered. 'Only for you.' He stumbled away, changing direction several times, before he settled on a destination to aim for. Joe beamed and turned around to receive Anne's praise, only to find she was walking away with her friend. He noticed Frank watching him with a big grin on his face.

'Thought she was going to fall right into your arms? You've got a lot to learn about English women, pal.'

'You could've kept them engaged. Haven't you learnt anything from our training exercises?'

Joe jogged after them. 'Hey! What's your name?' He knew already but it seemed the right thing to say.

Anne's friend halted, forcing Anne to do so too. He caught them up, quickly followed by Frank.

Her blonde friend answered for them. 'I'm Betty. This is Anne.'

A short silence followed as they studied each other. Betty and Anne wore similar coats, each with a handbag hanging from their forearm and a gas mask slung over a shoulder. They both wore hats, with neat curls around their necks; Betty's neat and sculpted whereas Anne's looked more natural and soft to touch – the sort of curl that would naturally spring back to shape should he take a moment to tease it straight.

Joe cleared his throat. 'Where are you going? Can we buy you ladies a drink?'

'We have to get home. We've a lift to catch,' Anne replied, staring at his boots.

'We could walk you there … make sure you aren't bothered by some other guy,' suggested Frank.

To Joe's relief, Betty agreed before Anne could refuse. They fell into step beside them, Frank walking next to Betty and Joe following behind with Anne. A silent message passed between Frank and Joe by way of a glance. *Joe owed him one.*

They walked in silence. The sound of their echoing footsteps and Frank and Betty's easy banter ahead of them made the silence feel far longer than it was. Two couples, one pair relaxed without a care for the future, the other taut with tension. Joe had an overwhelming feeling that this moment could make or break what was to come. Anne was staring at her feet, so he did too. She wore white ankle socks and sturdy, but worn, shoes. She was feeling the shortages of the war, but the shortages of the war were not exactly a great chat-up line.

'You are probably wondering why that soldier had my photograph.'

He glanced up to find her looking at him. Another jolt to the chest.

'Yes. I guess I am.' It was a lie; he hadn't given it a second thought, although now she mentioned it, he was curious to know. He'd been too busy trying to think of a topic of conversation and had missed the most obvious one of them all.'

'My brother swapped it for a pair of stockings and some cans of fruit.' The same crimson flush rose towards her jawline again, but this time with a vengeance. He found her reaction endearing, amusing and utterly mesmerising. 'It was the second photograph he'd taken. He knew he would be in trouble if I ever found out so the peaches were for him and the stockings were to appease me.'

'And did they?'

There was that shy smile again; a smile that could embody teasing fun, joyful abandonment and seductive flirtation all in one, depending on the scene she chose to place it in – or the scene he wanted to imagine in his head.

'Yes. One was sheer bliss, the other will be an exciting novelty so I'm saving it for a special occasion.'

Joe thought about asking which gave her the feeling of sheer bliss but decided it didn't really matter. He knew it would be how he would feel should she ever decide to wrap a stockinged thigh around him.

'I could get you more stockings. Anything you want. I just have to have them shipped over.'

'There's no need.'

'I'd like to. It's no trouble. Name it and I'll get it. Chocolate? Candy? Nylons? Money's no object.'

Anne's steps slowed. 'You are very sure of yourself, aren't you?'

Joe frowned. Had he said something wrong?

Betty interrupted them before he could reply.

'Hey, Anne. Frank is Bob Hope's cousin!'

Joe scowled at Frank. Frank grinned at him and winked, before placing his arm around Betty and continuing their cosy, laughter-filled walk.

'Is he?' asked Anne. Her wide eyes looked up at him. He should play along and support Frank's fib; he'd done it before and it never caused any harm. It was just a buddy supporting a buddy, like brothers-in-arms and all that, but somehow this time felt different. Anne was different, which made him want to show her that he was different too.

'No. It's Frank's chat-up line. It's not even original. Half of our battalion probably claims to be related to Bob Hope.'

'And the other half?' she asked, falling into step beside him.

'The other half pretend they *are* Bob Hope. After a few beers, some even believe it.' And there it was. His cheap joke had done the trick and put her at ease. She started to laugh. Her laughter lit up her eyes and made them sparkle with joy, while the sound made him feel ten feet tall and want to laugh too. He was vaguely aware that Betty and Frank had turned to look at them before Frank eased Betty to walk on. At least that was what Joe guessed he was doing, for in that moment Anne's throaty, goddamn sexy laugh, was all that really mattered. Her laughter faded, but in its wake was a more relaxed and talkative Anne.

'You're the soldier in the truck, aren't you?' she asked, glancing up at him as she measured her steps with a relaxed, jaunty step. The sort of walk you used when you'd just had good news. The sort of walk he was using now.

'Yeah. And they were the best jelly sandwiches I've had in a long while.'

She frowned. 'Jelly?'

'Yeah. What? What did I say? Why are you laughing again?'

She shook herself sober. 'I'm sorry. Is that what you call jam?'

He realised what he'd done and nodded. 'It's a lot to get used to. Different words, driving on the wrong side of the road—'

'The right side.'

'No, the left.' They looked at each other confused, then broke into a smile instead.

'I'd like to see you again if that's okay.' He tried to gauge her response, but a veil of eyelashes shielded her downcast eyes.

'I don't think so.'

If she had socked it to him straight between the eyes he would have been less surprised than he felt right now. 'Why not?'

'You seem very nice—'

'Why do I feel there's a "but" coming?'

'—but …'

'There it is.'

She had the good manners to look uncomfortable as she tried to form her excuse for breaking his heart. 'Look Mr …'

'Joe. Call me Joe.'

'I understand how it must be for you …'

'Do you?' he asked. 'I'm impressed, 'cos I'm still trying to work that one out for myself.'

'American troops are arriving all the time. No one knows for how long or when the order will come. I could wake up tomorrow and you might have moved on. You want to have fun while you're here. Mr Hayward says you're all overpaid, over se—'

'I can guess what Mr Hayward thinks. Who is this guy? I'd liked to show him what we're really like.'

'He's an elderly lay-preacher in the next village.'

Joe shoved his hands in his pockets and found his cigarettes. He popped one out with a well-practiced tap of the base and offered her one.

She shook her head. 'My mother says a lady doesn't smoke in the streets.'

'Well, I'm no lady,' said Joe with a smile as he flicked his lighter into a raging flame and lit the end. He inhaled deeply as he watched the amber ember eat up the tip, then exhaled with an irritable sigh.

'I can see that.'

He glanced up to find her smiling at him; it was only then that he realised what he had said.

'I'm sorry, Anne. I don't mean to be grouchy, just wasn't expecting the knock-back.'

'Do women usually fall at your feet?'

He shook his head. 'No. It's not that.' He took another deep inhale, before watching the exhaled smoke catch on the breeze. 'Just can't help feeling that I've been lumped in with all of Bob Hope's relatives.' He smiled. 'Look, Anne, I like you.'

'You don't know me.'

'I *really* like you.'

'You *really* don't know me.'

'All I'm asking is for a chance to get to know you.' He pinched a small space between his fingers. 'Even if it's a little bit'—he closed the space again—'or maybe just half of a little bit.' Anne tilted her head as if she was seriously considering it. His hopes rose just a fraction.

Betty called her name, robbing him of her attention. 'Our lift is here! Hurry up.'

Anne looked back at him. 'I'd better go. I'm sorry—'

'Just tell me where you live? I'll call on you and we can talk some more. Just talk, nothing more.'

He saw Anne's hesitation to leave, before she relented and walked to the waiting car. It was just a fraction but he had seen it all the same and it told him that he was still in with a chance. He walked briskly to catch her up. The waiting car was full of young women. She answered his question before he asked it.

'Our neighbours pooled their petrol coupons to give the young people in our area an outing to Truro.'

'So, you don't live in Truro?'

Anne shook her head, but gave no further clues. The car door opened and a space was made for Betty and Anne to get in. To Joe's frustration, Anne got in first.

'If I go to the trouble of finding you, will you take a walk with me then?' he asked through the car window. The passengers took pity on him and encouraged her to say yes.

'Maybe.'

'Give me a clue? The name of the house. The name of the town?'

Betty got in and the car door was slammed shut. Joe was forced to take a step back as the car began to move forward.

'You said "Maybe"!' he called after her as the car drove away. 'I'll take that as a "yes" then.'

Joe threw his cigarette on the ground and used the ball of his foot to stub it out.

'So how are you planning to find out where she lives?' asked Frank. 'Didn't look that keen to see you again.'

'She's been listening to too many people. I just need a chance to prove I'm not like the rest.'

'Bit hard to do when you don't know where she lives.'

Joe slipped off his army cap and ran a hand through his hair. The beer, night air and long hours of training had finally drained him, or maybe it was the realisation that he might never see her again. Last time he could cope with it, now, after hearing her laugh and talking to her, he was going to find it harder.

'Just as well Betty took pity on you.'

Joe's heart lurched in his chest. 'What are you saying?'

'I'm saying that Betty told me where Anne lives.'

Joe couldn't believe his luck. 'Where?'

'Somewhere on Carrick Road. Her house is called River something-or-other. It's south east of the King Harry. Near a village called Free Hock'

'King Harry?'

'Sounds like a hotel or bar to me.'

Joe slapped his friend on the back. 'I owe you a beer, pal.'

'You sure do!' Frank beamed. The smile left his lips as quickly as it appeared. 'Look, Joe,' he said quietly. Joe braced himself. He'd heard Frank use that tone before, just before he detonated a pearl of wisdom. Wisdom that had helped him survive an alcoholic father.

'What?' he asked, not sure he wanted to hear.

'Be careful. We could be given our orders any day now. Don't let that broad cost you more than she's worth. Wherever we're sent, we need to hold it together. You can't leave half your head back here in

England. It might be the half you need to stop yourself getting killed. We have a war to win.'

Frank was right. 'It's okay. I know exactly what I'm doing. How about another beer before we go back to camp?'

Reassured, Frank brightened. 'Sounds good to me.' He walked towards the nearest public house, before noticing Joe hadn't joined him. 'Aren't you coming?'

'Yeah, course I am. Get the beers in, I just need a couple of minutes.'

Frank shrugged as he headed to the door. 'Okay, don't be too long. The beer's warm enough without it waiting for your ugly mug.'

Joe breathed in deeply and finally took a moment to look around him. He had blindly followed Anne, more interested in her than his surroundings, which were now cast in the soft light of the moon. He realised he was standing in the main high street at the point where the road forked into two narrower roads. Standing at the fork, proud in his uniform, was a bronze statue of a British WW1 soldier. He stood frozen in time, a rifle in one hand, his flat tin helmet aloft in the other. Was he waving for help or was it in sad farewell? Joe stared at it. The first had an aura of relief, the other of great sadness. *We have a war to win.* Frank's words were as clear as if he were standing beside him. Joe braced himself and studied the man more closely. His back was straight, his chin held high. Of course, he was celebrating victory. Joe smiled, preferring this take much more. One day that would be him, he told himself as he walked away to join his friend.

Chapter Seven

At first Anne ignored the soft rumble in the far distance. The recent rain had encouraged a rampant resurgence of weeds in the vegetable plot and Anne had the task of clearing it. Their vegetable plot was three times bigger than before the war, thanks to the Dig for Victory campaign which encouraged everyone to plough and sow any land they had available to produce food. Billy wanted to keep chickens, but as their next-door neighbour had some and was willing to share their eggs for help with their garden, her stepfather had seen little point.

The sound of the engine grew closer, causing Anne to pause in her hoeing and look up. She straightened as she searched for the source, her hand holding the hoe while the other shielded her eyes against the harsh summer sun. A dark silhouette of a man astride a motorcycle came into view, navigating his way down the narrow bumpy lane to her house at the bottom of the hill.

The bright rays suddenly disappeared behind a cloud. The motorcycle and its driver were clearly visible now; the engine was battered, worn and trailing grey puffs of smoke, the driver was in an American uniform. Anne's eyes widened as she slowly lowered her hand. It was *him* – the American GI she thought she'd never see again. Suddenly alert, she threw her hoe aside and crouched down out of sight. She looked a mess!

She examined her earth-covered hands in panic and lifted the neckline of her oversized shirt. A slight sheen of sweat covered her chest. She sniffed, wrinkled her nose in disgust and sighed. She couldn't let him see her like this. She'd have to hide until he went away. Tentatively, she craned her neck to see what he was doing. To her horror, he'd dismounted his bike and knocked on the door. He was going to come face to face with her mother! The door opened and a few words were exchanged before he stepped inside. Uncharacteristically, her mother had invited him inside to wait. She must be intending to question him about his intentions towards her daughter. How excruciating! Her horror changed to sympathy for the young man who was only looking for some fun to fill his day off. She suddenly felt duty-bound to rescue him. There was only one thing left to do: sneak into the back of the house, quickly wash and change, then liberate him from her mother.

Still crouching, she ran across the vegetable plot, jumping expertly over the deep furrows to avoid damaging the plants. Confident she was out of sight of the front room window, where her mother would be entertaining him, she straightened and followed the narrow slate path to the lean-to at the back of the house. Next to the lean-to was a water tank. It was used to collect rainwater to feed the garden and had seen better days, but the water was always clear and Anne would make use of it now. She dabbed her face, neckline and under her arms with quick well-practiced strokes of her fingers before using the windowsill of the lean-to to climb up onto the low slanting roof.

She hadn't climbed on the roof since she was banned as a teenager, but the route and footholds, learnt from experience and mishaps, all came flooding back – she just had to remember to keep to the areas supported by wood joists and take her time. The childish excitement she used to feel set her heart racing again. Only this time it wasn't because it was naughty or daring; it was because of the American waiting for her inside. He was rather too forward and way too confident, but he was tantalisingly different to anyone she had met before. Her interest was piqued, if nothing else.

Anne reached for her bedroom window. Fortunately, the sash was open as she'd left it ajar when she woke; a summer-long habit to chase away the stifling night air. She climbed through, contorting her limbs to a painful degree. It had been easier when she was a child. The next few minutes were spent frantically dragging off her clothes, rummaging through her cupboard for her best summer dress and quickly brushing her hair with speedy, rough strokes. Despite the lack of time to prepare, she was surprised at how presentable she appeared when she finally looked in the mirror. Her hair shone, her eyes sparkled and her skin glowed from the morning sun. Her gaze dipped to the packet of stockings on her dressing table. She was saving them for a special occasion, but this wasn't it – although it was tempting. Anne took a deep breath, mustered some courage and made her way silently down the stairs.

'No, ma'am. Just me.'

'And your parents?'

Anne heard a clumsy clink of a teacup.

'My mother passed away when I was ten. My father is a lawyer. He lives in Baltimore.' A painful silence followed, marked by the steady tick-tock of their mantel clock.

'This is a fine cup of tea, ma'am.' Another loud clink, then a rattle. Joe's discomfort reached out to where she stood on the bottom stair. Her mother's questions began again.

'What did you do before you joined the army?'

'I was a law student, ma'am.'

'You were training to be a solicitor?' Her mother was impressed.

'A lawyer, ma'am. It was what my father wanted.'

'And did you achieve it?'

'I joined up instead.'

'Oh.' Her disappointment was loud and clear. 'As a private?'

'Yes, ma'am.'

'Your father must be disappointed. Could you have entered as an officer once you qualified?'

'Maybe. I didn't tell them. It won't be the first time I've disappointed him, ma'am.'

'Do you disappoint him a lot?'

She couldn't allow his torture to go on any longer, even though she felt it might do him good to have his confidence taken down a peg or two by her mother's questioning.

Joe immediately stood as she stepped into the room, relief, then delight, sweeping across his face as his gaze settled on her bare legs. From the warmth in his eyes he liked what he saw. She felt her cheeks burn, which he appeared to find endearing if the smile on his lips was anything to go on.

From the slight raise of her eyebrow, her mother had noticed too. Anne felt her cheeks throb with the heat.

'Mr Mallory here—'

'Please, call me Joe, ma'am.'

'—wishes to take you out for the afternoon. I told him you don't date soldiers.' Her gaze dropped to Anne's best dress and cardigan. 'Unless you've changed your mind, Anne?'

Her mother was right, she had avoided dating soldiers as a few of her childhood friends had already died in the war. Such frivolity was on hold, as far as Anne was concerned. Why give your heart to someone when they could suddenly disappear from your life so traumatically? Her mother was waiting for her rebuff … although the American, with his smart uniform and brazen ways, seemed more amused. Suddenly, being placed in a predictable, stuffy box, set off her hibernating rebellious streak. Before she could stop herself, she found herself accepting. It made no sense.

'A walk would be nice.'

'Actually, I was thinking more of a ride on the motorcycle …'

Her mother was horrified. 'Oh no, Mr Mallory, not that dangerous thing. A walk through the village is more in keeping. Our neighbours can keep an eye on you both then.' She began to tidy away the teacups. 'We are grateful you are here to help liberate Europe—'

'Thank you, ma'am, I—'

'*—but* …' she said straightening with a teacup in each hand, 'you are a stranger and I have only just met you. It will take a few more visits before I entrust you with my only daughter … war or no war.'

'Do you think that was an invitation to visit again?' teased Joe as they stepped out into the sunshine. Anne watched as he slid his cap onto his head in a well-practised, precise manner. His optimism was endearing, but hopelessly wrong.

'No. Her daughter dating a service man is my mother's nightmare.' *It's mine too*. 'We know people who've died in the war and she also experienced it in the Great War. She doesn't want me to get hurt.'

'And what's your excuse?'

'My excuse?'

He tilted his head to look at her. 'For not dating a soldier.'

She shrugged. 'There seems little point.'

'There's a lot of point.'

'Why date when it might never lead anywhere?'

'Having some fun is the point.'

'Are you having fun? It didn't seem like it to me when I heard you being grilled by my mother.'

'Your mother is a skilled questioner; I'll give her that. She would make a great spy.'

Anne threw him a mock reprimand glance. 'You shouldn't make jokes about spying. Someone might hear you and report it.'

Joe whistled. 'I can see there's a lot more to get used to in England than I was expecting. Dating an English girl is more confusing than I thought.' They walked on in silence. 'Is this a date, then?'

She stopped to look at him, confused.

'You didn't correct me when I said we were dating.'

Anne tried to recall the conversation, then realised he was smiling at her. She would have to get used to his teasing if they were going to last the afternoon.

'This is not a date,' she confirmed, firmly.

They fell into step, following the lane that would take them through the village.

'I got to admit, setting up a date is usually easier than this one was,' said Joe, snatching a blade of grass from the hedge.

'That's because it isn't a date.'

'If it weren't for your pal spilling the beans, I'd never have found you. Although it took me two days to discover Carrick Roads isn't a road, King Harry isn't a bar and there isn't a village called Free Hock. And do you know how many houses have River in their name?'

'Lots. And the village is called Feock, not Free Hock.'

'Damn. That explains the crazy looks I got when I asked for directions!' He peeled the outer skin from the grass and popped the succulent end into the corner of his mouth. 'Your friend's directions helped, but I wouldn't use her skills of navigation to plan an invasion. We'd end up back where we started.'

Anne laughed. 'Betty shouldn't have told you anything at all.'

'But you're glad she did, aren't you?'

'I wasn't when she told me what she'd done.'

'And now?'

Anne threw him a sideways glance to find his smiling eyes coaxing her for some encouragement. 'Maybe.'

'More than maybe. I saw you down tools. Did you sneak into the back of the house to change?'

Anne stopped walking, horrified. 'You saw me?'

Joe turned to look at her. 'I wasn't sure it was you … until now.'

Joe had outfoxed her. Anne pretended she didn't care and shrugged. 'I felt I had little choice. You caught me by surprise as I didn't really think you would drive out to see me.'

'We could turn back if you like?' he offered, smiling. 'I wouldn't want my visit to spoil your day.'

Anne wrapped her cardigan around her and pretended to consider the offer. As the seconds ticked by his teasing smile faded.

'Although I'd happily follow a whole book of clues if I knew it was what you wanted me to do.'

He really did have all the Hollywood lines to go along with the Hollywood looks, thought Anne. His dark, warm eyes studied her as he waited, showing her a glimpse of vulnerability beneath that brash, confident exterior.

'No, there's no need to turn back.'

His smile returned – the relaxed, broad one which showed a row of perfect white teeth. The one that made her smile too and threatened to ignite something inside. She felt herself grow taller at the thought.

They fell into a steady walk, following a path lined by overgrown hedges bursting with towering foxgloves, red delicate campions and cheeky white daisies as they jostled for space. Anne plucked a flower from the hedgerow, nipped off a leaf and popped it into her mouth. To Joe's questioning look she offered him one.

'It's soursob. Sweets are on ration so the children like to eat this instead. It tastes nice.'

Joe held up a hand. 'No offence, but I think I'll give it a miss.'

'What's your home like?'

'Not like England, that's for sure.' At first, she thought he wasn't going to reveal any more, but her silence coaxed it out of him. 'I come from Baltimore City, that's in Maryland.' Anne wasn't sure where Maryland was. She tried to recall the world map on her old classroom wall.

'What's it like?'

'Busy. Large. Wider streets. Taller buildings. It's different . . .' He gave a hollow laugh, 'not like Cornwall at all.'

'Do you miss it?'

'Yeah, sure. At least there I could get a cold beer.'

Anne felt Joe was holding something back but didn't like to pry. Silence fell. They followed the path onto the narrow road which cut through the village and found they were no longer alone. Joe's uniform caught the villagers' attention as they passed the houses lining the street. Mr Rowe, the old man digging in his garden, lifted his gaze and paused to watch them pass. Mrs Piper, a housewife and grandmother, with her basket cradled in the crook of her arm, studied them briefly before stepping inside her daughter's house. The boy who lived at the top of the village, followed them on his bike until Joe eventually told him he was 'All out of gum'.

'I feel like an oddity, which is kinda strange since there are hundreds of us here and there'll be more to come.'

'Hush! Careless talk, haven't you seen the posters?'

Joe glanced at an old woman scrubbing a doorstep. 'She doesn't look like a spy.'

Anne felt herself bristle. She'd been living under the threat of invasion for four years and Joe seemed to be making light of it. However, she resisted snapping at him. He was new to Cornwall and politeness held her in check. Instead, she decided to change the subject.

'Where did you get your motorcycle?'

'I bought it from Tower's Garage in Falmouth.'

'For how much?'

Joe told her.

'You were cheated. Albert has had it for sale for months … at a cheaper price.'

'Damn. He saw the overpaid Yank coming.' They'd reached the top of the hill, with the village, and its mismatched cottages, spread out behind them. In front lay a road lined by a mixture of lush green grass and brown ploughed fields. 'I just can't get my head around the currency,' said Joe stopping to admire the view. He looked at her. 'It might be a heap of junk, but it's my heap of junk.' He smiled. 'I reckon the price was worth it.'

His remark hung in the air between them, a tantalising vision of what could be. He was glad he'd found her … and, as her throat grew dry and her lips grew tender, she finally had to admit, even if it was just to herself, that she was too.

She turned to look at Falmouth in the distance, its barrage balloons floating above the harbour and streets like silent, airborne guardians. He continued to watch her; she could feel it setting off her heart to pummel wildly in her chest. But it didn't stay there. The throbbing sent a surge of sensations coursing through her. And the feeling only intensified, as she came to feel it in every part of her; her neck, her wrists, her legs, until it turned to liquid sensations deep down inside her.

'Mother says the balloons stop Britain from sinking,' she said, brushing her face free from a stray strand of hair. Her hand accidently touched his sleeve as she lowered it. She hadn't realised he was standing so close. 'Sorry.'

'Shall we take off?'

'Take off?' she asked, looking at him. 'But they aren't that sort of balloon.'

Joe smiled down at her. 'I mean let's get out of here.' Joe jerked his head towards a house. 'Away from the Apron and Curlers Brigade.'

Anne followed his gaze. Two middle-aged women from the Women's Voluntary Service were staring at them. She could see what Joe meant. Standing by their garden fence, with sleeves rolled up, arms tightly folded across their ample chests and sharp elbows jutting out on either side, the two women were a formidable sight, despite their curlers.

'They're talking about us out of the corners of their mouths.'

Anne stifled a giggle. 'They mean well. They just care about me.'

'Is that a no to our escape, then?'

'Maybe …' She glanced at him. 'Maybe not.'

They continued their walk, their steps in time, both wearing a nonchalant expression on their faces – but it was all an act. As soon as they turned the corner and were out of view, Joe grabbed her hand.

'So where are you taking me?' asked Joe.

Anne thought wildly for a place to go. 'We could visit the river by cutting across the fields and wood.'

'And see the famous Carrick Roads alone with you. Will I be safe?' He tugged at her hand, eager to go.

She resisted. 'Are you ever serious?'

Joe sobered. 'I have never been more serious in my life.'

Minutes later, they were climbing over a stone stile in the hedge. Joe offered his hand to help her down the other side. Anne accepted his help, although she'd climbed it a hundred times before. They followed the boundary of the hedge down the hill towards the river. Butterflies danced across the flowers, noisy thrushes fed on dogwood berries lining the hedges, but Anne didn't notice. Joe's hand was still warm and firm in hers as he hadn't let her go. A dense wood framed the banks of the wide, tranquil river. They stepped into its shadows and carefully stepped over the bed of soil, twigs and decaying leaves. The earthy bank, knotted with tufts of wild grass and exposed roots, fell away sharply to the waters' lapping edge. They stood side by side in a small clearing and watched a flock of seagulls flying after a small rowing boat. Eventually the boat landed near the small beach nearby, where it was dragged up the pebbly shore to be stored with four others. It was a beautiful tranquil scene, if it wasn't for the American amphibious landing craft harboured on the other side.

'You have gulls too,' said Joe, surprised.

'Yes. Cornwall has a lot. They like our coast, fishing and ploughed fields.'

Joe frowned. 'They look like Herring Gulls.'

His observation surprised her. 'Do you know a lot about birds?'

He shrugged. 'No, not really. They interested me more when I was a kid. Probably because they looked … so free.'

His remark warranted more questions, but they would all be too intrusive for a man she barely knew. Instead she opted to play safe. 'Is that the ship that will take you?'

'Maybe, maybe not.'

She wanted to ask if he was scared, but the deep furrow between his brows told her it was a subject he'd rather not think about. He suddenly realised she was watching him and his face brightened.

'Hey, can you hear that? Someone is playing music. I think it's coming from the landing craft.'

Anne dragged her gaze away from Joe's face and across the blue sheet of water, glistening in the afternoon sun. The large landing craft, marked with *US* in white lettering, was formidable and unmoving, but lifting on the breeze from somewhere in its depths were the swinging notes of playful saxophones and trombones. A chorus of male voices sang, or rather shouted out, in timely, bonding unison, the words 'Pennsylvania, six, five-thousand.'

'Glenn Miller's great. Do you wanna dance?'

Anne laughed at Joe's suggestion. 'What here?'

'Why not? I'll teach you how we dance in the States.'

Anne haltingly nodded; after all she was running out of ideas on how to entertain him and the afternoon was still young.

Joe took both her hands. 'Feel the beat by just walking on the spot first.' Anne, feeling self-conscious and afraid of looking stupid, watched Joe tread the same spot in the earth, but a mixture of upbeat music and simple steps soon coaxed her to join in. 'That's it,' he said as she stiffly copied his rhythm. 'I can see you're going to be a natural.'

Anne wasn't so sure. Since the war started, a waltz was the only dance she'd learnt. Conscription hadn't helped, drastically reducing the number of dance partners available so she had to make do with Betty and take the male lead at any dances put on to raise funds for the war effort. She had a sinking feeling that those steps wouldn't help her now.

'And now step this way,' said Joe, stepping to the side and back again, while at the same time encouraging her to do the same with a gentle tug on her hands. She did so, belatedly, but by the third attempt she'd picked up the rhythm enough to do the steps with him.

'And now back,' prompted Joe taking a step back and stretching the space between them before squeezing it away as he stepped forward. She noticed he was holding her closer this time, his right hand slipping naturally behind her waist to graze the hem of her cardigan. She could feel the light pressure of his hand permeating through her dress and slip, to her heated sensitive skin beneath.

The pleasant sensation didn't last long, before their arms stretched away as they both stepped back suddenly. 'That's good, that's good,' he praised. Anne smiled back at him, her confidence growing by the second.

'Let's try a kick now.' They did. 'Now pass behind me, like this.' Anne followed his lead as he passed her hand from his left to his right behind his back. Suddenly they were facing each other again, repeating the same sideways and backward steps he'd previously taught her. 'I think you are ready for a twirl.'

'A wha—?'

Before she could finish, he was turning her around under the umbrella of their clasped hands. She faltered, feeling stiff and uncoordinated suddenly, but he didn't seem to care.

'That's it. You're really good!'

Anne stopped and stepped back. 'No, I'm not. That was terrible.' She reached for his hands. 'Let's try that step again. I want to do better.'

Joe's smile broadened. 'Now that sounds like fighting talk.'

As the brass notes of the swing band continued across the water, Anne's confidence grew, along with the swing of her hips and the complexity of their moves. She even joined in with Joe, the ship's crew and Glenn Miller's Orchestra by shouting out the chorus words 'Pennsylvania six, five-thousand!' When the music finally came to an end, she almost felt bereft. They slowed to a halt staring at each other, unwilling to let go, yet not quite knowing what to do next. When the loud trumpet call, signalling the start of "In the Mood", pierced the silence, they laughed with relief that the music hadn't stopped.

More experienced, relaxed and willing to just enjoy the moment, Anne needed no coaxing to dance this time. The beat was faster but it didn't matter. The moves seemed to come naturally to her now, each additional twirl or exchange of position requiring no direction or warning as, somehow, she instinctively understood him as he did her.

Soon they were laughing, teasing, twirling and joking; two young people enjoying the summer sun on the banks of Carrick Roads. For the first time she was experiencing something fun which was beyond the confines of Cornwall; something that the war had threatened to deny her, yet strangely had brought to her door. She was having fun again, the war briefly forgotten, as she learnt to swing dance with a handsome American, named Joe.

Several more tunes continued, all upbeat and perfect for their dance, but their steps gradually slowed as the minutes ticked by. He began to hold her a little closer, his breath fanning her hair. Their twirls had somehow changed too, morphing into gentle, slow turns, their linked hands above lowering to form a spiral of a protective embrace. Eventually they were not dancing at all, just swaying gently in each other's arms, the up-tempo distant music now a quiet backdrop to the sound of her beating heart. She looked up to find him looking at her lips and she knew without a doubt what he was thinking. He wanted to kiss her. She wanted him to, too. She waited, her breath catching in her throat, eager, yet terrified he would be disappointed in some way. He stepped away from her.

'I think we should be getting back. Your mother will be worried. Especially if someone in the village has told her I've taken you over a stile … I mean taken you away from the village.' He looked flustered. Was he embarrassed that he'd been caught wanting a kiss or did he just want to end the date and get back to his friends? Confused, Anne agreed.

They retraced their steps to her home, talking little and of nothing of importance. Finally, they reached her door. She turned to him. So, this was how they were going to say goodbye, with her mother probably peering out the window and her brother hiding somewhere in the bushes, aiming his catapult at them. Joe slipped his cap off his head and began to examine it in his hands.

'Morale has been pretty bad lately and Uncle Charlie has given new orders—'

Anne frowned. 'Uncle Charlie?'

He glanced up. 'Our nickname for Major General Gerhardt, the new commander of the 29th. He's strict. Tough. Likes things done his way. God help you if he catches you with your chin strap undone.' He seemed to realise he was rambling. 'Anyway, as I said, morale amongst the troops has been down. Seven days training a week gets a bit much, and those bloody moors aren't …' He realised he'd sworn. 'Sorry. Didn't mean to be disrespectful.'

Anne noticed he'd begun to turn his cap in his hands again. She'd not seen this side of Joe before. Unsure. Nervous. Less confident than her.

'Anyways, apart from insisting we learn to swim, although how swimming is going to help us when we're carrying our packs on our backs … packs which are heavy enough to sink any soldier above chest deep.' He must have noticed the growing horror on her face for he quickly added, 'Oh I'll be alright. I can swim, just a bit rusty and need more practice. What I mean to say is … I mean what I want to say, no tell you, is that he's given us three rest days a week. Done our spirits no end of good, I can tell you. It means I have more free time and …'

'And what?'

'I'd like to spend it with you.' Anne stared at him. '… if you're okay with that, of course.'

Anne felt a rush of relief sweep through her, sapping her muscles of the tension that had been building. She'd thought he was building up to say goodbye for good, not asking to see her more. As a woman who didn't date soldiers, she shouldn't care. However, perhaps there was another reason to date than being the only method to find the right husband. Perhaps the point of dating could be just fun after all.

She took a deep breath to calm herself. One date wouldn't hurt, although it wouldn't be right to look too eager.

'I'd like that,' she said, smiling shyly. 'We could go swimming next time. I know a good bay where you can brush up on your swimming. I used to go there in the school holidays.'

'Will you be joining me … in the water?'

'Of course.'

'Then that sounds like heaven to me,' said Joe, replacing his cap. 'So, when are you next free?'

Anne watched Joe ride away, waiting until she could no longer hear his noisy engine floating towards her from beyond the trees. A trail of black smoke still lingered in the air, ceremonially belched from a motorcycle which had seen better days and which he'd just officially named *Heapojunk*. Anne jauntily twisted on her heel and entered her house. She halted in surprise in the kitchen. Her stepfather was sitting at the table, talking to a solidly built, American soldier, who sat beside him. The man immediately stood to greet her.

'This is my daughter, Anne,' said her stepfather proudly. 'This is George. Billy and I had trouble with the cart and George came over to help, so I invited him home for tea.'

'There was no need to, sir. I was happy to oblige.' The soldier looked at Anne, immediately dropping his gaze to the floor at her feet. 'Nice to meet you, ma'am,' he added quietly in his deep southern drawl.

Anne smiled and returned the greeting. From his bowed head she had a suspicion he would rather be anywhere but with them. His nervousness, and quick, watchful glances, gave her the impression he was waiting for something to happen.

Her stepfather encouraged him to sit down again with a flap of his hand. 'There's no need to call us sir and ma'am. We're not royalty.'

Despite his reassurance, the soldier remained wary, lowering himself slowly into his chair but remaining stiff and straight-backed.

'What's the matter, we don't bite,' teased her stepfather.

'Begging your pardon, sir,' apologised George, 'but I've never been allowed to address white folk by not saying ma'am or sir.'

The admission temporarily stunned her stepfather to silence. He quickly rallied. 'Well, you're in England now, son, and we do things differently here.' He looked up. 'Ahh! Looks like tea is ready.'

All heads turned as Anne's mother came in with a tray of sandwiches and five dishes. Each serving had two slices of tinned fruit, lavishly coated with cream to fill out the serving.

Billy proudly followed. 'The fruit is from me,' he said, sitting next to George and staring at him in awe. 'What's it like? America, I mean. Do you miss it?'

'It doesn't rain so much where I come from. And I miss my wife and daughter. She was born last fall.'

'Does your wife fall down often?' asked her mother.

George frowned, slightly confused. 'No.'

'How old is your daughter?' asked Anne.

'Almost one. My wife thinks it won't be long until she's standing.'

'You must miss them both very much,' said Anne's mother as she offered him a sandwich.

He praised the food, carefully selected one and politely thanked her. He stared at the egg sandwich, causing Anne and her mother to exchange glances. The national wholemeal bread recipe, which the government insisted all bakeries now made, was still an acquired taste. Perhaps he didn't like the look of it. At least the eggs were fresh as they'd collected them from their neighbour only this morning.

'Is everything all right, George?' her mother asked.

George released a shuddering breath. 'You folks are being so kind. You all makes me think of my own family. And whenever I do,' he said, swallowing down his regret, 'it feels as if my heart will weep even more tears than it did the day before.'

George stayed for two hours. By the end of the evening they'd all fallen in love with him. Kind, courteous and a skilled storyteller, his humorous tales from his childhood had them laughing around the table most of the evening. 'I'm telling you all, a boy can run fast when he's dodging his mother's wrath and a whippin' from his father. Never stole an egg again'—he winked at Billy—'at leastways not on a Sunday.'

'Did your father whip you a lot?' asked Billy, intrigued.

George smiled sadly. 'Never. The threat was always there and it was enough to stop us boys misbehaving. There were others who used it, though. But I have come to believe that unjust punishment will only breed resentment and that applies to all ages, be it man or boy.'

It was only later, as Anne settled under her blankets, did she wonder why George had been so wary of them in the beginning and who was he talking about at the end.

Chapter Eight

Overgrown hedgerows, peppered with rich summer flowers, hugged the narrow Cornish lane from either side. The peach coloured honeysuckle blooms, vibrant yellow buttercups and proud purple foxgloves, with their hanging trumpet flowers, merged into one continuous splash of colour as Joe navigated the twists and turns on his motorcycle. Fortunately, thanks to some concentrated effort and a promise of a beer, Marty from his company had fixed the engine so it no longer left a stream of black smoke rising in the air behind him. Now he was able to arrive and conceal his banned motorcycle, without raising Anne's mother's polite, but overly protective, bloodhound senses.

Joe pulled into a gateway and stopped, kicking the stand out from underneath with a well-practiced flick of his boot. He rocked the motorcycle onto it and looked out onto the field on the other side of the low hedge, carpeted with innocent white daisies with their yellow centres facing the sky. *Damn! England was quaint!*

He'd been looking forward to seeing Anne ever since he waved her goodbye and what better way to spend a hot summer afternoon than brushing up on his swimming skills, not that he needed to as the army had arranged visits to the local, freezing cold, swimming pools for the troops to practice. If you didn't learn to swim, you were out, simple as that. However, he wasn't going to let on about those swimming trips to Anne and miss out on seeing her again. Especially if she was going to wear a bathing suit too.

The front door opened before he reached it. Anne stepped out. Joe felt a pleasant jolt in his chest as she turned her fresh smile upon him.

'Has anyone ever told you you're very pretty?' he murmured as she approached. A light blush coloured her cheeks, making him smile. Her soft curls bounced as she turned briefly to call out a goodbye to her mother and swung obediently back into place as she looked at him. She was picture-perfect, with her pin-up poster cute face and a rose-kissed complexion just ripe for kissing. But he would hold off. Best not rush. He didn't want his first attempt, and maybe his only chance, to be shot down because he'd moved too fast. She was worth the wait and he was in it for the long haul – however long that long haul lasted. Why waste time trying to pick up other English girls when one checked all the boxes?

'Hi.'

'Hi to you too,' said Anne, smiling.

Joe realised the smile she was flashing at him was going to make it a whole lot harder to stay as cool as he wanted.

'Got your swimsuit, hun?'

'You don't need to use your American sweet-talk on me. And yes, I do. Where did you park your motorbike?'

He frowned. 'Around the corner.' He hurried after her. 'Can't say I know what you mean?'

'Babe. Hun. Sweetheart. Sugar. Women aren't confectionary or children.'

He watched her hips swinging gracefully in front of him with each step. He wanted to disagree with her. She was as sweet and tempting as candy to his eyes, *and* he had the urge to protect her. It would make a pleasant change. He spent most of his time cheek by jowl with dirty-mouthed men who had no manners. He suspected he was no different. A guy only realises how lapse they have become when a lady steps into the room. Nothing got the Blues and Grays to stop lounging, cool the swearing and clean up the innuendo like the presence of a pretty lady. Yet despite all this, his way of talking might seem a bit … brash to an English woman.

'I meant no offence. I just thought—'

'Oh, you haven't offended me.' She stopped and turned to face him, as if she was waiting for someone. He realised who. They'd reached his motorcycle, and she was waiting for him.

He searched for the key. 'Are you trying to confuse me? Only you're saying one thing, but your expression is saying something else.'

She tilted her head to one side to study him.

He found the key and indicated towards her with a quick nod of his head. 'There's a definite twinkle in that eye.'

'Only one?'

'Now you come to mention it …'

'All I'm saying is that your way of talking is different.'

Yes, there was a definite twinkle in both eyes, thought Joe; in fact they were almost smiling at him, even if her full lips weren't. For someone who didn't date, she knew how to keep a guy on his toes.

'Different … as in a good way?' he asked, as he climbed on his motorcycle.

She finally smiled. 'Yes … in a good way.'

The tautness in his shoulders fell away and his heart lifted. For the first time he felt he was nailing this walking out lark with her. She was definitely flirting. He would take that.

Anne arched an eyebrow at him. 'Just don't overdo it, Joe Mallory. Quality not quantity is always best.' If it weren't for the twinkle still lingering in her deep blue eyes, he would have thought he'd blown it.

He rocked the motorcycle off its stand and flicked it upwards out of sight. 'I can see I'm going to have to raise my game with you.'

Silence fell at the implication of his words. He'd practically laid his cards on the table. He wanted more than a couple of dates. He wanted to stay around. Yet somehow, he didn't mind her knowing. She looked at him, absorbing each detail in his eyes, as he was with her. A primal attempt to examine a little deeper the new interloper in one's life. To discover who they really were. The other person's character, trustworthiness, past and hopes for the future.

An array of questions rose in the ether between them, far too many to ask and answer on one summer's afternoon in the midst of a war. He was tempted to find out all about her, but the future was uncertain … they could be parted in the blink of an eye. He must not think too far ahead. He must only think of today. And today, he'd glimpsed her sassy side and liked what he saw.

'We better go,' she murmured, breaking away first. 'I said I'd be back for tea.'

Suddenly he was back in the here and now, not an unknown hour ahead, or a day, or a year. Here, now, with her. He kicked the motorcycle peddle and the engine roared into life.

'Climb on.'

Anne briefly hesitated, before climbing on behind him. He felt her place her bag between them, nestle up against his body and wrap her arms around his waist in a comforting embrace.

'Have you ever been on one of these before?' he asked over his shoulder, enjoying the necessary closeness of her body next to his.

'Never, but I've held onto a tailgate of a moving lorry while on my bicycle,' she replied matter-of-factly as she repositioned her bag. 'It's the best way to cycle uphill.'

Joe found himself laughing as they pulled away. Sassy, brave and a little bit crazy. Why did Anne's reply not surprise him any more?

Conscious of her warm body hugging his and her mantra of quality rather than quantity still running through his mind, he refrained from showing off, but drove carefully and steadily along the narrow back roads. She had defied her mother's concerns about riding on his motorcycle and had placed her trust in him – a foreigner she barely knew, and he wanted nothing more than to keep that trust. *Her* trust, inexplicably, made him feel ten foot tall. It was not a familiar feeling to have. It was something the army was trying to drill into them. Trust. Trust your superiors. Trust your army buddies. Trust America will win. But Anne trusted *him*. A guy she hardly knew from Baltimore. And it felt good.

Anne shouted directions to her favourite bay, her words so quickly snatched by the passing wind that he had to concentrate. Their communication reminded him of his navigation training on the damp, dark moors where instructions were understood, confirmed and accepted within a blink of an eye. Yet most of the journey was in silence, the war and his fractured family all but forgotten, as he enjoyed the freedom of driving in the countryside, with the wind raking their bodies. Glorious views of lush green fields, scattered with a patchwork of swaying golden harvests still ripening in the blazing sun, added to the contentment flooding through him. And he knew Anne must be feeling the magic too, as her body gradually softened against him with each mile that passed.

The roads were quiet, except for a group of young men. They stood out from the usual land workers. These were fighting age, but instead of guns they held pitchforks and large square-shaped spades. Anne let go with one hand and waved at them. They saw her, their faces breaking into smiles as they waved back. He didn't blame them; he would have waved too if greeted by a pretty young woman with her hair flying in the rushing wind. He felt no jealousy. Anne waving, and their returning smiles, didn't change the fact that Anne was with him and not them.

Joe parked the motorcycle where Anne indicated and they both climbed off. The hidden cove below was one of Anne's favourite bays. It emerged gradually as they descended the narrow path cut through the rocky cliff, its beauty and uniqueness unfurling to his eyes like the petals of an exotic flower. They'd planned to visit another bay, but were quickly reminded that the larger beaches, with good road access, were not only considered beautiful, but vulnerable to invasion. Access points had been blocked with scaffolding and rolls of concertina barbed wire, while the more exposed sandy beaches were scarred by grotesque alien military defences to prevent potential enemy attack. However, this hidden secluded bay, Anne's secret oasis, appeared untouched. The perfect place to forget the war and hide from the ugliness of the world. It was as if mother nature herself, in her eagerness to steal some Cornish soil, had reached out and grasped a fistful of coast and dragged it away, leaving behind a deep, secluded bay, carpeted with pebbled sand. This was the place a lonely child, seeking comfort from his father's coldness, would have longed for if he only knew it existed. A place to escape to, learn to swim in safety and have the peace and freedom to just be himself. Unable to access the more public beach nearby, Anne had shared her secret cove more out of necessity than a plan. It was the perfect spot for lovers, as it was shielded from the westerly winds and had tempting sapphire blue waters waiting to gently lap at young thighs. She seemed almost embarrassed by the seclusion. He found her reaction endearing, as he silently celebrated the isolation.

They claimed their own perfect spot, near a rock. It provided both shelter and a smooth place to lie rather than the wet, recently exposed sand from the outgoing tide. Anne wanted to just watch, but he persuaded her to change into her bathing suit too. It seemed hardly fair, he told her, if he was going to change alone. She finally relented. Contorting under threadbare towels, they changed into their bathing suits and headed down the gently sloping beach, where the deceptively cold, and initially shallow water, eventually deepened to surround them.

Anne's vibrant blue one piece matched her eyes and the sea, reminding Joe of the morale boosting pin-ups which had been painted on the fuselages of the Air Force's aircraft. He tried not to stare, dragging his eyes away from her, time after time, yet he always found himself drawn back to her, as she laughed and twisted away from each gentle wave. He advanced into the water further, enticing her forward, so the water surface rose higher to circle her waist. The water rose and fell around her, caressing her hips, as if it had a breath of its own. Anne refused to go deeper, so he swam for a bit then returned to her, teasing, circling and encouraging her to swim.

'I can't,' she finally confessed. 'I came here for you to practice. But you are good. You don't need to!'

'I'm rusty.'

'But better than me.'

He swam towards her, found his foothold and rose up through the water to stand before her.

'You're too tense, you need to chill.'

Her body twisted as she thrust her hip against the incoming, gentle wave. 'Chill? I'm already chilled. It's colder than I was expecting.'

He found himself smiling as he watched her gnawing her bottom lip. *Damn she was cute.*

'If you just go with it the coldness will go away. Lie on your back and relax. If you rest your head back, you'll float. I promise.'

Anne looked doubtful.

'I'll hold you,' he coaxed. 'Everyone learns front stroke first, but I think back stroke is easier.'

He placed a hand behind her neck without thinking and her body grew rigid. 'It's okay. I'll just hold you here and maybe in the small of your back. Lean back …'

Anne pulled away, embarrassed – even scared, he couldn't quite tell. His hand momentarily lingered in the air, grieving the loss of the warmth of her skin.

'I almost drowned as a child,' she explained, embarrassed. 'I don't like it when I can't touch the ground with my feet.'

Another side to her. Vulnerable Anne.

'But it will be okay. I'll be holding you.'

She thrust out her chin. Stubborn Anne. Her face an open book for him to read and learn from.

'It's okay,' he said softly. 'I won't make you.'

A small crease developed between her brows. Uncertain Anne.

'I'll never make you do anything you're not ready to do.'

She dared to look at him, checking his sincerity with a sharp intensive glance.

'I'm sorry,' she muttered miserably. 'You must think me a terrible coward.'

'I'd never think that. Some things are best not rushed.' And he meant that. Especially where Anne was concerned. Her body softened. She believed him. 'You're looking cold. You've got goose bumps. Let's climb up on that rock and soak up some rays.'

They emerged from the water, climbing up onto razor sharp rocks, crowned with lush green fields above. They lay for some minutes in an invisible pool of warmth, as the droplets of saltwater on their skin dried one by one in the sun.

Eventually the ocean chill was successfully chased away, leaving limbs and thoughts languid, and minds free to listen to the symphony of the coast. Pebbles were the percussion as they rolled onto the beach. The sea was the string, as each wave, growing louder and in size, strummed across the water's surface to take centre stage. The gulls' caws the woodwind, screeching notes high and low, while a child's far-off laughter reminded Joe of the joyful unpredictable notes of a brass piccolo trumpet.

He turned on his side, rested on his elbow and looked down on Anne's closed eyes. Her soft, full lips turned up at the corners telling him she knew he was watching her … but didn't mind.

'You're pretty.' The colour of a pale rose bloomed on her cheeks. 'You're blushing again. Surely, fellas have told you that before?'

'Only you.' She opened one eye. 'Twice.' She closed it again. 'English boys are—'

'Stupid to not notice?'

' —more reserved.'

He watched her for a full minute, his gaze trailing along her lashes, the slope of her nose, the outline of her lips. 'Those guys you waved at weren't too reserved to wave back.'

'That's because they're German.' When he didn't reply, she threw him a glance. His expression must have showed his thoughts, for she burst out laughing as she turned her face towards the rays of the sun. 'They're prisoners of war put to work on the land.'

'Aren't folks worried they'll escape?'

Anne shielded her eyes with her hand and looked up at him again. 'Where would they go? Back to the war? They know they're better off here. They're content to wait for the war to end. They know that at least they'll have a chance of being alive at the end of it. Then they'll go home.'

Silence fell.

'I'm sorry. I didn't mean to—'

He waved her concern away. 'It's okay. I don't intend getting killed.' Only a few minutes before they'd been listening to the symphony of the sea and the war was all but forgotten. A distant war that made no sense. Even now there were guys back at camp who didn't understand why they were even here at all. Japan had attacked them, so why fight in Europe?

'What's America like?' Her words dragged him back to the here and now. He lay on his back as she turned to face him, mirroring the position he'd held only moments before.

He closed his eyes. 'Too big for me to be able to answer. I only know the part I grew up in.'

She nudged him. 'The part you come from then. What's it called?'

'Baltimore.'

'Where's that?'

'I told you, in the state of Maryland.'

'Where is the state of Maryland?' He opened his eyes to look at her. Didn't everyone know the states of America? A pair of earnest eyes, framed with a concentrated frown, stared down at him, waiting for an answer. Realisation dawned on him that his knowledge of England was no better. He hadn't known there was another "Cornwall". He thought there was only one, a town in Orange County he'd no desire to visit. Now he knew there was another. Anne's world. He smiled at her; how could he not?

'Maryland is on the mid-east coast and surrounds Chesapeake Bay, which is an estuary, just like Carrick Roads … only bigger. A lot bigger.' He closed his eyes again to bask in the warmth of the sun.

'What's Baltimore like?'

'Busy. Tall. Louder than here.' He felt her hand nudge him. 'What?' he asked in mock indignation.

'You're infuriating!'

'Is that a quaint English saying for "I think you're amazing"?'

'No, it is not!' She wriggled herself back against a rock and folded her arms mutinously as she stared out to sea.

'Now you're angry with me.' When she didn't reply, he tried not to break into a smile.

'Okay, okay.' He moved to sit next to her. 'I'll tell you about Baltimore.' He searched his memory for what to say. How do you describe something that's all you've ever known?

Start at the beginning, before his mom had died. Before his older brother left. His first home was in the leafy suburbs of the great city. Memories of playing baseball in their white picket fenced garden came flooding back. Michael teaching him to pitch with a glove far too big. His wisecracking neighbour and his equally wisecracking son, who's sister seemed to swing constantly on their creaking veranda swing. His mother smiling at him as she poured lemonade, with its homemade zesty kick, from her favourite white pitcher. Her sweet-smelling, soft kiss on his forehead, before she wished him goodnight and turned out the light. His visits to the centre of Baltimore, with his brother, to watch ships in the harbour. He'd been so young that he could only peep through the railings that towered above him. Then one day, in their garden full of flowers, his mother sat her sons down, poured lemonade from the same white pitcher and told them she had cancer and wouldn't live to see the end of the fall.

Everything had changed after her death. Everything.

'Father moved us from the neighbourly suburbs to the city.' His gut heaved at the memory, as it had done a thousand times before. 'The apartment was closer to his work but away from my friends.' The isolation he'd felt swept over him all over again. It felt as raw now as all those years ago. Too raw.

'Losing your mother and your friends must have been difficult for you.'

Anne's voice felt like a smoothing balm. 'Yeah. Like a Chimney Swift fledgling on a city sidewalk,' he murmured, thoughtfully. Time to retreat from that dark subject and try a lighter one – the holidays. 'Every Christmas, the wide-open streets are packed with people, everyone carrying packages and scurrying like ants. But it's always busy in Baltimore. Lots to do and buy.' He shared his memories of the streetcars, crammed with people hanging from brown leather straps, trundling beneath wires as they threaded the streets. How sidewalks were as wide as a narrow Cornish lane, and how the shops had large glass windows and were fit to burst with goods. And how at night, from his father's office, he could see most of Baltimore; a grid of blocks, carved by streets, each district unique with its own history, problems and successes. And how, as night fell, tower-block windows lit up like toys, casting their warm illuminations across the deep harbour water, while keeping the secrets of the lives inside. They stood silently and proud, as if waiting – almost daring for a giant to walk amongst them and tear the city to bits. And how the skyline waited in shadow against the distant dark sky, waiting and observing the madness beneath. And how, at such a young age, he realised he didn't know his father at all.

The confession came before he had a chance to censor it, breaking out, like a captive free at last. And, strangely, it felt only natural to explain a little more, perhaps hoping to recapture the confession and put it back in its box. Yet, he soon realised that the more he spilled his guts, it was he who felt freer, for Anne's non-judgemental silence allowed him the space to relive it.

‘My father was a cold man. *Is* a cold man. As a kid I accepted it. I knew he wouldn’t be that proud dad cheering in the crowd when his son hit his first homerun for the school. I knew he’d be too busy to attend the end-of-year school play. I knew he didn’t like his home, *our* home, to be filled with other people’s kids, so I didn’t invite any pals home. It was just how things were. But it still felt wrong. It felt as if I was wrong. Wrong for him. Not the son he wanted. He already had Michael. He didn’t change, not even when Michael left. I thought, if I was more like Michael, perhaps … At least that’s what I thought then.’

‘But you don’t any more?’

‘No, I don’t.’

‘What changed?’

‘I learnt that even a man like my brother has his flaws.’ He turned his head to look at her. ‘It took me a few more years to realise that it’s best to be your own person rather than rely on someone else’s ability, or inability, to love you.’ He turned away from the concern on her face and stared out to sea. ‘I remember the very day I came to that conclusion. I was on the verge of graduating from law school. I walked into my father’s office and told him something … and he did nothing.’ He shook his head at the memory. ‘He didn’t try to change my mind or show any pride. He simply did nothing … and that was when I knew.’

‘Knew what?’

‘That no matter what I did or said, we’d never have that father and son relationship I always wanted. And that I no longer wanted to keep trying to achieve it.’

Anne lay her hand on his arm. ‘What did you tell him, Joe?’

‘That I was going to war. That I’d signed up and would never come back.’

He turned his head to look at Anne and saw the glistening sheen in her eyes that had been so blaringly absent in his father’s.

‘I had even prepared a speech which included principled phrases such as fighting for freedom, be Britain’s ally, doing the right thing – I think the truth was less brave and heroic. After that I went home and packed my things. Stayed with a buddy for a short while. Entered the army the day after graduating.’ He smiled broadly to lighten the mood. ‘So here I am. A soldier in Company B, 175th regiment of the 29th Division.’

‘Sounds confusing. Explain it to me.’

‘Nah.’ He glanced at her and realised she was serious. Her interest surprised him and his sudden desire to teach her even more so. ‘Well’—he lifted his hand as if he was pointing to a graph in the sky—‘there’s a squad, maybe four to ten soldiers. Above that is a platoon, which is made up of … I dunno, maybe up to forty soldiers.’ His hand swept upwards. ‘Above that is a company, made up of probably three to five platoons. Above the company is a battalion … made up of probably four to six companies. Then there’s a brigade …’

‘Made up of three to five battalions?’

He smiled at her. ‘Yes. Or maybe two to five.’ Near the top is a division. In my case the 29th. Which is made up of three brigades.’

‘The army is quite a machine.’

‘Which is probably why we’ve a nickname for our division. The Blues and Grays after the blue uniforms of the Union and the grey of the Confederates.’ And he was just a small part of it … as all soldiers were in whatever war they fought. Significant or insignificant, he wasn’t quite sure. He smiled again, his cheeks hurting in the effort. ‘It’s not all bad. I’m here with you now, aren’t I? Enjoying this beautiful day with the prettiest girl in England.’

‘Now you’re just being daft.’ Anne smiled, nudging his arm playfully.

Her touch and reaction made him laugh. It felt good that it was genuine.

‘Daft is good. Life is too serious sometimes. Are you up for another swimming lesson?’ She nodded with more enthusiasm than he was expecting, so he quickly slipped into the water before she changed her mind. Anne carefully took the hand he offered as she eased herself in too.

‘Are you ready?’

She nodded and took a deep breath. He placed his hand behind her neck, her drying curls tickling the back of his fingers as he tried to concentrate. The warmth of her skin cradled into his palm almost made that impossible. He took a deep breath, instinctively aware that he was on some precipice he couldn’t see – the end, or perhaps the beginning, of something new and exciting – or scary.

He couldn’t really tell.

‘Just relax, there’s nothing to fear,’ he murmured half to himself as much as to Anne. Their eyes met as she laid her head back into his open hand. With a light touch to the small of her back, he lifted her body until she lay floating in front of him, horizontal, half-naked and caressed by the surrounding water, her skin pale and translucent just beneath its surface, like a Hollywood goddess on a flickering screen. He dragged his eyes away to meet hers and for a moment they silently watched each other, all too aware how the water sensually enveloped their bodies. He wondered if she was thinking the same as he was – feeling the same as he was. Was she aware of this connection, this invisible chord, which had been slowly growing? He'd not realised how strong and out of control it had become, until it appeared from nowhere and struck him speechless.

This was what he wanted, wasn't it? A good time with a girl like Anne? So why did he feel scared to death this time? Because '*when a girl gets under your skin you're vulnerable, take my word on it, she'll twist ya round her little finger*' the other guys often complained during their drunken laments. Falling for a woman was a gamble. *Lay your bet and take a chance.* Joe knew a man could win the jackpot or lose it all. On the other hand, the connection, the bond, the chord, whatever this damn thing he was feeling right now, felt too strong to resist.

Anne smiled and he realised that today he didn't want to resist getting more deeply involved with this woman. Tomorrow was too far away to worry about. This woman was special. Differences in culture or experience, nor a battle in some far-off land, could change how he felt about her right now. It was scary, but kind of exciting too. As her smile faded, her sultry eyes darkened and her soft inviting lips appeared to invite him to taste them. He warned himself not to overplay his hand. He wanted to. God knows he wanted to, but he also didn't want to lose it all. Not with Anne, because how she felt mattered.

Her body softened in his hold. He gently eased her to standing, determined to play the role of an English gentleman, whatever that was, yet somehow the distance between them had gone, sucked up by the current and swept far out to sea, leaving her shy and embarrassed as her body buffeted into his. He steadied her so she didn't fall, although he felt unable to step back. He expected her to move away, keen to put some distance between them, but she didn't. He knew then that she felt it too, and in her own quiet way, she was telling him. He wanted more, a kiss from her lips. Dare he? She looked up at him and he saw she wanted that too, wrapping her arms about his neck as if he was in some hazy dream. And when he felt her lips beneath his, he knew he'd gamble everything he owned on her, for he had finally hit the jackpot and come home.

Chapter Nine

Anne fidgeted with the waist of her new dress, just bought with some of her precious clothing coupons. She was tempted to buy a jacket but had eventually resisted. A new winter coat was more important so she'd keep her coupons for later in the year. She turned around and strained to look at the view from behind. It's practical, she told herself as she smoothed the material over her bottom, as she'd be able to wear it in all seasons. It was a bit simple, but that was the requisite for all the fashion nowadays. She turned around, warming to it. It was rather stylish and reminded her of Greer Garson, who'd worn something similar in *Mrs. Miniver*. She had watched the film twice, as it seemed to capture what everyone was going through, yet also had a hint of Hollywood glamour mixed in. She was meeting Joe again tonight and wondered what he'd think of her dress. She smiled. He'd probably say something cheeky and forward, with his usual charm.

She should have declined meeting up with him again. She'd promised herself not to date a soldier as the very nature of war took them away and did not always return them whole physically or mentally. She couldn't bare her first experience of falling in love to be treated so brutally. Yet here she was, twisting and turning in front of the mirror, hoping an American soldier liked what she was wearing.

Joe had been teasingly insistent when he'd asked her on another date, reminding her that they should enjoy the here and now. He'd be leaving soon and after the war would return to America. Why not just enjoy each other's company while he was around. His argument made sense. If they both knew the plan, there was no risk to dating … and kissing. Just fun, and she certainly needed some fun in her life where fashion, food and luxuries were so limited. She tilted her head as she studied her reflection in the mirror. Perhaps she just needed to bring a bit of Hollywood glamour to her outfit? She could do something with her hair to spruce things up a bit.

Anne was attempting to tame her curls when she heard the familiar rumble and rattle of an American Jeep approaching. The sound grew louder as it trundled down the stony lane to their house, with a trail of fumes snaking in its wake. She opened her window and leaned on the sill, wondering if it was Joe. A coil of nervous tension tightened her stomach as she remembered her mother was at home. She hadn't told her mother she was meeting Joe again. Her parents would read too much into their daughter dating a man and would either start planning a wedding in their heads or ban her from seeing him. Neither seemed a desirable outcome. Anne sighed in relief when she saw there were two men in the Jeep and neither was Joe.

Without slowing the vehicle, the driver circled the yard in a 360-degree turn, churning up a cloud of dusty earth, like a flamboyant swirl of a cloak; it rocked to an abrupt halt. Before the cloud had settled, a tall, uniformed officer jumped out. He glanced up at the house. Anne recognised him and quickly withdrew before he saw her; it was the same officer who'd warned her against doing menial jobs for a soldier. His three knocks on the door reverberated through the house, demanding attention. Anne waited. Her mother opened the door. Anne inched her head out of the window to watch.

'Good evening, ma'am,' the man said as he slipped his hat from his head. With his hat removed, Anne could now see his sharp, neat, well-balanced features, albeit at an angle. He turned his head to look around at the garden, the outbuildings and the climbing rose threading its way up towards Anne's window. Once again Anne darted inside, instinct overriding confidence yet again, much to her frustration. She waited, her heart thumping, until she heard his voice. She eased her head out to watch the conversation unfold beneath her.

'Mighty fine-looking place you have here.' His southern drawl was almost lyrical, yet it still jarred against the lush green country fields beyond the hill. His considered gaze swept across the water of Carrick Roads, before finally returning to her mother again. 'Kind of reminds me of home.'

Her mother smiled. 'Can I help you?' She stepped into the sunshine, furtively closing the front door behind her. Anne knew her mother had been polishing the family's shoes and that boot polish and brushes littered the kitchen floor. Her mother was a proud woman and would be horrified if the American soldier caught a glimpse of the mess.

'My name is Lieutenant Hammond. I was just passing and wanted a kindly word regarding the service unit based up yonder.'

Her mother smiled knowingly as if she understood.

'The thing is, ma'am, we consider the men under our command as a grand experiment and the last thing we want is to see it get out of hand.'

Her mother continued to nod, but her smile was faltering.

‘It’s come to my attention that you’ve been offering hospitality to one of my men.’

Her mother shielded her eyes against the blazing sun as she looked up at him. ‘Do you mean George?’

The sergeant braced himself against the sound of his name, as if a waft of stench had caressed his face.

‘I do. The thing is … they have a hankering to be like us. Now I’m sure he was as happy as a dead pig in the sunshine, sitting at your table and being part of a family …’

‘Yes, he seemed to have enjoyed himself. He’s a nice young man.’

The lieutenant looked at his cap, turning and brushing it with a quick flick and pass of his hands. ‘I’m glad to hear it ma’am, but none-the-less’—he looked up sharply—‘he did accept *your* invitation.’ He suddenly smiled, tilting his head as if he were indulging an innocent child. ‘We believe it’s best the invitation isn’t offered in the first place.’

Her mother frowned.

‘Now, ma’am, I know you don’t understand our ways—’

‘I certainly don’t.’

‘And I bet he was full as a tick on your home cooking—’

‘Which I was happy to serve up to him.’

‘Now you see’—he waved a finger at her knowingly—‘that’s the problem right there, ma’am. We need to keep discipline. I can’t have my soldiers mixing with decent folk like yourself.’

‘Oh!’ Her mother smiled. ‘I see what you mean. I wasn’t aware inviting a soldier into our home was against orders. I’m sorry.’

The lieutenant visibly relaxed. ‘I see you understand my meaning.’ He placed his hat back onto his head and smiled at her. ‘So, no more invitations?’

Her mother smiled and nodded in agreement. ‘No more invitations,’ she repeated obediently.

He replaced his cap on his head and smiled. ‘We can’t have whites serving negroes. Don’t want them getting all … uppity’.

Anne could see, from her mother’s horrified expression, the true meaning of his warning had finally dawned. Her mother watched him bid her a goodbye and stroll back to his Jeep. He climbed in with a well-practised swing of his body. Still her mother hadn’t moved, not a turn of her head or a lift of her hand, she was so rooted to the spot. Anne felt sick. Her mother was in shock. If the sergeant felt inviting George into their homes warranted a warning visit, what punishment had they inflicted on him? Her mother's angry voice tore her from her thoughts. At last her mother's paralysis had been replaced with explosive anger; a side of her mother Anne had only seen once before when Billy and his friends had used her best girdle to sieve for brown shrimp in the estuary. She sat on the sill for a better view. Her mother, stiff limbed with rage, marched towards the Jeep.

'George was the perfect guest! Never in my life have I met a more polite and gentle man. You should be proud to have him under your command, as proud and honoured as I was to have him at my table.' She came to a halt, squaring up to the two men as if she were ten feet tall. 'If all men were like George, we wouldn't be fighting this *bloody war*! Shame on you for your wicked thoughts and deeds and I hope that when the day comes and you have to answer to your maker, he'll show more mercy and kindness than you have just shown your fellow man!'

Anne gasped in delight. Her mother never swore! The sergeant looked around, his gaze lifting to finally rest on Anne. This time she felt no instinct to hide, only pride for her mother for taking a stand. She thrust her jaw out in an act of defiance; raising an eyebrow in what she hoped showed contempt for his behaviour.

The lieutenant turned to his driver. 'Thought this place reminded me of home, but I was wrong. These folks have a lot to learn. Drive on.' The Jeep roared off, leaving a cloud of pale, dusty earth to envelop her mother. Her mother harrumphed, spun on her heels and marched back inside, slamming her front door so loudly that it would provide fresh gossip for the neighbours to circulate for the remainder of the week.

Anne pushed her bike to the top of the lane and was about to mount it when her brother marched around the corner, swinging a crooked stick at protruding brambles from the hedge on each alternate step. He had a smudge of blackberry juice on his chin and his pockets bulged with crab apples.

'Where are you going?' he asked focusing his attention on her front wheel and tapping it with his stick.

'Don't do that! I'm going to the movies.'

'Movies? Why are you calling the pictures movi—'? His eyes widened. 'You're going to the pictures with the American!'

'No I'm not!' snapped Anne, frustrated with herself that she'd slipped into Joe's way of speaking.

'Yes you are! It all makes sense now. Pinching mother's lipstick. Washing your hair in Father's home-made beer.'

'It adds shine and don't tell him!'

'I will as soon as I get home.'

'Well you can't. He's not home. He caught a rabbit this morning and is giving it to the new family who moved into the requisitioned house at the top of the village.'

'Which one?'

'Oak Cottage. Their house was bombed two days ago. They arrived late last night.'

Billy pointed his stick at her legs. 'And you've stockings on!'

The boy was like a dog with a bone! 'I can wear stockings if I want. What's the point of having them if I don't wear them?'

Billy stood in front of her bike, widening his stance and pointing his stick at her as if he was a swordsman. 'The boys at school have names for girls who date G.I.s,' he said, twirling it in an accusing swirl.

Anne sat back in her seat. 'What sort of names?' He was determined to waste her time or keep her company. She didn't always know with Billy.

'*Loose Lou.*'

'Do you mean Louise who works on the pig farm?'

Billy nodded. '*Open Your Legs May Peg.*'

Anne brushed his stick away. 'I'm not listening to this. That's just mean. Now get out of my way.' She was about to stand on her pedal to push off, but paused, her curiosity getting the better of her. 'Is that May from the grocery shop?' Billy nodded. 'I didn't know she was seeing a soldier.' Suddenly it seemed that every girl in the parish was dating an American. If Joe got bored with her, there'd be plenty willing to take her place. The thought was unsettling, as if she'd discovered something that was precious and unique was not so special after all.

She straightened in her seat. 'I'm going to the pictures with a friend, not a soldier.'

'*Bet A Dollar On Betty*?'

'Oh! Stop messing around!' snapped Anne as she attempted to manoeuvre her bike around him. It was one thing to call people they knew names, but Betty was her friend.

Billy danced out of her way. 'Okay! Okay! Go and enjoy your *movie*!'

Anne scowled at him as she passed. She loved her half-brother dearly, but sometimes she could throttle the idiot. A thought struck her …

'And don't tell Mother!'

'What about? The beer you waste washing your hair or the Yank?'

'Both!' she shouted back.

Billy laughed as she pedalled furiously away. Anne found herself smiling too, confident Billy wouldn't tell tales. He knew she had plenty of ammunition to retaliate with should he start this. His back catalogue of antics and secrets far outweighed anything she'd ever done. Besides, Mother was still in a mood following the lieutenant's earlier visit and Billy had a nose for when it was best to lay low.

Anne met Betty at the crossroads. Together, they cycled their way along narrow roads. Since their last visit to Falmouth, they noticed some of the hedges had been bulldozed back, making the roads wider for large military vehicles. It was just another reminder, of many, that something was brewing. Anne could feel it in the air, almost palpable, thick and tenacious, just waiting in the wings to engulf them all. Betty chose that moment to scream as she rode through a rut in the road, dragging Anne away from her dark thoughts. They looked at each other, relieved she'd not fallen off. They laughed, eyes shining for the evening ahead, as they imagined parking their bikes, fluffing up their curls, giving each other a quick check-over before catching a lift around Restronguet Creek.

The Odeon cinema had opened a few years before the war started. In Anne's opinion, the Art Deco building, clad in cream faience tiles, was as grand as the Magistrates' court next door. The cinema was large and impressive, its bold Odeon sign a magnet for all the young people in the area who were desperate to escape the confines, regulations and rationing of war. Joe was waiting for her, leaning on one of the pillars at the entrance as a queue of excited couples snaked away to his left. It was at that moment it began to rain. A collective rebellion of groans rose up as scarves, umbrellas and jackets were removed to form tents over girlfriends not dressed for wet weather. Joe took off his jacket and ran out to greet her, shielding her from the rain as they ran under the pillared entrance for shelter. They came to a breathless stop, shaking the raindrops from their clothes and hair. All her preparations for the evening had been ruined in one downpour of rain.

'You look great.'

Three simple words, accompanied with an intense softness to his eyes, were all it took to make Anne feel on top of the world again.

They looked at each other in silence, unaware the heavy shower had ended as quickly as it had begun. She found herself eager to soak in his features in the hope of locking them into her memory for a time she needed comfort. His eyes, brown as dark oak, with black centres so large she could almost fall into them. His lips, not too thin, not too full, just right, with a softness she wanted to touch. His nose perfectly shaped, its bridge peppered with raindrops and threatening to drip. He brushed them away with a sweep of his hand.

'We better line up or we'll miss out on a seat,' said Joe.

'Yes. Yes of course,' she said, noticing for the first time the rain had stopped. She took his offered arm and joined the others, waving at Betty as she passed her in the queue.

The cinema was simply decorated inside and held both stalls and a circle of seats. The majority of seats were quickly filled with excited couples, many made up of American soldiers in uniform. The familiar notes of "God Save The King" were played by an older man on the piano in the corner, signalling for the audience to stand. The British audience, and a few experienced soldiers, did immediately. The less experienced, including Joe, were slower to stand, bemused and a little awkward for what was about to happen. "God Save The King" was patriotically sung, the words reverberating around the cinema. Respect from the soldiers grew at the emotion it evoked in the singers. Some of the soldiers even tried to sing along, trying their best to anticipate the lyrics to a song they didn't know. Joe was just content to watch Anne, with a tilt of a smile and warmth to his eyes, as she belted out the words to the out of tune piano.

The Farmer's Wife, released two years earlier, was doing the cinematic circuit again. Its plot, seen through a cloud of cigarette smoke which continually hung in the beam of the reel lights, was far too predictable, but Anne didn't care. She was in the company of Joe, who'd reached for her hand at the beginning, but by the end had slipped his own around her shoulders so she could snuggle against him as she shared the bag of sweets he'd brought along.

The summer evening light had faded by the time the film and obligatory newsreel had ended. The audience spilled out into the dark, blacked-out street; light purposely made absent in order not to attract bombers. The crowd gradually dispersed around them, romantic couples peeling off to enjoy a moonlit walk along the water's edge, cheerful groups of friends to hunt down the nearest pub. Anne's heart began to hammer in her chest as she wondered which way Joe would take her.

They strolled side by side along the pavement, lined with earth-filled sandbags and taped up shop windows. It all looked so drab; a constant reminder that Hitler was just across the water.

'I wish you could see Cornwall how it really is … like it was before the war.'

He glanced across and raised an eyebrow. 'I could always come back after the war is over.'

She smiled, but inside her heart felt suddenly tender and susceptible. Such a plan would depend on winning – and surviving the war.

'I'd like that,' she replied seriously, as she threaded her arm through the crook of his.

'So which way is it to the harbour?' he asked as he squeezed her arm against him. 'I feel a romantic stroll coming on.'

A loud crash, quickly followed by shouting and screaming, erupted from inside a nearby pub, halting them in their tracks.

'What's going on?' asked Anne.

Joe frowned. 'Sounds like a fight in the Prince of Wales.'

A stool crashed through the pub's window, and although Joe had instinctively protected her from the accompanying shower of glass with his body, the unexpected violence still shook her. She stared at the broken, splintered stool in the middle of the road as the sound of the fight inside grew. She'd never witnessed a fight before.

Joe took her trembling hand. 'Let's get out of here.'

The words had just left his lips when the doors burst open. A band of fighting soldiers fell out the door. One on one, two on one, three on two. To Anne, there appeared no rules to rein in the frenzy of punches, kicks and chokeholds.

Joe pulled at her hand. 'Come with me.'

Their hands were suddenly ripped apart as two fighting soldiers fell hard against Joe, causing him to stumble away from her. She screamed in horror as someone punched his head from behind. Instinctually he turned around and landed a punch of his own. Joe returned and grabbed her hand to pull her away from the brawling mass.

'Come on!'

As he led her away, she turned to see another stool crash through another window and land where she'd stood, smashing on the ground in an explosion of splintered wood.

Two American military police trucks approached at speed around the corner. Joe pulled Anne into the dark recess of a shop doorway. They watched in breathless silence as the police jumped out and efficiently rounded up the culprits, let some go and arrested the others, ordering them into the back of trucks with the point of their guns.

Anne frowned. She was still shaking, but it was no longer due to fear for herself or Joe.

'Why would soldiers fight soldiers?' she finally asked, perplexed. 'They're on the same side.'

'It's nothing. Just guys letting off steam.'

Anne looked at Joe, surprised by his reply as if what had occurred was nothing out of the normal. She could tell he was tense, in fact taut as a bow ready to fire, so why didn't his words, which brushed off the incident, reflect that tension? After all, the fight was now over, wasn't it? She turned back to look at the street again, grey and colourless, like a sinister black and white scene in a film. It was almost deserted, as the trucks, loaded with mainly African American soldiers, quietly receded into the distance; the crowds had already dispersed. It had taken less than two minutes to clear up the mess. Anne realised the American army was efficient when it wanted to be. Keeping up good relations with their hosts was paramount, even in a small Cornish town like Falmouth. The fight was over, as if it had never happened, the only evidence being gaping holes in the pub windows and the bewildered pub landlord being offered money by an officer to repair the broken glass. Somewhere in the distance she could hear the boasting of heavily accented voices, high on drink, adrenaline and victory that they'd walked free.

She felt a tug on her hand.

'Let's go.'

'Why did they arrest more black soldiers, Joe?' She looked at him, but he wouldn't meet her gaze.

He quickly lit a cigarette, inhaled deeply, then studied its red embers. Anne continued to wait for his reply. In the end, to fill the silence, he shrugged. 'Perhaps they started it.'

'But how would the military police know that? They didn't ask any questions.'

‘They will back at base.’ He looked up and smiled a little too brightly. ‘Look, when a whole bunch of guys are cooped up together, tensions boil over.’

She studied him as he flicked his ash and inhaled and exhaled in quick succession, blowing the smoke up into the star-studded sky littered with silent barrage balloons. Perhaps Joe was right, she thought. What did she know about being a young man, his life ahead of him and far from home, waiting for orders that would send him into battle?’

He stubbed out the cigarette with the heel of his boot. ‘Now how about that walk by the river?’ he asked reaching out his hand to her.

Anne looked at it, his slim fingers were tempting, his grazed knuckles a reminder of what had just happened. She slipped her hand into his. She may not understand what it was like to be a man waiting for battle orders, but she knew what it was like being a girlfriend. She realised, with a certainty that she couldn’t explain, this time with Joe was special; a time to store away memories that would never be tainted and she could live on for the rest of her life – in the event he never returned. So, she didn’t press for more answers, but followed him where he led. The evening was still theirs, and their time together was too precious to turn it into an interrogation on something she didn’t, deep down, want to know.

Chapter Ten

'You heard – whites on odd dates, blacks on even. And as today is an odd date'—Frank grinned as he slapped Joe's arm—'tonight, pal, is our lucky night!'

Frank and Joe stood up from the long wooden bench and began to file out of the Nissen hut. They had just been dismissed from a tactical training session on ambushing, where it had been drummed into them that working together was imperative. The day had concluded with an update on the new rules, passed down from on high, made up with the intention of quelling the rising tensions between the segregated US military personnel which were manifesting itself throughout England. The soldiers were only allowed to go into town according to the date and the colour of their skin. So much for working together, thought Joe. He looked at Frank who had a silly grin on his face. He either found the new rules reassuring or was simply looking forward to heading into town. Joe, on the other hand, was less so – on both counts.

The rules reminded him too much of home to feel reassuring, while Anne's questions about the arrests had played on his mind for several consecutive nights. Her innocent questions made him feel dirty somehow, as if he'd something to do with how things had to be. At least he wouldn't have to cancel his date with her tonight, although he could hardly avoid telling her about the new rules. She had a brain and would soon cotton on to the fact he was only seeing her on dates with odd numbers.

'It's for the best,' Frank was saying, 'The guys aren't happy when they see how the negroes are behaving. Bolton being one of them.' They looked over at their nemesis, waiting his turn to leave, his left eye still badly bruised by Joe's fist. 'He's still not forgiven you for the shiner.'

Jo shrugged. 'He's a jerk. Shouldn't have started the fight in the first place.' Anne had been right to question the arrests. From what Joe had heard, the street fight ignited when an African American began to chat up a land girl. He must have been doing a good job of it as it riled up the white troops, faster than a spark on kindling. Bolton threw the first punch. The rest, as they say, is history.

'Mallory!' Joe turned and found himself facing Bolton, his gum visibly nestled on the right side of his jaw as he chewed loudly. His cocky smile matched the arrogant tilt to his chin. 'Didn't realise you were the sort of fella to not have your pal's back during a fight.'

Joe's gaze settled on Bolton's bruised eye. 'I am,' he replied in a measured tone. The implication was clear.

'Didn't look that way to me last Saturday. Chose to fight on the side of laundry workers not'—he turned to smile at his friends—'real soldiers. Guess it won't be long before you're *dropping the dime* on your pals too.'

'I'm not listening to this,' said Joe, turning away and shouldering himself through the milling troops. Frank followed.

'Ahhh … forget about him, Joe. He's an idiot.'

'I know.'

'Well if his griping isn't bothering you, what's been eatin' you up lately?'

Joe and Frank left the hut and headed to the waiting truck that would take them back to their temporary home.

'Didn't know I was bothered.'

Frank tugged his shoulder and stopped him in the tracks. 'Hey, I'm your pal. You can tell me.'

'To be honest, I don't know.'

'Has this fight reminded you about your brother?'

'Maybe. Maybe not.'

Frank slapped him on the chest with his hat. 'What you need is a nice soft green sheet to lay down on.'

Joe laughed as he turned away. 'Sex is your answer to everything.'

Frank feigned being hurt. 'Well isn't it? England has a lot of fields to lay down in. Might as well make use of them.' He paused, placed his hand on his heart and looked up to the sky. 'In fact, I see it as my duty, as a citizen of the United States of America, to accept what this beautiful country has to offer.' He opened his eyes to discover Joe had walked on ahead. He swiftly caught him up, pleased to see a slight smile on Joe's face. 'I'm serious. Show me one fella who would disagree with me?' He tugged at his shoulder, 'Just one.'

Joe raised an eyebrow at him.

Frank waved his reply away. 'Nahhh … guys like you don't count.'

Joe came to a halt at the end of Anne's lane and turned off the engine. He remained seated on the motorcycle and glanced at his watch; he was five minutes early but was happy to wait. Wasn't he? Any normal date would see him driving to her house and waiting in the hall for her to be ready, but for some reason Anne wanted to play down their relationship with her parents. At first, he was okay with that. What guy wouldn't be happy to avoid the stilted, overly polite conversations as they tried to navigate the tricky path keeping their girl's folks onside? Yet strangely he felt relegated. That things weren't that serious between them. But that was a good thing, wasn't it? What guy would want to get too serious with someone just before they go off to war? Yet, he realised he'd have liked to have driven down the lane and be welcomed by her parents. To feel part of a family … a normal family … for once in his life.

He looked up, silent and alert, his sixth sense kicking in as a hammer thumping through his veins. He was being watched; the hairs on the back of his neck knew it and so did his head. He studied the panoramic view. Crops, grazing animals, smattering of villages and towns, an increase in military ships since his last visit, but he couldn't see anyone watching him. However, he was sure there was someone. A tree, not four yards away, was the only thing blocking his view. And there he discovered the culprit. Hanging from one of the branches were two muddy shoes, grey socks and bare grimy knees of a boy.

'Are you waiting for Anne?'

Joe lifted his gaze, attempting to see the boy hidden in the leafy branches. 'Who's asking?'

'Her brother.'

Joe smiled to himself. So, this was Anne's photo-swapping brother.

'Now that's top-secret information.'

'Why?'

'Because you might be spying for Hitler?'

The boy swung his legs off the tree and hung momentarily from the branch. 'I'm not!'

Joe pretended to study him. He looked about thirteen, maybe fourteen in age, and reminded him a bit of himself at that age.

'How do I know that? What's your name?'

'Billy.' The boy let go and landed with a thud. He nodded to a lump in Joe's jacket. 'Is that gum?'

Joe dragged the packet from his pocket. 'Yep. You don't miss a thing, do you?' He offered him the pack. 'Do you want some?'

The boy puffed out his chest, nodded and selected a stick. 'Thanks, mister.'

Joe took one too and watched Billy through his brows as they both silently unwrapped their sticks. He's feeling all grown up, thought Joe, talking and eating gum with a real soldier.

'You can call me Joe.'

'I've never called an adult by their first name before,' said Billy, popping the stick into his mouth. He chewed closed mouthed and a little too noisily, as if it was a lump of beef. He would have to learn how to chew it right if he wanted to look cool.

'We aren't so different in age. What are you? Thirteen?'

'Fourteen. Well almost.'

'Thought so.' It was a little bigger age gap between him and his own older brother, but not by much.

'So, Billy, what do you do with your spare time? Do you play any sport? Are you in any teams?'

The boy's smile faded a little. 'No. Go fishing. Swim sometimes. Spend most of my time at school or doing chores. I mess around with my mates a lot too.'

Joe wondered if he'd inadvertently made Billy feel inadequate somehow. He should have realised, before he'd opened his big mouth, that there weren't a whole lot of sport facilities around here.

'Cool,' he replied cheerfully. He was pleased to see the smile return to Billy's face. Maybe he hadn't blown it after all. 'When I was your age, I played a lot of baseball. I don't think you play it over here, but maybe I could teach you?'

Billy's smiled broadened. 'Cool.'

Joe suppressed the laughter threatening to rise up inside him. This kid was so keen to be a man, that he was absorbing and mimicking every little thing he did. He hoped, for his family's sake, the war would be over before he came of age to fight.

To his surprise, Billy, all long limbs and knees, began to scramble up the tree.

'What are you doing?' asked Joe, bemused.

'Anne's coming and I don't want her to know I'm here.'

'Why?'

'Because she'll know I was spying on her. I wanted to know who she was getting ready to see.'

'So, you are a spy!'

'Sort of, but not for Hitler.' He thrust his head through the leafy branches. 'You won't tell her, will you?'

'As long as you don't tell her parents about us until she's ready to let them know.'

'Only if you keep your promise to show me how to play baseball.'

'I'll do better than that. I'll get you a leather baseball glove so you can learn how to catch when I'm not around.'

'Cool!' On hearing Anne's greeting as she neared the top of the lane, he said hurriedly, 'Bye Joe,' before disappearing from view.

Anne arrived, beaming. She was like a breath of sweet summer air, brightening his day and chasing the fog and grime from his mind. He kicked the starter of the motorcycle and the engine immediately roared into life.

'Ready to climb on Heapojunk?'

She nodded, climbed onto the seat behind him and wrapped her arms about his waist, just how he'd wanted her to since waking at dawn. She snuggled even closer and tapped him on the shoulder. He turned his head. She wanted to say something under the cover of the engine noise. He moved his head closer to catch her words. A sweet strawberry-laced fragrance infiltrated his nostrils as she spoke.

'Is that my brother hiding in the tree?'

Joe pressed his lips together. He'd just given his word to Billy that he wouldn't give him away. What should he say? His hesitancy was all Anne needed.

'Thought so, the rascal,' she said, smiling. He returned her smile; relieved Anne didn't appear to mind. After all, he liked the kid and didn't want to see him get into trouble with his older sister. He had the feeling it was because he saw a lot of himself in the kid and Anne's kindness towards her brother was … in a strange way … a kindness towards him too, at least the lost boy he'd been in the past. If only he'd had someone like Anne around at the time.

'Are you okay, Joe?' She looked worried. Was he such an open book? He kissed her on the cheek, which made the leaves of the tree groan in adolescent disgust. Anne laughed at the noise, and so did Joe, but he knew, as they drove away with the wind in their hair, he'd have to be more careful. Anne may be able to read him like a book and he feared how she would feel about him, once she knew him better.

This is how life should be, thought Joe, as he stroked Anne's hair. They'd found the perfect spot, quiet, isolated, but with a fine view of a tributary river to Carrick Roads. The sun shone down, but its warmth was gentle here, not like back home, where the heat was hot and humid, temperatures reached beyond 100 degrees Fahrenheit and the pavements shimmered with rising heat. They sat in the shade of an old oak tree, Anne snuggled between his legs, her rounded hips touching the inside of his thighs and one of her soft, warm cheeks against his. They sat for some time, simply admiring the view together. Yes, this is how life should be. Peaceful. Safe. With a beautiful girl in your arms.

He brushed his lips against her soft, shiny hair and breathed in deeply, filling his lungs with its faint aroma that reminded him of hops.

'Will I see you again?'

It was the first time Anne had asked *him* about the next date. 'Yeah, sure,' he replied and kissed her cheek to seal the pact. She was growing in confidence, ready to plan, to make the first move and he liked that. He enjoyed watching her change and become more settled in his company. She'd been so wary at first, or maybe it was a cover for shyness. A thought struck him: maybe he was the first guy she'd ever dated. He liked that idea too. Being her first. Maybe even her only. This was why he was taking things so slow – not like the other guys who boasted of their exploits on their return from nights out and got through packets of rubbers as if they were gum. Was he missing out? He tucked one of her curls back in place and leant back on the trunk of the tree, taking her with him. He didn't think so.

'You didn't tell me you had a brother.'

'I'm sorry he was waiting for you. I'll tell him off when I get home.'

'Don't. I like the kid. Promised him a baseball glove.'

Anne laughed. 'I bet he loved that. I swear Billy and his friends are actually enjoying this war.'

'You think?'

'Yes I do. They can identify the make of every plane that flies overhead, the location of every new encampment and they seem to make friends with every soldier they meet. I wouldn't be surprised if they've some bootleg enterprise going on with all the stuff they find or are given.'

Joe chuckled. 'Sounds like a lad after my own heart.'

'Last night he benefitted from the build-up of ships in Carrick Roads. He beachcombed Loe Beach and came home pulling a trolley filled with washed-up rations. Mother was mad.'

'Why?'

'Because he smelt of diesel and had trodden in oil.'

'I'm sorry our ships are washing up so much oil and diesel.'

'Father says the water will clear again when the ships have gone.'

They fell into silence. When the ships were gone, so would he be. He tried to comfort himself that they were together now, with another date to meet on the horizon. He stroked the fine, light hairs on her forearm, marvelling at how they delicately moved under his touch. Best live for now.

'I'm free Saturday.'

He did a mental calculation of the potential date. 'I can't make Saturday.'

'Why?'

His heart sank. He'd wanted to avoid this conversation yet had blundered into it while daydreaming. *Fool.* How do you explain to a girl like Anne about the army's new rules? But he'd have to. It wasn't something he could hide.

'The 29th can't go out on even dates. They are for … some of the … service units … and others.'

'What a strange rule. Why?'

He rested his hands on his bent knees, as if to anchor himself where he sat. 'You saw the fight in Falmouth last week. Well, similar fights have been popping up all over the place. The army wants to crack down on it.'

She half turned to look at him, with a cute frown on her face. He'd rather be kissing her than being pinned down by incoming questions.

'Why?'

He shrugged, as if to lighten the subject. 'Tensions have been rising. The regular soldiers don't like what they're seeing. It's to be expected.' He looked away, focusing on a stray root of the tree breaking through the rich soil. He ran his finger along it, back and forth, back and forth. 'You can't mix people who don't usually mix. Fights are bound to flare up.'

'Mix people who don't usually mix? You mean black and white soldiers?' Anne turned and knelt before him. 'We had an army officer call on us the other day. He warned us not to invite black soldiers into our home. He said some terrible things. Is he ordering this?'

'No. It comes from higher up, but most agree.'

'Do you?'

He stared at the root and dug his nails into it, avoiding her puzzled gaze.

'You don't, do you, Joe? You can't think this is really necessary.'

'Back home things are done differently, Anne.'

'Soldiers are usually kept apart?'

'I mean black and white people are usually kept apart.' There was nowhere to hide from her now. From the look on her face, she'd never heard of segregation, let alone lived with it. 'Don't look so horrified,' he said more irritably than he intended. 'Every country has their divisions. This country is divided by class, ours by—'

'The colour of a man's skin?'

'You don't understand.'

Anne stood up. 'Explain it to me so I can understand, because right now'—she shook her head—'I just don't. I heard that a man wasn't allowed to enter a church because of his skin colour, but I thought that was an isolated case.'

He stood up. 'No. It's how it is. Segregation—'

'Segregation? What's that?'

'They've their own schools and churches.' Joe could see from Anne's face she wasn't buying his carefully chosen examples. Examples she might understand. Private and state schools. Catholic and Church of England churches. These were examples of division she could relate to. But he could see from her face that she feared there'd be more. Best tell her what she wanted to know. Or at least some of it. 'They have their own neighbourhoods. Seats on buses. Coaches on trains. Fountains to drink from.'

'Do they want this?'

'It's what the whites want.'

'But they don't.'

'I thought we were here to enjoy the day. I didn't know you were going to put my country under a microscope.'

'Are they banned from places?'

'Some. The others they have their own entrances.'

'Jobs?'

'Some.'

'Places to live?'

'Depends on the landlord or the neighbourhood.'

'How do they get on in life?'

'Why do you care?'

'Don't you?' Anne shook her head. 'George hinted at things like this, but we never asked too deeply. Didn't really want to believe it.'

Joe rolled his eyes. 'George! That man knows your parents better than I do! What do you want me to say? We're over here, aren't we? It's us who'll be on the front line and getting killed, not people like him. He'll be safe well back from enemy lines.'

'And whose fault is that? Besides, he wasn't allowed to fight on the front line. He had to serve in the service unit and now I know why. They didn't want him to experience being equal to white men. But the frontline soldier can't do anything without support. Just like the air force can't do without people like me – a woman who can't fly a plane and, God willing, will never see battle. I may be behind the frontline and only one of many, but I help to provide them with a plane to fly. Without the support, Joe, there is no frontline. But this isn't about me. This is about everyone pulling together and respecting the fact that we all have a role. We all bleed red blood, Joe.'

'I'm here fighting *your* war. Don't make me feel bad for something I have no control over.'

'*Our* war! We're in this together. It doesn't matter what class, what age, what country we come from … or the colour of our skin. We're in this together. We have to believe that or we'll never defeat Hitler!'

'That's easy for you to say.' He reached for her arm, but she avoided his grasp. He sighed. 'What do you want me to do? Change something that's been going on since before I was born?'

'What happens if they break the rules? What happens if they enter the wrong building or sit in the wrong seat?'

'Trouble. Look, segregation stops things escalating. Believe me, I know what happens when things get out of hand. You saw it yourself.' He didn't want to fight with her. This was not how today was meant to turn out. 'Look, Anne. I know it sounds bad. Seeing it through your eyes … well the way things are back home don't look good at all, but it's how things are. There's a lot of history. History you don't understand, and it comes with a whole heap of baggage. There's a lot of mistrust and fear between the two.'

'People are people. George was so nice. Polite, funny, a real family man.'

'Why are you telling me this?' He could feel his anger rising, stoked by defensiveness, jealousy, and frustration.

'How can you get to know someone if you've never had the chance to sit down and talk with someone like George? Have you ever spoken to a black person?'

'Of course I have!'

'I don't mean a few words in passing. I mean a conversation, so you come away learning more about them than you knew before.'

Joe fell silent. As a child he'd never been encouraged to, not even by his mother. Since Michael left him, he'd no desire to. In his life he had never held a deep conversation with anyone not white. The realisation didn't shock him, and perhaps it should have done. He pulled out his cigarettes and busied himself lighting one.

'I have, Joe. Twice. They were both respectful.'

Joe inhaled and exhaled deeply through tense lips.

'They didn't catcall at me, like the other soldiers,' continued Anne.

'I'm sure they didn't,' bit out Joe as he focused on his cigarette in his hand. He rapidly flicked the ash clear.

'They didn't try to drape their arms over me. I've seen some soldiers do that to women they hardly know, as if they're some tramp they've just picked—'

Joe swung to face her. 'And do you know why they don't? Because at home they'd get *lynched*!'

Anne flinched as if his words had slapped her in the face.

'Lynched? What do you mean, lynched?'

Joe shook his head. 'You don't want to know.'

'Yes, I do.'

He looked at her through furrowed brows. 'No, Anne, you don't.'

'Tell me or I will ask someone … like George.'

He turned and stepped away from her. 'A lynching is when a man is strung up by the neck from the nearest tree and left hanging for their family and wild animals to find.'

He heard Anne gasp behind him.

'It's a crude form of justice,' he muttered, in an attempt to explain it away. Only, there was no explanation that would make it right. He knew it. Anne knew it. And in reality, despite the perpetrators claiming otherwise, the whole goddamn world knew it too. But even now, Anne couldn't quite comprehend what he was telling her.

'By trial?'

'Not the sort you're thinking of.'

What he was telling her, bit by bit, finally dawned on her. He heard another gasp, fainter than the first, but broken with despair.

'But … that's terrible!'

Joe threw his butt away with a flick of his fingers and swung round to face her. 'Yes, it's terrible! It's more than terrible! And that's why it's best they're kept away from us.'

'There should be no *they* and *us*, Joe.'

'Well there is and there's nothing that can be done about it! And to be honest, I'm not sure I want something done!'

Anne snatched her cardigan off the ground. Small twigs and grass hung limp in its wool, but she didn't brush them off or even care.

'I want to go home.'

Joe frowned. 'Look this doesn't have to come between us. We're still good, aren't we?'

'I thought it was just the lieutenant prejudiced or some elderly preacher in a narrow-minded village … I didn't realise the army was. Or America.'

'Some parts more than others,' he muttered.

'I didn't realise *you* were. And I don't think I want to be with a man who thinks it's all right to treat another so badly, as if they're some animal that has to be kept in check.'

Joe picked up his cap and brushed off the twigs with angry swipes. 'Is that it? Are we done now? Do I have a say in this?'

'There's nothing to say.'

'Well if that's what you think …' He fetched the motorcycle, swung his leg over and kicked the engine into life. 'Climb on. I'll take you home. There's no point wasting the rest of the day.'

Chapter Eleven

Anne ducked under the wing of the spitfire to examine the underside. The plane was almost fixed; it just needed the final panel and it would be ready to go.

Her supervisor's legs came into view. She knew it was him as he was the only man who walked and talked with authority in the factory. 'How's it going?' he asked her hand, the only thing showing. Anne emerged from under the plane and stood up.

'Almost ready. The last panel's on its way.' Her eyes travelled along the elegant wing, which was almost stripped to a carcass only a few hours ago. 'It was torn up quite badly. I didn't think we could salvage it.'

'Waste not, want not.' He noticed Betty on the other side of the workshop, her growing frustration barely concealed. 'Betty looks like she could do with some help. Give her a hand will you Anne? The others can manage this Spit from here.'

Anne glanced over to her friend. She was working alone, attempting to strip a damaged panel off another wing, only the panel had other ideas. Although, she couldn't hear Betty cursing, she had a pretty good idea that she was, and from her animated expressions, she also had a pretty good idea which curse words she was using. She rushed over to help. Betty immediately brightened.

'Oh! Thank the Lord! The bugger just isn't playing ball.'

Anne ran her hand around the edge, while Betty, hands on hips, stood back for a rest. 'I think it's still attached. Yes, I can feel it along here.' They both immediately began to work on the area together and finally it came free, just as the supervisor arrived.

'Just had these delivered.' He dropped a wooden box of bolts in front of them. 'There might be some bolts we can reuse. Our supply is dwindling. Sounds like the factory took a hit this week and they're trying to catch up. In the meantime, see what you can find in this lot.'

Betty and Anne carried it to a vacant workbench and began sorting into distinct piles – unknown object, useable bolts, useable miscellaneous and items for scrap which could be later melted down and reused.

'When are you seeing Joe again?' asked Betty. It was the first time they'd had a chance to chat for days. A forty-five hour week, dating and family gave them little time to be together, especially since the supervisor had decided to separate them for two weeks due to talking too much.

'I'm not sure. We had a fight.'

Betty's rate of sorting slowed. 'What about?'

Anne shrugged. 'To be honest, I don't know.'

'You must know.'

'You wouldn't understand.'

'Try me.'

Anne took a deep breath. 'It was about how black soldiers are treated by the army and his country.'

'What's that got to do with Joe?'

'I wanted him to be different. I wanted him to change it. He said he couldn't. He even admitted he wasn't sure he wanted to. And it was the last part we had words about.' Anne glanced at Betty. 'Oh, don't look at me like that! I know. It sounds stupid. Me asking him to change how his country behaves. But what he told me was awful. How could he be part of that? I saw a side of Joe that I didn't like and I'm not sure I want to be with someone like that.'

'And you told him that?'

Anne nodded. She looked at the rusty bolt in her hand. 'And I know I've done the right thing. It's not as if there's a future for us. He could leave any day …'

'But you miss him.'

Anne nodded, tears choking her throat. She swallowed them down. 'Does that make me a bad person? To still have feelings for someone who could be so callous?'

Betty squeezed her hand. 'Of course not. Maybe he'll see things differently now. However'—she picked up a rusty bolt, matched it with a nut and threw it in the "to reuse" pile—'asking him to change the world was a bit of a tall order. The man has other things on his mind at the moment. There's the little problem of winning a war for you first.'

Anne found herself smiling.

'That's better!' said Betty. 'Although …' She smiled at her, 'there're loads of G.I.s around. Why just settle for one?'

'Oh, I don't know if …'

'The trouble with you, Anne, is you're too loyal. We could all die tomorrow, so why not have some fun dating first?'

Anne wasn't sure she wanted to date another American and said so.

'*Anne.* You're going through a blip in your life, that's all. Just a blip. There are loads of men who'd cut off their right arm to be on a date with someone like you.'

'I'd question his sanity if he thought of doing that.'

Betty nudged her playfully. 'You know what I mean. We're surrounded by young eligible men. Mother says it's like an invasion, only a friendly sort. "There'll be no room for a German army to land",' mimicked Betty. 'You know the wood up by Goose View?' Anne nodded. 'It's full of military vehicles. Rows of them. Hidden under the trees.'

'Everything has changed so much. I never thought my mother would join the WVS. She always saw her role as being a wife and mother. These days she's so busy that I don't know where she is half the time. I can't see her being content with just a housewife and mother role again. I wouldn't be surprised if she announces she wants to go out to work when this war is over.'

'What did your father say when she joined up?' Betty asked.

Anne thought of her stepfather spluttering on his cup of tea like a drowning man.

'Initially shocked, but when Mother reassured him that her voluntary work wouldn't affect the running of the house and he'd still get a hot meal on the table, he was incredibly supportive … and I think quite proud.'

Betty sniffed. 'Honestly, men! All they think about is food and sex.'

Anne noticed Betty break into a smile as she returned her attention to sorting the bolts.

'Are you trying to tell me something, Betty Skewes!'

Betty raised an eyebrow, her hand juggling from tray to tray. 'Maybe.'

'You have, haven't you!'

She stopped what she was doing and turned excitedly to her. 'Several times. I've been dying to tell you, but old bossy boots over there'—she nodded to the supervisor—'keeps sticking his oar in.'

'Who was he?'

'Would you think badly of me if I say there was more than one? Oh, don't look so shocked. It was just two. Several times.'

'If your dad finds out he—'

'Well it won't be from me.'

They fell into silence, returning to their sorting and a companionable rhythm. Eventually Anne could bear it no more.

'So … what was it like?'

'Bit of a disappointment if I'm honest. All a bit clumsy and messy and I had my worst underwear on. And it was over so quick.'

Anne was horrified. It must have showed on her face as Betty patted her arm.

'It was better the second and third time.'

'What about the fourth?'

Betty grinned. 'I'll tell you after tonight.'

Anne threw a bolt in a tray. It rattled loudly causing a few of their co-workers to raise their heads. One by one they began to refocus on their work.

'It'll be your turn one day,' reassured Betty. 'And it will be better for you as I can tell you what to expect.'

'I'm not sure I want to know. Besides, I'm no longer with Joe and I can't imagine doing it with anyone else.'

'There are plenty more Joes out there. Your time will come.'

Anne wasn't so sure. Joe was different, or at least she thought he was. 'I plan to wait until I'm married.'

'That's very admirable, but just in case the passion takes you by surprise, I intend to prepare you for the big moment.'

'And how do you intend to do that?'

'Teach you all the things your parents wouldn't dare, and all the things I learned myself.'

'You're hardly Mata Hari.'

'Who's that?'

Anne shook her head. 'It doesn't matter.'

'No, it doesn't, because, Anne, my dear friend, I'm determined that when you do it for the first time, you'll enjoy it much more than I did.'

'Is that possible?'

Betty nodded. 'Oh yes! The first time I did it was in Father's chicken coop collecting the eggs! Lesson number one, dear friend, is select the right setting where you won't be disturbed by ferocious clucking!'

Chapter Twelve

Crammed together like sardines in a 36ft by 11ft can, thought Joe as he looked about him. Everyone appeared eager to leave, after being packed tight into a mocked-up Higgins boat only a short time ago. Every jaw held tight, every pair of eyes focused to the front, their equipment-bound bodies rubbing shoulder to shoulder, with a layer of dark green helmets crowning the lot of them. He caught Frank's eye on the other side of the dummy landing craft. Frank winked at him with a stupid grin on his face. This was close to what they'd been training for and Joe could see, from the surrounding faces, some like Frank and Bolton, were taut with nervous excitement and keen to see battle. Joe felt more sombre. Once the makeshift ramp fell away, they'd finally be able to see what waited for them on land.

'Now be ready, men,' yelled their lieutenant. 'When the bow-ramp is lowered you run like hell! Do you hear me?'

'Yes sir!' replied a chorus of soldiers' voices.

'If you're lucky you'll hit sand. But there are no goddamn guarantees in life. There's every chance you'll get a face full of water. Keep your rifles high and those damn legs moving. The sooner you get out, the sooner you can find cover. Do you hear me?'

'Yes sir!'.

'Get ready!'

Thirty pairs of hands tightened on their rifles.

'Go!'

The ramp fell away and landed with a thud on the grass, the ropes used to pull it open now lay flaccid amongst the green blades. The men poured out onto the moor; their rifles kept above their waist as they tried to gain ground. Someone fell, tripping up the one behind.

'Run, you bloody fools!' shouted the lieutenant. 'You're being shot at by enemy fire! Half of you won't even make cover. Damn you!' He dragged a fallen soldier to his feet. 'At this rate, most of you'll be dead before you hit sand! Back inside, the lot of you! You're going to do this again and again, until you get it right! And once you have got it right, we're going to do it goddamn again!'

Despite the swearing and shouting, the training session was soon abandoned. A rough-hewn mock Higgins boat was a poor substitute for real amphibious training. Training quickly turned to a five-mile cross country run with full army kit. It was brutal, with no rests, and a sudden downpour of rain to add weight to their journey. The session finally came to a mud-splattered end. The platoon gathered in a subdued group, easing off their haversacks, gasping for breath as they lit up much needed cigarettes. The silly grins and nervous excitement felt earlier in the day, exercised out of them. The day had been a message to all of them: war was not a game where they could play at being soldiers. It was repetitive, exhausting and motivationally sapping. One trip, one off day, would mean not keeping up with the others, turning you from a soldier into a hindrance, a liability and no help at all.

'Okay you guys, put out those fags and fall in,' ordered the lieutenant. He waited as his men formed several straggling, disorderly lines in front of him. 'You think today was tough?' He let his needle-sharp gaze rake every miserable face in front of him. 'Well I got news for you … you ain't seen nothing yet.'

'Don't use the john on the left. The others are still useable though. Do you think we're going to win this war?'

Joe wiped the soapy water from his face and glanced at Frank, who'd joined him in the communal shower tent. Naked men lined each shower row, washing bodies and hair, amidst banter, chat and throwing soap.

'Thanks for the heads-up. I'm not even sure *we're* going to survive it.'

'What's that supposed to mean?'

'We've never trained for assaulting a heavily fortified enemy coastline. Today started out as a crude attempt at amphibious training. We're not going to arrive on a ship and walk down a gangplank at a port, Frank. We're going to be landing in a flat bottom tin can. That's not an orderly arrival; that's an assault.'

'Jeez, man!' said Frank. 'Give me a break! I was looking for some positivity.'

Joe turned off the tap and dragged his towel off the rail. 'Not sure I'm the right guy for a dose of positivity right now.' He wrapped the towel low around his hips. 'Had a fight with Anne last week.'

'Well, I hate to say it—'

'Then don't.'

'—but you breaking up with Anne is good news for me. My drinking buddy is back!' Frank smiled broadly as a lather of soap ran down over his face. He swiped it away with his hand, turned off the tap above his head, grabbed a towel and hurriedly followed Joe to the changing area and long wooden bench where new laundered uniforms waited for them in neat piles.

'Do you know how much it broke my heart …' Frank lamented as he thumped his chest dramatically with the side of his fist, '… to see you riding off on your motorcycle every time we got a pass? You should have stayed closer to camp with your pals! There are loads of pretty girls in town.'

'I know what you're trying to do, Frank. And I appreciate it.'

'Appreciate what?' Bolton was behind them, no doubt with his usual posse. Joe had heard him but didn't turn.

'None of your business,' he said, pulling on his trousers.

'Maybe I'll make it my business.'

Joe secured the remaining buttons as he turned to face him. 'Or what?'

The two men stared at one another, mentally calculating the odds if it became more than just words. They were the same height. Same frame. Same weight. They were well matched. Joe realised he'd be happy to oblige and fight the son of a bitch, should a challenge come his way.

Bolton looked him up and down with contempt, chewing his gum noisily. 'What did that girl see in you?' He looked back at his friends, who were indeed with him, with a toothy, wide smile. 'Or maybe I got it wrong and she wasn't with you. Perhaps she likes them black.'

Joe tightened his fists but didn't move.

'That's funny, Bolt,' egged on one of his mates, his laughter grating on Joe's nerves.

'Bolt.' Joe jerked his chin forward towards Bolton's friends. 'Is that what they call you?' He looked back at the man opposite him. 'Is that because you like to … run?'

Bolton lunged at Joe. A roar erupted from the men around them as they fell backwards over the bench and onto the ground. The men circled around, cheering, with a few consolatory voices advising them to 'settle down'. The fight didn't last long, at least not long enough for Joe. They'd only just found their rhythm before they were pulled apart and pushed their separate ways.

'What the hell are you thinking, Joe?' snapped Frank as he half-guided, half-pulled him towards the opposite exit to the one Bolton was heading for.

Joe dabbed his bloody nose with the back of his hand as he watched Bolton being escorted away. 'I was thinking, let Bolton throw the first punch.'

'Why? Are you crazy?'

He looked at Frank. 'It's easier to claim self-defence if the first hit isn't yours.'

'You *wanted* to fight. You've been building up to it all day,' said Frank as he watched his friend shrug into his shirt.

Joe buttoned the front up with well-practised fingers. 'Yeah. I wanted a fight. It just happened that Bolton was the first to step up.'

Frank returned to the table with two pints of bitter. 'I swear they warm this beer up when they see us coming. That's one thing I really do miss, the weather and cold beer.'

'That's two things.'

Frank batted Joe's comment away. 'It's one thing in my book. A hot, lazy summer and a cold beer should never be parted.'

They drank deeply. Frank wiped his mouth with the back of his hand and let out a satisfactory sigh as Joe sat back in his chair, wishing he was anywhere but in the crowded pub. He'd been lucky. The captain had given him a dressing down, warning him that if not for his exemplary record and witnesses, he'd have been punished. The reprimand had been measured and concise, executed by a man who'd no reason to stand, preferring to remain seated behind his well-organised desk. However, his casual delivery didn't diminish his meaning. If Joe stepped out of line again, he was risking more than latrine duty. Bolton, on the other hand, had his 48-hour pass removed and was put on latrine duty for two weeks.

He was preparing to be dismissed, when he realised he wasn't going to escape a dressing down after all. He'd kept this part of the meeting from Frank, but now recalled it silently to himself as he nursed his beer. Strangely, he understood the captain's words more clearly now than he had at the time.

'I've seen your type before, Mallory,' the captain said as he studied him with narrowed eyes from across the desk. 'Controlled, focused … always wanting to be the best. Don't think I've not noticed you standing out from the rest. We want that type of man in the army.' He'd stood then and began to shuffle through the neat pile of papers sat on his desk. He continued to talk as if he wasn't even there any more. 'Men who want to win every race, succeed every personal best, achieve the tasks given to them more efficiently and faster than the last time. That type of men can help win a war.' He stopped shuffling and looked up at him. 'But grit like that means doodly-squat if you don't have every man in the platoon on your side … because, mark my words, there'll come a time when you might need one of them. And it won't matter if you hate them or like them – they might be the only one around to save your goddamn ass. And it don't take a genius to work out that they're more likely to risk their life to save yours if they like you.' He dropped the pile of papers onto the desk with a thud. 'Now having a competitive streak is a good thing … but fighting with your buddies is not. And in my experience men who do that have a past they need to come to terms with. I don't care what it is, Mallory. I'm not your nursemaid … So … sort yourself out.'

Frank's abrupt laughter dragged him from his thoughts and he smiled, in a lame attempt to pretend that he'd heard his friend and found it funny too. They continued to drink, Frank becoming more boisterous and welcoming with each sup of his drink. Joe watched bemused at his friend's social skills, as the number of his new-found friends multiplied around him. At first, Joe attempted to keep up with the banter and the songs, but his heart wasn't in it. He looked around the pub: old men playing shove ha'penny in the corner, American soldiers playing darts in the other; a table of elderly, disapproving women, wearing their best hats, drinking something resembling port in short glasses. However, most of the saloon, no *pub*, with its mismatched wooden chairs and tables, wonky stools and dour decoration, had been taken over by young G.I.s. And despite the noise, the camaraderie and the recklessness, Anne was always there, lurking at the back of his mind, a constant reminder of what he might have lost.

Had she gone to Falmouth tonight? Was she with some other guy at this very minute? Was she thinking of him … or was she glad to see the back of him now she knew the type of guy he was? Or at least she thought she did, which was quite an achievement as Joe didn't really know himself.

Frank leaned towards him, the movement impeded by the fact his right arm was draped around the shoulders of a girl; a girl Joe hadn't even seen arrive.

'What the hell is up with you? I'm telling you, we've got it made tonight!'

Joe looked at him blankly. Frank rolled his eyes.

'Forget about *her* and enjoy what's lined up right in front of you. Sally here says she's meeting a friend. I'm telling you, Vera sounds right up your alley.'

Joe realised it was time for him to leave. 'Sorry pal. I'm off back to the hall.'

'Whoa there!' said Frank as Joe stood unsteadily. 'Don't go!'

'You stay and enjoy yourself. I'm not feeling too good.' It was a lie. He felt fine, it was just the room that was swaying. He left the pub and stepped out into the street. The cold fresh air, sharp and intense, hit him in the face, but failed to sober him.

I don't think I want to be with a man who thinks it's all right to treat another so badly.

He walked in the direction of 'home'. The steep gradient of the street stretched ahead of him, lined with an assortment of architecture, each building a symbol of the decade they were built. Some were old and fancy, some sleek and minimal, many tired and in need of a lick of paint. It accurately summed up the war-weary country and its people. At the top of the hill he flagged down a service lorry and hitched a lift back to camp, preferring to sit in the rear so he could avoid conversation; he pulled down the troop bench, sat down and watched the pitted country roads slip away from beneath its rumbling wheels. The open back, with its draping curtains of tarpaulin, framed the countryside view, reminding him of a silent movie playing at an old English picture theatre. The cold air was more sobering, the time alone to think was even more so.

Have you ever spoken to a black person?

As if her words came to life, they passed a black soldiers' camp sited several hundred yards away from their own. He knew it was there; it had been for several weeks, but the two camps never mixed.

I don't mean a few words in passing. I mean a conversation, so you come away learning more about them than you knew before.

Joe thumped on the side of the truck, next to where he sat. The driver must have heard him, despite the roar of the engine, as it slowed immediately before coming to an abrupt, rocking halt.

'What's up?' called the faceless driver through his open window.

'I'm jumping ship here,' called Joe, climbing down from the overhang and onto the road. 'I'll walk the rest of the way from here. Thanks for the ride.' He hit the lower side of the truck to signal he was clear and watched it drive away, the driver's shadowed hand raised out the window against the violet sky in a casual farewell.

The camp was not too dissimilar to some of the training camps he'd been on. Smaller, perhaps; it was hard to tell in the fading light. He'd decided to stop without thinking ahead, a reflex to get away from Anne's taunting words. Not that Anne was bad. Anne was anything but bad. Did he miss her or did he miss her respect? He had earned the latter without doing anything extraordinary. He'd just arrived in her country with a smart uniform that was given to him, money he felt he'd yet to earn, the extrovert character of his culture and a mystical allure because he was foreign. She liked all these things, but did she ever really like the man beneath? Joe Mallory from Baltimore – the guy with no idea what the hell he was doing these days. Perhaps walking into a camp full of black soldiers was exactly what he needed. He doubted they'd be happy for a white soldier to walk into their territory. Segregation might just work both ways and tonight Joe was happy to take whatever they dished out. What would Anne think then if he turned up at her door with the crap beaten out of him? Maybe, if they were successful, he wouldn't even turn up at all.

The faint cascading notes of a harmonica drifted towards him from beyond the hill. He found himself rocking from his heels towards it, partly swayed by the gentle music, partly off balanced by drink. 'Don't drink too much,' his brother once said, 'it tends to make you act with everything but your head'. Joe ignored the warning and walked unsteadily towards the sound.

As he reached the brow of the hill, he could see the distinct red glow of a fire. Circled around it, shoulders hunched and looking inwards, sat four silhouettes, toasting food over the flames. The fifth sat slightly away and played the harmonica, his hands skilfully moulding the sounds like a magician, while his companions talked with deep southern accents. Joe searched for the camp behind him. It was some distance away, too far to be seen in detail, but still within shouting distance if they were needed to be roused. Did he have anything to fear? He wouldn't blame them if he did. He was in their neighbourhood now.

Only the other day he'd overheard one soldier from his division warning an English girl to stay away from people like this. 'They've tails didn't you know,' the laughing soldier had said. What would Anne think if he told her what he'd overheard? Would she laugh or be horrified that a man could spread such slander about his brother-in-arms? He was fairly sure he knew the answer to that question.

Come away, learning more about them than you knew before.

Joe swayed slightly as he watched the scene ahead. 'Well, Anne, I'm about to do what you wanted me to do,' he muttered to no one in particular. 'I hope you think it's worth it because I sure as hell doubt it.'

Chapter Thirteen

Joe had twenty-five yards to go when the first man looked up. He continued walking, steady and slow, concentrating hard in the dim light so as not to stumble on the rutted field. The others sensed something had changed and in unison their heads lifted and turned in his direction too. The lyrical notes of the harmonica quickly faded away.

It was only when the glow of the fire reached his body and illuminated his skin, did the first man brace himself. He stood up abruptly, his arms slightly out and bent, the grip on his skewer a little tighter. It wasn't the friendliest greeting Joe had ever received.

'What do you want?' asked the man as he looked past Joe for his friends. Joe stopped his advance. It was reckless to come here alone. What had he been thinking? He rocked slightly on his feet, a silent reminder that he wasn't sober just yet.

'Don't rightly know.' What else could he say? It was the truth after all. He shrugged. 'To sit. To talk.' He casually reached into his jacket pocket. The movement was too sudden for his audience as it set them all on alert and brought them to their feet, skewers held in readiness for what might unfold. He raised his brows in exaggerated innocence as he lifted both hands in surrender. Making a show of his forefinger and thumb, he slowly withdrew the cigarette packet from his pocket. 'Do you want a smoke?' he asked, clumsily offering them one.

'We don't smoke,' replied the second man coldly. 'I think its best if you just turn around.'

The first man, added, 'This is our base ... unless you're after a Yankee whipping.'

'Now settle down,' said another. 'He's just being friendly. Can't be easy walking into a black neighbourhood.' Someone chuckled. Was it a genuine attempt to ease the tension or a secret code to ratchet it up? Joe couldn't tell. He thought his brain was sharp, but maybe that was just the drink playing tricks.

An engine roared into life somewhere in the distance, reminding him that although he was outnumbered here by four, not far away was their unit who would all feel just like these men ... suspicious as to why a lone white soldier would seek out their company. Decisions and choices lay before him, suspended in the wind by an invisible thread. The consequences of what he chose to do next was less clear. He decided to do what he always did when unsure how to proceed. He withdrew a cigarette for himself and leisurely lit it. It gave him a moment to think and his audience time to realise he meant no harm.

'Why are you here?'

Joe exhaled loudly and smiled. 'I told you. Came to talk.'

'About what?'

'Nothing. Everything.' Although barely visible in the fading light, their expressions changed. No longer wary of his sudden appearance, they now stared back with passive contempt. Joe realised that a steady gaze of a stranger can be more unnerving than the scorn of someone you know. He might as well come clean or they'd be here all night. 'I'm here to see if we have anything in common.'

'I know what we don't have in common,' said the first man. He's the one to watch, thought Joe. Every muscle in his body had yet to relax. This man didn't just dislike being interrupted by a stranger, his anger, probably nurtured for years, went far deeper than that.

'If you need to come here to find out,' interrupted a voice, 'then maybe that's the problem right there.' The man who'd spoken was the fourth in the circle. He had been content to remain silent until now, yet Joe had the feeling that his role in the group was much more than just a quiet observer. This man, who was slightly older, gathered his wisdom by listening and learning, then shelling out valued nuggets of advice for others to devour. His face had no vanity, yet proudly told his life story of hardship, laughter, and sorrow. And from the number of lines on his face, Joe reckoned he'd seen quite a lot of all three.

Joe shrugged. 'Maybe it is, but can you blame me for trying?'

'And what's prompted you to do it tonight?' asked the wise man as he reclaimed his seat and removed a billycan from the fire. He examined the beans warming inside, before glancing up at him. 'Or perhaps I should ask who?'

One seated – just four more to go.

'A girl.'

The five men, bonded by more than war, didn't respond. It was unnerving to be the centre of their attention. Joe, feeling under pressure, felt he had to elaborate.

'We had a fight about segregation. She didn't understand it.'

'She's not the only one,' someone muttered. Joe's gaze scanned the men. The man who'd rebuffed his offer of a smoke was now rearranging his seat. Satisfied it would be as comfortable as he could make it, he sat down with a thud.

'She asked me if I'd ever had a conversation with …'

'Someone like us?' It was a sarcastic challenge to be truthful, made by the only guy who'd no wish to become friends.

Joe nodded. 'You could put it that way.'

He could no longer hold their gaze. He stared into the fire, feeling fully sober for the first time. Somehow, he'd dug himself into a corner and hadn't seen it coming. Did they see him as a voyeur now, visiting their camp as if they were oddities who could be teased and poked? This was not why he'd come. Why was every good intention, obscured and twisted when viewed through a prism of prejudice? Someone else's prejudice. *Only it's not someone else's as it's happening now and you're accepting it*, Anne's voice berated him in his head.

The man with the harmonica sat down, blew a few notes and added with a half-smile, 'Sounds like you have a smart woman, there.'

A fourth man decided to join him and sat down too.

Joe felt the tension leave his shoulders. Being truthful had been the right call to make, even though the words were hard to hear … even as he spoke them. Only one was still standing. Four out of five was a good sign of acceptance, although he knew this change between them remained fragile and could still turn on a dime.

'I did have a smart girl. I'm not so sure now.'

The older wiser soldier turned his half-cooked sausage to the fire. 'Well that's something we all have in common.'

'What do we have in common with *him*?' asked the aggressive one.

'Being on the end of a woman's tongue whipping.' A ripple of laughter circled the fire. The man who'd been standing finally smiled too and sat down on an upturned billycan. Joe wanted to join in with the laughter, but remained where he was, unsure whether to approach or to just say goodnight and walk away while they remained on good terms.

'Want something to eat?' In the fading light he couldn't make out who had spoken, but did it really matter? The invite was there and ready for the taking; it was now his call as to whether he accepted it. He had never sat down and ate with an African American before. He had never refused – he'd just never been asked. The situation of eating together had simply never arisen … or been encouraged. 'I'm not going to ask twice.'

Joe approached them. An empty, beaten up billycan was kicked his way. It rolled towards him in a lumbering fashion. He stilled it with his boot, righted it and sat down. A sausage, pierced with a long metal skewer, was offered to him. He took it with a quick, 'Thanks'.

The harmonica player smiled to himself, closed his eyes and cupped his instrument in his hands. Sliding his lips across its wooden plate, he instantly produced a soft mellow tune that had the power to thaw the atmosphere more rapidly than any dialogue could.

'So where are you from?' asked the third man. This man was the pacifier of the group, thought Joe. He was loyal, a homemaker, with probably a wife and child at home.

'Baltimore. You?'

'Me too. Druid Hill Avenue, Old West.'

Joe nodded as if he knew it, but in reality, he'd never visited the neighbourhood. It consisted of approximately 175 city blocks, directly northwest of downtown Baltimore. It was densely populated, made up of largely African-Americans; a melting pot of those who'd risen to the grand heights of the doctor and lawyer professions, despite the education system offered, yet lived alongside rows of boarding and alley houses densely occupied by poor working-class tenants. No, he didn't enter that neighbourhood, coming from the all-white Bolton Hill area. And they all knew it, which is why the silence that followed said all there was to say.

'I'm originally from Mississippi, but I heard there was work going in the harbour and brought my family with me.' Joe nodded in acceptance. He'd been right; this man was a family man and his story held truth. Since the outbreak of war in Europe, numerous emergency shipyards had been established to build cargo ships for the U.S. and Britain. The Bethlehem-Fairfield Shipyard on Baltimore Harbour was one of them, and was soon building cheap Liberty cargo ships, at great speed, to replace those lost to German attacks. To build a lot of ships at great speed needed a lot of men, men who came from far and wide to seek employment. Every war has an economical benefit to someone, and initially it was America.

'And then you were drafted?' asked Joe.

'Yes, but I'd already volunteered the week before I got them.'

Joe fell silent. Why would a family man with regular employment, want to fight for the country where he was treated as second class citizen?

‘I know what you’re thinking, but we all had our reasons. I wanted some respect from my community, from my pastor. I wanted my family to be proud of me.’

Joe was still digesting what he’d said when the more aggressive man joined in.

‘I joined because I heard Hitler didn’t shake hands with Jess Owens at the Olympics. The day I received my draft papers I marched right down to the office. I had to go three times before they accepted me. Didn’t quite match up with what they were looking for.’ He pinned Joe with a resentful stare. ‘Face not pale enough.’

The last four words hung in the air between them, all with an arrow pointing right at Joe. This man considered Joe partly responsible, lumping him in with the draft system and every other prejudicial barrier he had faced. Joe remained silent, for anything he said would not be enough to wipe away those beliefs.

‘I’m fighting for freedom …’ the second man broke in, ‘in Europe and at home.’ Joe frowned, surrounded by reasons that were far from his own. ‘I’d been hankering for a holiday from Jim Crow for some years and decided it was high time I took one …’

Someone murmured, ‘Amen.’

Joe stared into the fire, feeling his gaze upon him.

‘You see … ’ he continued, ‘when this war is over, I’m hoping the white folks back home won’t be able to treat me as if I’m no more than mud on their shiny shoes.’ Joe glanced up to meet his gaze. There was no accusation there, just hope. ‘I want to be able to look them in the eye and say that we fought, shoulder to shoulder, white and black together.’

‘It’s hardly together. Did you notice when we were boarding the ship to come over here? A line of correspondence reporters, with their neat hats, pristine notebooks, and cine cameras, waiting to record the occasion. Not one wanted to interview any of us. I’m telling you all, they’re going to erase us from history, you wait and see.’

‘Nu huh.’

‘Hmmm. Yes they will.’

‘Oh sweet land of bigotry.’

‘Soon found being in the army wouldn’t change anything. Not equal enough to train together, travel together, eat together, drink together. Tried to join the marines. The officer would have none of it. He says to me, “Do you see any of your kind here, boy?”’ He shook his head as he remembered. ‘He was a swine of a man.’

Joe remained silent as they appeared to forget he was there and continued to talk, excising their pent-up resentments on how they'd been treated in the army so far. How the army segregated them from the white troops on board ship. Had they known they were even there? How they were allotted hammocks in the depths of the ship, closest to the noisy engine rooms. How they were given separate "black only" sittings to eat their meals. How, on their arrival to England, they were wary, conscious they were about to step onto another country's soil and unsure of the reception they'd receive. Would it mirror their place in society at home or would it be even worse?

Joe was seeing into their lives by way of stark images of mistreatment and demoralisation, intimately painted by the witnesses who were there. Disgust churned in his belly, robbing him of his appetite. Did they see him as a representative of what they had to endure? Would they want him to pay when they remembered he was still there? The tension was returning, sliding unseen into their little group and coiling up by the fire ready to strike.

'Perhaps I should go,' said Joe placing his sausage carefully on a stone to avoid the dirt. He didn't want to be accused of wasting their food.

'Perhaps you should,' someone said. Joe didn't need to know who had said it, the message was clear. He was not wanted here. He half stood as the music stopped.

'There's no need for that. Sit yourself down.' The player examined his harmonica, brought it back to his lips and looked over his cupped hands to his friend. 'It's not his fault, Rivers, if your grandaddy was a slave.'

To Joe's surprise, there was another ripple of laughter. It was a strange response to such a statement, yet it sounded genuine. Had he read them wrong? He seemed to be doing a lot of that lately.

'Depends what he wants us to call him,' said the man who still seemed to hold a grudge against him. However, it was an olive branch, albeit edged with thorns. No man of colour was encouraged to call a white man by their Christian name.

This time, Joe knew how to respond, as it was how he genuinely felt. 'Call me Joe.'

The invite to sit down was offered again by a wave of a hand. 'I joined the army to change peoples' minds about me. About us,' said the shipbuilder. 'I guess we can only start one man at a time.'

That was enough to soften the tension. He sat down.

The wise man took up the introductions. 'That's Rivers,' he said, pointing his skewered sausage at the man who'd been spoiling for a fight. 'He's Homer.' The musician acknowledged his introduction with a slide of blues notes along his harmonica. The man's skewer dipped towards the shipbuilder. 'Jessie.' The man acknowledged the introduction with a half-smile. 'And that ugly one is John.' John laughed; his earlier serious manner now gone. 'And I'm Charles.' Joe nodded to each man in turn. Charles turned the meat over in the flames. 'I signed up because I wanted to escape my daddy's belt. He was a *hard* man. Beat me regular as a child and when I turned an adult it still didn't stop. Well … I'd had enough. Left home with just a bag, a pocket full of coins and not a clue in my head which way to go. Then over the hill came a bus. Me, being adventurous—'

'Stupid, more like,' someone interjected, with a wily smile.

'—hopped on and rode it for miles. Felt like a man of the world.' He laughed to himself, shaking his head at the memory. 'First stop was outside a draft office. The officer, well he looked me up and down and said "You have a choice, boy. You can come back in two weeks or get on that bus over there and it will take you straight to training". Home to my daddy's belt, sleeping rough or straight in the army. Well, for me there was no choice. Next thing I knew, I was signing the papers. Got on that bus feeling some proud of myself. Later that day I heard the news that Pearl Harbour had blown up. Realised I'd signed up for war. Should have gone home for a belting.' A ripple of laughter circled the group, even Joe found himself smiling. 'What about you?' asked Charles.

'Same sort of thing, only my Father … well let's just say he shows his displeasure in the freezing out kind of way.'

All the men nodded. It seemed they all knew someone like that.

'But it ain't been too bad here,' said John. 'The British have been warm and friendly, on the whole, and treated us with respect.' They began to eat the food they'd cooked, similarly baring their teeth to avoid the spurting fat, as they bit into their sausages. Joe followed suit. The sausages were good, a secret gift from a local farmer. The information was one shared in confidence and Joe dared to believe that sometime, somehow he must have passed some test and was no longer considered their enemy.

'Not sure what it will be like when the war is over and we finally go home,' said Charles, his wise low tones bringing a sombre air to the gathering as he chewed on some gristle.

'What do you mean?' asked Joe.

'Once you've tasted a little respect, Joe … it's hard to want to give it up and go back to what it was like before.'

They all nodded in agreement, as they gnawed on their charcoal-coated meat. They had all entered for different reasons, with the idea of fighting for their country, but had found themselves excluded from many combat units, ending up in service or labour units, logistics, communications, anti-aircraft defence or truck transport. Their attachment to divisions was only temporary, brought in as needed and then just as quickly withdrawn. They remained segregated, even in this.

'I hope you get it,' said Joe. They lifted their gazes to study him over the amber flames of the fire and found it was sincerely meant. Their nods of acceptance, almost indiscernible in the darkness, allowed the thaw between them to grow in earnest, where past resentment and beliefs faded away and no longer existed, just six men with tales to tell. Tales of childhood adventures, fanatical preachers, family moments and the girls they'd met. Gradually the conversation changed again to their lives in the here and now, but this time it flowed freely, without the barriers placed between them by history and those who still wanted to preserve them. One by one, they moved from the hard billycan seats, to lay before the fire, heads resting against rolled up jackets, blankets or utility sacks. Cigarettes were finally passed around and lit, as they speculated on what plans the military might have in store for them. In turn fears were shared, interrupted only by comic tales of overzealous drill sergeants and the soldiers' revenge. And as the fire gradually burned itself out, leaving only ash and smouldering embers with narrow grey ribbons of smoke, the moon shed its light as a backdrop to their silhouettes, where the colour of a man's skin could not be observed, and where only their laughter and conversation could be heard.

Chapter Fourteen

Late summer, 1943

Joe had been right. The US army, ill-trained for a coastal attack, was going to rectify the situation in a more organised way. Rumour had it that an assault training centre was being hurriedly built in Devon to help train the troops in amphibious assault. In a matter of weeks, it was said, units from the 175th would be sent to the centre for training. In turn those units would train subsequent ones. With no signposts to direct us, Frank joked, it would be a miracle if any unit got there at all. Joe realised he could be deployed there at any time, but it was the fact he still hadn't made things right with Anne which unsettled him the most. It was something he had to do, even if he risked being turned away. Yet despite his determination to set things right with her, his hand still shook as he finally knocked on the door of her home.

It was her mother who opened the door, and although he towered above her, he had the distinct feeling it would be her he'd have to convince first.

'Good afternoon, ma'am.'

'It's Mr Mallory, isn't it?'

Joe smiled, pleased she'd remembered him from his one and only visit to her home.

'Yes, it is, ma'am.' He touched his cap in a casual salute, then remembered his manners and slid it off his head. 'I promised Billy I'd get him a present.' He indicated to the roughly wrapped parcel in his left hand. 'I was hoping I'd be able to give it to him in person.'

'I'm afraid Billy isn't here.' She looked at the parcel cradled against his body. 'I hope Billy hasn't been making a nuisance of himself by asking for gifts.'

'No. Billy's a great kid. It was my idea.'

Joe fell silent. He'd hoped Billy's presence, with his friendly chatter, would help him during the visit. He hadn't planned on Billy being AWOL.

'Would you like to leave it with me?' asked Anne's mother. He nodded and gave it to her, their hands and arms somehow becoming tangled as the parcel transferred from one to another. 'What is it?' she asked as she secured ownership of it. She turned it over in her hands, silently judging his inexperienced wrapping.

'A baseball glove and ball.'

The woman nodded, but the appearance of a puzzled frown told Joe that she didn't have a clue what he'd just said. Her bright smile, which didn't quite reach her eyes, told him that the end of his visit was looming large and fast.

He cleared his throat. 'I was also wondering if Anne was at home and if she'd like to take a walk with me?' A slight movement in the shadows caught his eye. It was Anne, dressed in overalls, and she'd been watching him all the time.

'Do you want to, Anne?' asked her mother, without turning around. Anne subconsciously touched her head, searching for her beautiful hair which was mostly hidden under a brightly coloured scarf. She looked embarrassed to be caught dressed in her factory clothing, and this, strangely, gave him hope.

'I'm happy to wait, Anne, if you wanted to change.'

She hesitated, then nodded. 'I'll be back in five minutes.' They listened in silence to her footsteps as they ascended to the next floor.

'Would you like to come in?' Joe smiled, pleased to be asked, only she didn't step aside. 'I'm entertaining. Mrs Friar is here. She is living in the requisitioned house in the village.' She mouthed the last words, 'And is feeling rather lonely.'

Joe understood. The invitation was offered out of politeness, but it would not be polite to accept it. Why didn't the British just say it how it was?

'No thank you, ma'am. You've such a beautiful home here that I'm more than happy to wait outside for Anne and admire the view while I wait.'

Anne's mother smiled and shut the door in his face.

Joe stepped away and wandered down the side of the house, his eyes scanning the undulating horizon of the hills until it led to Falmouth's docks in the distance. The barrage balloons still floated above the town and harbour, but the number of ships had increased since his last visit. It felt like everyone knew his future, the whens, the hows, the wheres, but him.

'Is that the American you were telling me about?'

Joe looked about him to find the source of the voice and found it by way of a slightly open sash window. A window that Anne's mother had, no doubt, forgotten was left ajar.

'Yes. He's a handsome man, there is no doubt about it. Americans can be very charming. This one could charm the birds from the trees if he had a mind to.'

Joe smiled to himself. Maybe he didn't have to win her mother over after all. Maybe that battle had already been won.

'Did you know they were still seeing each other?' said the first female voice. It seemed Anne's mother had spoken the truth about Mrs Friar after all. She was visiting and, no doubt, setting the world to rights over a steaming cup of tea and her mother's best cake that her rations were able to make.

'No. She told me they were finished. Anne has been quite secretive about it all, which is a worry in itself. I only found out last night that they were once courting when I heard her crying.'

Joe straightened. The thought of Anne crying felt like a blow to his chest. He hated the idea that he'd not been there to comfort her … yet if their fight had caused her to be so upset, that could only mean …

'Of course, I didn't like seeing her upset, but to be honest I was relieved it was over. He could be gone tomorrow for all we know. Think of the heartache that would cause.'

'She would spend her days worrying.'

'Exactly.'

'And if he's killed, they won't tell her as she's not his next of kin.'

'She'll spend the rest of the war worrying about him.'

'And if he's lucky enough to survive, what will happen then?'

'He'll go back to America and she'd just be a fleeting memory. Unless they marry and she goes to America to live.'

A short silence followed. 'Do you think that might happen?'

Another short pause, he could almost hear Mrs Friar nodding. 'But I'll never see her again. She'll be alone in a foreign country without her family around her.'

'Ssshhhh!' warned her visitor. 'I think Anne's coming.'

Joe heard Anne's quiet voice in the distance. He tilted his head to listen as he imagined Anne standing in front of the two matriarchs waiting for their opinion.

'You look nice,' they chorused in harmony.

'Thank you, Mrs Friar. Mum.'

'Handsome lad, that Yank of yours. Had a good look at him through the window while he was talking to your mother.'

‘Is he still outside?’ Joe imagined them nodding to confirm that he was. ‘I won’t be long,’ said Anne.

Joe’s heart sank. It seemed that Anne had already relegated him to a short conversation and no more. He returned to the doorstep, making it just in time to greet Anne as she opened the door. He greeted her with a smile, as his stomach churned inside.

‘Hi.’ He looked her up and down with what he hoped was a sultry, but appreciative glance. The former he had to work on, the latter he didn’t at all. ‘You look nice.’

‘Hello, Joe,’ she replied, ignoring the compliment and walking past him. It appeared that his “American charm” wasn’t going to be of any use here. He fell into step beside her.

‘I hope you don’t mind me calling on you. How our last date ended … well it wasn’t great. We were good together, right?’

‘I thought we could walk through the village and down to the river. It will be quieter there.’

Joe realised she wasn’t going to make things easy for him. ‘Sounds good to me,’ he replied, following her lead.

The silence that followed was uncomfortable even for Joe, who’d always been happy to observe life rather than feel the need to talk about it non-stop. He glanced at her. She looked fresh and vibrant, not like someone who’d lost any sleep over him. He wondered if she smelt as fresh as she looked. He fought the urge to pull her close and find out.

They followed the short lane, which soon morphed into a narrow road. As it neared the top of the hill, it became marginally wider, lined with quaint houses with small windows hiding cluttered, cosy rooms amongst dimly lit shadows. They turned left onto a road that passed the church bell tower. The church itself was sited a little distance away, nestled at the bottom of a sloping embankment, overlooked by rows of silent, grey headstones. Joe felt the urge to pull Anne into the shadows of the arch-covered gateway which framed the start of the footpath to the church’s oak door. They needed to talk and he wasn’t sure if he could wait. By the time he plucked up the courage, they were already past it and heading down a gentle slope. Perhaps it was best to make small talk first.

‘Is Mrs Friar a friend of the family?’ he asked, not really caring if she was or wasn’t.

‘She lives in the requisitioned house just over there.’ Anne pointed to a small house, hidden by two trees and set aside from the others. ‘She comes from Bristol, but her house was bombed so she was sent here with her three children. But she's finding it difficult and misses her family who still live in Bristol.'

Joe nodded. The silence threatened again. There was no use pretending their last argument hadn't happened and he might as well cut to the chase.

'You were right. I've accepted how things are back home ... and in the army, too easily.'

Anne turned right onto a narrow footpath which, he assumed from its sloping gradient, would finally take them down to the water's edge and a dead end. Soon they'd be able to talk in earnest, but not yet as the breadth of the path was no wider than a man's shoulder, forcing him to walk behind her and follow in her footsteps. It abruptly stifled the flow of any meaningful conversation between them, yet the moment would come eventually.

High hedges lined the path. Occasionally these were interrupted by garden gates guarding small flights of stone steps. The steps guided visitors into handkerchief-sized gardens and up to cottages with brightly painted front doors. Despite the pretty surroundings and the view of Anne walking ahead in her dress of sunshine yellow, Joe felt a growing sense of concern as to how their conversation would go. One misspoken word, a meaning taken the wrong way and she could hate him more than she did already.

The path ended in a set of curved brick steps, which fanned out onto a landing of sloping, smooth, grey rock. This natural mooring area wasn't large, just enough for three, maybe four rowing boats to be hauled onto, however it remained bare, a quiet oasis but for the gentle lapping of the expanse of river at its foot. Anne looked about her. Anticipating her next move, Joe quickly slipped off his jacket and lay it on the rock for her to sit on. His quick thinking surprised her, however she thanked him, albeit reluctantly, and settled herself down upon it.

He sat beside her and looked around at the vast expanse of blue water, dotted with well cared for rowing boats waiting for their owners to return.

'This is a beautiful spot,' he said, as he followed the surface of the water with his gaze. On the far right was Falmouth harbour, with its ships and buildings protected by barrage balloons, then empty water, then the native rowing boats, each with their own characters and colours. Finally, his gaze settled on one abandoned rowing boat, which had beached on the nearby narrow, earthy bank sometime in the past. Despite lying several yards away, he could still clearly see its rotted wood, the green algae and the gaping holes shaping its hull. Abandoned, it no longer played its part in the working flotilla of boats bobbing round it.

'Why are you here, Joe?'

He turned to look at her. 'To make things right between us before I go away.'

'Away?'

'I could be called away any day now. The thought of leaving on an argument doesn't feel good.' He rested his forearms on his knees. 'I just want you to know you were right. I've just accepted how it is back home without questioning. It's not an excuse but it is all I've ever known. And things have happened in my life which helped make sense of it.'

'What things?'

He shook his head, a humourless smile masking how he felt inside. 'Things a kid shouldn't have to deal with.' He searched for his cigarettes, fearing he'd left them back at the base.

'What things?' When he didn't answer she prompted. 'Will you tell me?

He stopped searching and glanced up at her. 'And have you hating me more than you do already?'

'I don't hate you, Joe.'

'You might after I tell you. It's not a pretty story.'

'I can handle it.'

His silence told her otherwise. Anne lifted her jaw. 'I'm not as fragile as you think I am, Joe. There's nothing weak about being horrified that a human can treat another so badly. To feel nothing is surely worse.' Joe looked away, but she roughly tugged at his arm forcing him to return his attention to her. 'We've been at war for almost four years now. My life has changed in a way that I could never have imagined. You think this is a quaint country, with strange backward ways and stiff hosts, but we're more than that. *I* am more than that.'

Anne took a deep breath. 'I've lost two cousins, Joe. Both were killed within months of each other. Three boys from my class at school had barely reached adulthood when they received their conscription. All three died in Italy. They are never going to grow old. My neighbour has lost her son … he was her only child. There's a man from this parish whose family have not heard from him for almost a year. They're desperate and refuse to believe he is dead. They carry on, because they hope that he will one day come home and they want the family business to be ready for him when he does.' Anne looked towards Falmouth. 'We may not have suffered the bombings like London, Bristol or Plymouth, but we've still had bombs fall on us. I've heard them in the night, falling on Falmouth, or nearby fields as planes struggle to fly home and empty them to ease their load. The threat of death or invasion is always there. Sometimes the threat is worse, as it keeps you awake at night and makes you suspicious of everyone who behaves differently. Even now, when there's hope on the horizon, I worry that one day I'll wake up to find German soldiers patrolling our roads. I sometimes wonder if I will ever be truly free of worry again. So I'm not going to fall apart if you dare to share something that happened in the past which might explain how and why you feel a certain way. I'm made of sterner stuff than you give me credit for, Joe.'

'It's not that I think you won't be able to handle it.' He searched for the right words to use, to explain. 'It's because it's not easy to talk about.'

'What isn't easy to talk about?'

He searched for his cigarettes again, patting his pockets with an urgency he'd not felt in a while. She stilled his hands with hers, forcing him to give up and look at their layered hands.

'Or should I ask *who*?'

He dragged his gaze away from them and up into her blue eyes. He saw no accusation or anger, just warmth and tenderness which swallowed him whole and made him want to talk.

'I've not told you what happened to Michael, have I?'

Anne shook her head. He reluctantly withdrew his hands from under hers and returned to face the expanse of water stretching away from his feet. It would be easier to talk if he wasn't facing her. He noticed a piece of wood. It was rotted and soft from its time in the water. It had probably once belonged to the decaying boat, but now lay at his feet, washed up on the tideline like a dead fish. He picked it up. It was no bigger than his finger, but it would give him something to focus on. He rested his forearms on his knees and examined it, turning it over and over as he spoke.

'He was five, almost six years older. He always seemed like an adult to me. As a young kid, I thought Mike was so worldly and knew everything there was to know.' He smiled. 'He was great. Kind of took my father's place in a way.'

'Where is he now?'

'Nowhere. Everywhere. Depends if you're a believer.'

Anne remained silent. Did she understand what he was trying to tell her, but couldn't quite say? He glanced at her, then quickly sought comfort from the stick in his hand.

'When he was eighteen, he decided he'd had enough of our father. He'd always looked forward to the day he was old enough to leave home and experience life a bit. He came to my room to say goodbye. He was excited.' Joe found himself half-smiling at the memory. 'He was real happy to be finally leaving. I missed him like hell.' He threw the stick in the water and watched it bob away. 'Eight months later he came back. But he wasn't the same.'

'What do you mean?'

Joe frowned. 'He'd changed. Didn't smile any more. Didn't sleep. And he began to drink. He'd got himself a job but soon lost it and couldn't hold another one down after that. Finally, I think he just gave up looking.'

'What did your father say?'

Joe tried to laugh but this time failed. 'Father was no help at all. They had several bust-ups and Mike moved out, but by then it was too late. Mike was on a downward spiral and he'd listen to no one.'

'What brought about the change? Did you ever find out?'

Joe nodded. 'Oh yeah, I found out.' He pinched the bridge of his nose and sighed as the memories came flooding back. Memories so clear and filled with emotion that it was as if he was back there again, a fourteen-year-old boy, sick with disappointment. He'd visited him to ask him to play baseball, but instead found the brother he'd once idolised lying on a stain-marked couch, dishevelled, unwashed and as pathetic as his father told him he would turn out to be.

'I went to visit him. He'd been sleeping on a pal's couch and was drunk as a skunk. So drunk that he started to talk and didn't stop to think if it was something his younger brother should hear.'

'What did he say?'

'He told me where he had been and what he'd been up to.' Joe braced himself. He should have kept the rotting wood because it would have been something to hold on to. 'When he left us he'd travelled to Mississippi. Found himself a job cutting and stacking wood for a local wood delivery company. He found himself a place to rent … a cabin. Made some new drinking buddies … men he worked with. For once he was enjoying life. He thought he'd found a place he could call home … somewhere south of Clarksdale. He said everything was going well for him … until a young woman's body was found on the banks of the Sunflower River.' Joe smiled to himself. 'Funny the details you remember. Why would I remember the name of a river when the rest of his story was so sickening?'

'*Because* it was so sickening,' Anne said quietly. 'Sunflower is not something that should be connected to someone's death. How did the woman die?'

'Raped and murdered.' He glanced at Anne, to check she was happy for him to carry on. She nodded. 'Mike said every stranger to the area was a suspect, and he was worried fingers would soon point at him. Then someone said they'd seen a young black man in the area on the day it happened. A meeting was quickly called and Mike, relieved to have their suspicions move elsewhere, went along to be part of it. It didn't take long. Soon a crowd of two hundred men or more had gathered and they set off to where the man was last seen. It took several hours, but their bloodhounds were good and found where he lived.'

'What happened? Did they arrest him?'

'That's what Mike thought they were going to do. But he soon found out that's not what they had in mind.' He fell silent.

'What did they do, Joe?'

'Mike said he was just a boy. Maybe even the same age as me at the time. He wasn't old enough to think about raping and killing, just a kid who'd wandered on the wrong side of town. He hoped the men would see sense and leave him. After all every boy makes a dumb choice once in a while and this one had probably just been in the wrong place at the wrong time. But then he realised, as he watched them take him from his home, that his dumb choice was no excuse to this mob and it might just cost him a whole lot more.' *They dragged him to their truck, Joe. I tried to tell them he might be innocent, but they just didn't want to know.* 'They took him to the nearest wood.' *They hogtied him and threw him in the back of a truck. I should have tried to stop them, Joe, but I was too yellow inside.* 'They refused to believe he was innocent.' *They tortured him, Joe. I can still hear him in my head ... begging for his life. And I did nothing to help him, Joe. Nothing. God forgive me, I did nothing.* 'And they hung him from the nearest tree.' Joe no longer saw the water in front of him. Now he was back in the stuffy, humid room with Michael in front of him. His brother rocking on the couch. Fast flowing tears marking dirty tracks down his face as he hugged a bottle of cheap whisky to his chest. *If he'd stayed in his own neighbourhood, Joe, he'd still be alive. He should have stayed away. Dear God forgive me. Forgive me. Forgive me.*

'Mike took it bad and I didn't know how to help him.' He took a shuddering breath. 'I *wanted* to.' He glanced at Anne. 'But what does a fourteen-year-old kid know?' He lay back and blocked out the sun with the crook of his elbow. 'The brother I knew was gone. I no longer knew the man he'd become. In his place was a drunkard who spent his days crying. I didn't know how to handle it, so I told him I was going out to get us some candy and left.'

'What happened?'

'I didn't go back until the next day. I just couldn't stomach it. Just kept putting it off, hoping he'd sleep it off. When I finally went round I knew, straight away, that something was up. His friend said he hadn't seen him and didn't seem too worried, but I was. I searched their garage then went out the back and that's when I saw him. He'd hung himself from the red maple tree at the end of the garden. It was autumn and the leaves were bright red. They looked like a cloud of blood floating above his dead body.'

He waited for usual platitudes of sympathy, that neither comforted nor brought closure. Anne remained silent beside him. He couldn't bear to look at her in case he saw what he felt inside mirrored in her face. Disgust and failure that he'd not helped his brother when he needed him most. To his surprise she took his hand. He raised his elbow to look at her.

'You were just a child, Joe. No child should have to deal with something like that.'

'I didn't understand Mike's breakdown when I was a kid, but I also didn't understand it as an adult. I grew up with segregation and never questioned it. Mike's suicide even made sense of it. All I knew was that if the boy hadn't wandered into a white area, he'd not have run the risk of being falsely accused … and he and my brother would still be alive. It seemed to me that if everyone just stuck to the rules, there'd be no conflict.' He sat up and faced Anne, cradling her hand in both of his. 'But I was wrong. I should have *questioned* it before and Mike's experience should have made me question it even more. I should have asked *why* can't a boy walk along any public road he chooses? *Why* should a boy be accused of a crime with no evidence to back it up? How can it be possible for a mob to try, convict and execute another human being … and get away with it? And why didn't I think of *his family* at all?'

'Why didn't you, Joe?'

Joe thought for a moment. 'Because if I thought too deeply, because if I saw that young boy as being just like me, what happened, what was happening every day, was just too terrible to accept. And then I'd be forced to question what sort of person that makes me, and what sort of people my family were, and my neighbours and teachers were. Because only a bad person would treat another so badly, right? So, to avoid those questions, to avoid accepting the fact that our differences are less than what makes us similar, we kept our distance. We don't want to discover that deep down they're just like us because the truth is too painful to bear.' He looked up. 'Is any of this making sense? I hope it is to you because it confuses the hell out of me. And I am ashamed.'

'Ashamed?'

'That it took a war, a journey to another country and seeing the disappointment in the eyes of someone I really like, to make me face what has always been there, but I just didn't want to see.'

'I won't pretend to understand what it's like to grow up in your country.' She smiled. 'What do I know? I've never travelled further than Plymouth. But I do know that you're not a bad person. And I also know that we all have to work together to fight Hitler. If you're wounded, it could be a black soldier who saves your life. And I want you to stay alive, Joe. I don't want you to die.'

'I won't die.'

'That was what my cousin said. All I know is there's no room for prejudice in war or peacetime. A bullet or bomb does not see the colour of a man's skin, but the more we all work together, the stronger we'll be.'

Chapter Fifteen

Autumn marked its arrival with a vibrant, ever-changing display of trees laden with gold and copper leaves. Along with it, Anne felt, came a new, more settled phase in her relationship with Joe, where she no longer felt wary of his American confidence, dazzled by his movie-like looks or disappointed with his past failings. Had she been the one to change or had Joe? Whatever the cause, she believed they'd reached a new understanding, which brought with it a sense of relaxation and absence of doubt. They were together, fixed, solid, where compatibility blossomed and flirtation could be indulged without fear.

Joe visited her as often as he could, his noisy motorcycle a welcoming signal of his imminent arrival. His mode of transport and petrol supply, which he kept hidden in a can buried behind the village hall where he slept, was their lifeline and gave them the freedom to meet when miles of countryside separated his billet from her home. Anne's heart would lurch without fail, whenever she heard Heapojunk in the distance, which allowed just enough time to grab her coat, ignore her mother's tuts and check the mirror before running outside to greet him.

At first, the unusually warm temperatures for the season added to the atmosphere of calm for it provided the perfect conditions for long, meandering walks through woodlands and lanes, where kisses, hidden from prying eyes, could be indulged beneath swaying canopies of rustling leaves.

Some days, Joe would spend his time teaching Billy how to pitch and catch. Their laughter and good-humoured, but competitive slights would often make her smile, while Joe's athletic prowess warmed her inside and out. Joe and Billy didn't seem to care about the cold, as they dived and made tracks in the carpet of fallen leaves by the wood near the river. Anne was content to watch and wonder, snuggled deep in an oversized woollen scarf round her neck, if Joe was remembering his own teenage years and trying to right things somehow.

Their impromptu trip to the beach of Loe, where numerous rowing boats nestled around the small bay, resembled more of a summer excursion than a day snatched before winter. A day when, to her surprise, Anne learnt Joe's only experience of travelling *on* water was the sea voyage that brought him to her.

‘It was the first time that most of my division had seen the sea,’ he said as if it was of no concern. ‘America is big. You can travel for days and not hit the ocean.’ She trailed her hand in the water and smiled back at him as he made a valiant attempt to navigate the ebb and flow of the incoming tide. His strength helped him to handle the cumbersome oars, but he was no skilled boatman. However, Joe, just as it seemed to be with most young men in uniform, had boundless energy and confidence to believe that nothing was unachievable if he put his mind to it. She knew she was falling in love with Joe, and that made it worse somehow. Her smile grew heavy, then faded. He saw the journey across the sea as no more than an adventure, but one day he’d be leaving her by the very same route. She once had the confidence to believe she could accept their relationship as being only temporary – she wasn’t so confident any more.

As the temperatures dropped, their time together moved indoors. They attended dances, held by the American military who were eager to show their appreciation to their hosts, while at the same time keeping their troops occupied and under control. The dances provided the perfect opportunity for Joe to introduce her to his friends, which he proudly did. His manner of introduction sent them a silent message and instantly elevated her status from a casual date to “Joe’s girl”. The message was received loud and clear and she was warmly welcomed into their fold.

Anne knew she would remember those winter dances for the rest of her life, for they were a comforting salve to a fun-starved generation. A time when they could mingle, make friends and laugh, beneath haphazardly strewn bunting of red, white and blue, and dance, dance, dance as if there was no war at all.

Anne looked across to Betty’s abandoned bench. She glanced up at the clock; Betty had been gone for almost ten minutes. Anne grabbed a cloth, wiped the excess oil from her hands and went in search of her. She found her in the back room, emerging from one of the toilet stalls and looking very pale. Betty watched her approach the cracked wash basin, turn on the tap and sluice her face with water.

‘Are you okay?’ asked Anne.

Betty cupped one hand beneath the flowing cascade, filled it with water and brought it to her lips. Now Anne knew there was something very wrong, Betty was always warning her not to drink the water as she swore it was laden with rust deposits.

'Betty?' She came closer, slipping herself between her friend and the basin. 'Have you been crying?'

Betty shook her head. 'No.'

'But your eyes are red. And I can see tears.'

'I've not been crying,' said Betty as she turned away. Anne frowned. Something wasn't right. She watched Betty as she dried her hands on the threadbare towel hanging from the wall. It seemed like forever. As soon as she finished, Anne turned her by the crook of her elbow to confront her again.

'Are you ill?'

'I'm not ill.'

'Then what is it, Betts?' she pleaded. 'Tell me.'

'I've been sick.' Her face crumpled, like a heartbroken child. 'I think I'm pregnant and I don't know what I'm going to do.'

Betty seemed to grow smaller before her very eyes, as if with finally telling, someone had dismantled the scaffolding within. Anne wrapped her arms around her to both comfort and support her, as Betty sagged against her in a sobbing mess.

'How far gone are you?'

'I don't know for sure. Maybe almost three months.'

'Does the father know?'

'No. No one knows … except you.'

'Do you think he'll marry you?'

Betty pulled away from her arms, searched for her handkerchief and roughly began to dry her eyes.

'I don't even know who the father is, so I can hardly tell him.' She blew her nose and realised Anne was looking at her. 'Oh, don't look at me like that, Anne. There were only four. Well three, the third I don't really count.'

Anne felt the urge to ask her to explain but thought perhaps the time wasn't appropriate.

'Besides, they were all American and I can't see any of them offering to make an honest woman of me. They've a war to fight. It was never like you and Joe. You two are a proper couple. It was different for me.'

'What will you do?'

'I'll have to tell my parents at some point. I'm dreading it. I know they will be so ashamed.'

'And what about the baby?'

The question brought tears to Betty's eyes again. As they silently began to flow down her cheeks, Anne reached for her. They held each other close as Betty cried. Anne's heart broke for her. Eventually Betty's crying subsided, but they remained embraced, both too exhausted and drained of emotion to risk standing alone.

'I don't know what I'll do,' she said eventually as she stared into the mirror. Anne turned her head to look at their reflection too; two women holding each other, Betty's head resting on her shoulder, her eyes glazed with tears.

'I'll be here to help you,' said Anne.

'Thank you … but I don't think anyone can help me now.'

Anne knew she was being unusually quiet when Joe came to call, but he didn't seem to object, being in a melancholy mood himself. They strolled along the country lanes, wrapped up in heavy coats and scarves against the blustery winter winds. Betty's pregnancy continued to play on Anne's mind, but she'd promised to keep her secret. She paused to watch the clouds chase across the sky. Joe joined her.

'I'll be going away tomorrow.'

Anne felt her heart constrict in her chest. She had dreaded this moment. 'Are you going to war?'

He smiled. 'No. Just for training.'

'For how long?'

'Two, maybe three weeks.'

'Will you come back here?'

'I hope so.' He wrapped her in his arms. 'Try keeping me away.'

'But you can't be sure.'

'Sometimes I wonder if the army knows.' He held her at arm's length and looked at her. 'Don't look so glum. I'm sure we'll be back.'

'But you're not certain.'

'No one can be certain of anything any more.'

Anne wanted to cry, but instead scuffed some fallen leaves with her boot and resolved not to appear too needy. A girlfriend falling apart was not what Joe needed right now.

'I suppose I shall miss you.'

'I suppose I shall miss you too,' he teased.

She ceased moving her foot, all energy drained from her. She stared at the leaves as she fought to control the rising tears inside her. Eventually she looked up at him. They were no more than an arm's length away and she wondered if this would be the last time she'd see him. A physical ache racked her body at the thought, but she lifted her chin bravely and locked away the memory of his image to the deepest recess of her mind. Her determination must have triggered something in Joe, for his smile disappeared and his steady gaze grew intense. She had never seen him like this before. Something had changed and it both frightened and excited her. He stepped forward and framed her face in his hands, his gaze tracing every feature as if he had newly discovered some precious treasure. The kiss that followed was different too – heated, urgent and as intense as his gaze. And Anne found herself responding with equal urgency, for this might be the last time she would ever feel so loved again.

Chapter Sixteen

Joe watched the passing countryside through the train window, a mixture of snaking hedges dissected by stations and road crossings, with fleeting glimpses of fields and towns beyond. The view was a stark contrast to the scene inside the crowded carriage, heaving with booted soldiers, dressed in large winter coats, and multiple haversacks filling every available space. He still missed his brother, but this odd-ball unit of men were fast becoming his family now, and he shared their feelings of excitement that he too was heading somewhere new, with exciting experiences ahead, albeit for just three weeks. They had boarded the train energised and rowdy, despite the early hour, but the rattling journey on firm, threadbare seats, lulled many into late-morning naps and mellowed boredom.

His thoughts turned to Anne. He was already missing her. He'd attempted to reassure her that he'd be back, but it was only when they received their last orders of "pack only essentials", did he allow himself to believe it was true. The relief he felt at learning that they'd be returning could only mean one thing – Joe Mallory, whose only experiences of loving someone resulted in them dying, *had* fallen in love. The revelation scared him as it would inevitably end in some form of heartache.

The train began to slow. Those who napped around him began to stir, while those awake took it upon themselves to warn others that their journey was finally coming to an end. It took several minutes for the impatient, hungry troops to disembark; the long train had to stop and start several times to accommodate the small platform that greeted them. To the delight of the hungry soldiers, teenage boys, eager to make a profit, were waiting to sell them fish and chips for inflated prices that only well-paid American soldiers would not question.

A convoy of trucks took them on the last leg of their journey. Braunton Burrows was one of the largest sand dune systems in the British Isles and would become their main training ground. Their permanent base was meant to be nearby, consisting of over five hundred Nissen huts, mess halls and shower facilities capable of housing over four thousand men. However, bad weather and complications had delayed its construction, so alternative plans resulted in the troop convoy heading towards Saunton, and the fields adjoining Braunton Burrows.

The narrow roads were inadequate to cope with two-way military vehicles, so a one-way system had been set up to cope with the influx of trainees. In some areas there'd been no roads at all, so temporary ones, made up of bitumen and steel mesh, had been hurriedly laid, while junctions, devoid of signposts, were numbered to help the drivers navigate their way.

Upon arrival, the troops jumped down from their trucks and were instructed to 'Fall in.' As the troops, stiff from the confines of their long journey, formed rows, they surveyed their new temporary base for the first time. Muddy fields stretched out in front of them, lined with multiple, neat rows of square, high pitched tents. This was to become their new home and just like other tented camps, it would dispassionately be named Tent City by all who stayed beneath the water-stained canvas roofs.

Training started the following morning and would last for three weeks. Although the initial introduction to the course comprised the usual safety regulations, it also included guidance on wearing heavy combat equipment and how to discard it if they found themselves in deep water. It soon became apparent that the training regime would be different to anything the land-trained soldiers had experienced before.

'It will be challenging,' they were warned gravely. 'Our standards are high. If a soldier does not meet them they will be immediately transferred to a non-combat section of the regiment. Lives depend on each and every one of you being the best. We will tolerate no flagging.' The warning was stark. Joe and Frank exchanged glances. They'd already survived one military culling by becoming confident swimmers and had, albeit naively, thought they were already the best, as did all the young soldiers present. Today they were firmly informed this wasn't the case. The threat of transfer would become their constant companion and spur them on, as no soldier wanted to be the one to fail. Their introduction had already taught them their first lesson. Only the best would be good enough and they had not proved their worth yet.

Normal divisional hierarchy no longer applied as the troops were divided into multiple assault sections, each commanded by a lieutenant and assisted by a sergeant. Each sub-section of the assault unit was made up of riflemen, rocketeers, wire-cutters, flame throwers, mortar men, machine gunners and demolition men. The morning sessions of the first week concentrated on undertaking drills, mainly embarking and disembarking the landing crafts which would transport the troops and vehicles from ship to land. Joe was soon to discover that the order in which they did this would be vitally important as the formation they formed would enable attack, while at the same time protecting those within the unit. Their main goal, as they left the craft, would be to assault an armed enemy position and destroy it. Joe and Frank were riflemen; they would be the last sub-section to embark and the first to disembark and face enemy fire.

The early drills were initially carried out amongst the undulating sand dunes of North Devon, using scale-size outlines for the landing crafts, but by the end of the week, the drills moved to the sheltered waters of the Taw and Torridge estuary. The beaches provided ideal sheltered loading areas for the troops to practice, although there were several incidents when the landing crafts became beached on the sand and had to be pushed out to sea, as a direct result of the extra weight from the troops on-board. They disembarked on several nearby beaches, names of which Joe didn't know or care, but they were all glad to reach firm ground again when their boots hit the sandy shores. It was the first time many, including himself, had experienced such debilitating sea sickness that threatened to turn a soldier's stomach inside out. Those early days highlighted the absurdity of war, where a man came to believe that a coastline, which resembled a holiday destination, was hostile territory and that seasick, pale young men, most who'd never shot live ammunition in combat before, could be battle-hardened soldiers. Who was lying to who? The military to them … or were they just lying to their selves?

Throughout the first week, they were also taught the tasks of each sub-team. To Joe, the implication was clear: should any soldier be incapacitated, someone else could take his place.

Each assault section was made up of thirty men. They were fast developing into a fully coordinated unit. The aim of the next two weeks was to ensure they had the skills to tackle all the practical obstacles they'd face as they advanced inland and, ultimately, do it well while under enemy fire.

The training was well planned, a concerted effort to prepare them for war. Here, beaches were sectioned into areas, each with a specific training role in mind. Numerous ranges were arranged to perfect individual skills with the aim of soldiers having the necessary skills and fitness levels to overcome beach defences, establish beachheads, clear them of obstacles, such as wire, and clear minefields.

The obstacle course stretched over eight-hundred yards of sand dunes, consisting of an array of fortified defences for them to get through, including tank defences, concrete walls, ditches filled with barbed wire, tripwires, thick coils of barbed wire and concrete horned scullies used to tear the hull of boats. Each assault team took the course in turns, a fast-rotating rota which allowed no one to flag. Those that did were immediately hauled away. Their sudden removal was a reminder that only spurred the others on.

Area C was where Joe's assault team spent much of their time. Divided into numerous sections, it concentrated on rocket, demolition and practice assaults, including mines and booby traps, using live ammunition. Each session lasted an hour. Along with Area C were ranges 39 and 40, where Joe and Frank, along with other rifle men, honed their shooting skills. They were each given twenty-four rounds to shoot at silhouette targets, their skills constantly assessed and marked for accuracy.

'If you don't score a minimum of eighty per cent you're not wanted here!' barked the officer.

'Jeez!' muttered Frank as he reloaded his gun. 'Give us a break.'

Joe took aim and fired at the target. 'Don't think he's listening, Frank. You'll just have to cry into your pillow tonight.'

Frank smiled at him. 'Cocky bastard,' he said before firing at the target himself.

The training course covered a vast area of coastline, with multiple units from different disciplines at work. Grenades, controlled explosions, bazooka launching and rifle and machine gun firing dotted the area with plumes of smoke and a cacophony of yelled commands. Critiques and reviews were undertaken periodically so lessons could be learned and problems overcome, but the main instruction given to the assault units was to not be too cautious of mine-strewn beaches.

'The longer you're not under cover, the more likely you'll be shot. So if you want to stay alive … KEEP MOVING!'

The training course culminated in two full-scale multi-assault unit exercises, one held during the day and one at night. This time they landed on the three mile stretch of Woolacombe beach, with clear instructions to advance inland against resistance. The Atlantic waves rolled in, unhindered by rock, and brought the landing craft, laden with men, near to the shore. The exercise, which involved a mixture of blank and real ammunition, was the closest scenario to what they might face in the future. It was exciting. It was adventurous. But it was also terrifying. By the end of the intense training course, every muscle in their bodies ached, including several they didn't even know they had … but they had survived it. The men who designed and developed the course had been successful in their goals. Once completed, the inexperienced soldier came away with new perfected skills, confidence in their abilities, a greater understanding of the battle ahead, physically fit … and the belief that maybe, just maybe, they were untouchable by death.

Chapter Seventeen

'Anne! Betty is here to see you!'

Henry would often say that his wife's yell was loud enough to be heard by the cows in Devon. For the first time, Anne wondered if her stepfather was right. She efficiently tucked the last corner of the bedspread into place and went down the stairs to greet her.

Betty smiled brightly when she saw her. 'Fancy coming for a walk?'

Anne stared at her in surprise. Countryside walks were not Betty's favourite pastime, yet here she was suggesting the very same. Anne quickly accepted and grabbed her coat.

'Take the keys to Oak Cottage and check if Mrs Friar has left any taps on. She turned up this morning with the keys, said she was missing her family and was leaving. She left so suddenly I wouldn't be surprised if she's left a tap dripping.'

Anne took the keys from her mother's open hand and followed Betty outside. They strolled up the lane together.

'Is it your mother's house?' Betty asked.

'Oh no. The owner died and it was requisitioned by the government. I think Mother feels it's her duty to look after it until after the war.'

They paused at a closed gate to admire the view.

'Saw Billy earlier,' said Betty. 'He's grown. He is as tall as a man now.'

'Yes, but he's still a child at heart. This morning he found a stash of new treasure a couple had left behind in a bomb shelter. He came home, arranged it all on the kitchen table to proudly show us. He couldn't understand why Father burst out laughing and Mother started screaming. He's in his room now, sulking.'

'Why? What was it?' asked Betty.

'French letters,' replied Anne with a smile.

Betty rested her folded arms on the top of the gate and sighed. 'Well, I hope the owner of the stash used one to protect his girl, although I'm a living example that they don't always work.'

Anne joined her at the gate. 'Did you do it?'

'Tell my parents?'

'Yes. You said you would this weekend.'

Betty nodded. 'Yes. I couldn't keep it quiet any longer. It's not easy to hide a five-month bump.'

'You've done a good job so far.'

Betty shrugged. 'Winter helps. Lots of big cardigans and coats.'

'How did they react?'

Betty's eyes filled with tears as she recalled the memory. 'They were shocked. Angry. Devastated.' She looked at Anne. 'Everything you don't want your parents to feel. I'm a disappointment to them.'

'No, you're not.'

'Yes, I am. They told me so.'

Anne hugged her and would have comforted her all afternoon if it was needed, but it was Betty who ended it first.

'Well what is done is done. They've arranged for me to stay with an aunt. She's not my aunt really, just a family friend. Staying with a family member sounds less scandalous. In reality, my parents don't want my aunts and uncles to know. They say they don't want to dump my sin on their door.'

'I'm so sorry, Betty.'

'Don't be. It's my own stupid fault.'

Anne fervently disagreed, but Betty wouldn't have it.

'What will happen?'

'With the baby?' Anne nodded. 'I'm told there's a mother and baby home nearby. I'll have the baby there and then come home.'

'And the baby?'

'They'll find a family to adopt it.'

Anne frowned. Betty seemed oddly disconnected from the baby inside her, calling it 'it' as if the child was an object and something quite separate.

'How can you bear the thought of giving your child away?'

Betty's jaw tightened. She swallowed deeply. 'I don't think. I try not to think. Because if I do, I will die inside.'

The familiar sound of Joe's motorbike broke into their thoughts and set Anne's heart racing as over three weeks had passed since she'd last seen him.

Betty looked at her. 'That must be Joe's bike.'

Anne raised her eyebrows in innocence. 'What makes you say that?'

'Because your face has just lit up.' Betty smiled. 'You are so lucky to have a man who loves you.'

'He has never told me that he does.'

'He behaves like it. I don't have a soldier visiting me so often.'

Anne smiled, secretly pleased to have an objective view telling her what she hoped in her heart.

'But be careful, Anne. Don't end up like me. Mother and Father hope to brush everything under the carpet, but I'll always know what I've done and that there will be a child out there who I will never see grow up.'

'You could keep it.'

'No, I can't. My parents don't want me to keep it and I can't do it on my own without their support.' Joe appeared on the brow of the hill. 'Don't tell Joe.' She hugged Anne tightly, her firm swollen belly nestled between them under her outsized coat. Anne's eyes began to smart. Betty held her at arms-length. 'Don't cry, Anne. You'll set me off.' She hastily brushed away her own tears and sniffed loudly. 'I came to say goodbye. I'm leaving in the morning and won't be back until it's all over.'

'I'm afraid that it will never be over for you, Betty.'

Betty hugged her tightly again. 'I know, but there is no harm in pretending it will. It's all I've got to keep me from falling apart.'

Anne watched Betty walk away, her head bowed as if she was fearful Joe would guess her condition and take the news back to his division.

Joe parked his motorcycle and ran towards Anne, immediately sweeping her up in a dramatic embrace. Lifting her feet from the ground so she couldn't resist his antics, he spun her around in his arms. 'Now this is what I've been missing!' he said, smiling broadly. He slid her down his body, like an intimate dance, until her feet retouched the ground.

'Don't! Someone might see!' She laughed, feeling both delighted, yet anxious that his overly affectionate greeting would be seen by someone who would tell her parents.

'Who cares? I don't.' He tried to kiss her, but she twisted away.

'You seem rather … excited.'

'You would if you were me. I've just spent three weeks with hundreds of hairy, sweaty men for company. Believe me, I've been dreaming of this moment.'

He tried to reach for her again but Anne braced herself against his chest. She raised a reproachful eyebrow at him.

'You dreamt of being spied on by Mrs Oates?' She indicated in the direction of their observer with a jerk of her head. Joe's eyes followed the direction she'd indicated. His eyes met those belonging to an elderly woman who was staring at them through the opposite cottage window.

'Hmm … I get your point. Is there anywhere we can go to be alone for once? I'm getting a little tired at being constantly observed by the village Gestapo.'

Anne felt the key to Oak Cottage in her pocket. 'I might just have the perfect place.'

Anne had known Oak Cottage all her life, yet she had never been inside until now. The door moved easily on its hinges and welcomed them directly into a small room, with two comfortable chairs, a table and a set of wooden chairs in the centre. An open fire grate was prepared with knotted newspapers and carefully laid kindling. Anne stepped through to the back room. A neat and tidy kitchen welcomed her – not a dripping tap in sight. She returned to Joe. He was looking at a picture hanging on the wall. He moved on to an ornament, picked it up and turned it over to look at its base as if it was the most natural thing to look at other people's things. It was as if he lived here and the house was theirs. It was an exciting glimpse of what their future could look like. He glanced up and caught her staring.

'Everything seems to be in order here,' she said, making a show of looking around the room.

He replaced the ornament. 'Quaint place.'

Anne was pleased he was finding the visit of interest. 'Shall we look upstairs?'

His eyes darkened. 'I'd like that very much. But are you sure? What if someone comes?'

'No one will come. My key is the only one and no one knows we're here,' she confidently reassured him.

She climbed the stairs, eager to see the bedrooms. The top windows were the only ones visible from the road as the rest of the house was shielded by trees. There were only two rooms, one leading straight into the other. The wallpaper was dated and faded, but the rooms were still furnished. Mrs Friar had even left the beds with clean linen, ready for the next family to arrive.

Anne quickly looked around, approving, and disapproving the décor as if she'd just moved in herself. Joe came up behind her, eased her blouse from her neck and nestled kisses into the crook between shoulder and neck. At first, his kisses tickled, but as his breathing deepened, she recognised her own had too. Consumed by a wave of luxurious fatigue, her head lulled away, exposing yet more. It was not an intentional invite, but Joe took it for one. His hands began to explore further, sweeping over the curves of her body in a way a man had never done before. She had yearned for this moment, in the days before war, and the days she was not with Joe, but now it was here she was unsure if she could cope. Her experience until now was no more than a whispered discussion with Betty and see where Betty's dalliances had led her. What did she know about sex? It was a taboo subject, something no decent girl should know about until her wedding night.

'The best gift you can give your husband,' her grandmother had once preached to her, 'is your virginity. No decent man will want someone else's spoilt goods.'

Anne twisted away from his touch and pretended to laugh. 'My! You are full of it!'

Joe laughed too, unaware of her mounting hesitancy. 'What can I say? You are one sexy lady.' He reached for her again, eager not to have space between them. He cupped her face, his gaze lingering on her lips. If he would only look into her eyes, he'd see she felt troubled. But he didn't. They were on two different plains, and his looked far more fun.

He kissed her deeply, sending melting shivers of excitement to every intimate part of her body. Her body felt alive in a way it had never done before. A flush of desire filled her up, heating her skin and making her head race. This was how he was feeling, yet he was welcoming it and enjoying the ride. And she was tempted to too, yet a battle for supremacy began to rage in her mind. On one side every moral lesson, religious sermon, nugget of malicious gossip about some tart seen in town, on the other a very real desire to explore every part of Joe's body with her hands and lips, welcoming his touches, his kisses and everything else he had to teach her. Anne pushed him away.

'I can't. I don't want to get pregnant.'

'It's okay. The army has given us rubbers.' He patted his pockets to locate them.

Anne felt any desire instantly drain away. 'I hadn't realised having sex was part of the army's training.'

Surprised at her sharp tone, he stopped searching and looked up. 'It's not. Are you okay?'

She moved away from him. 'I'm fine.'

Joe tilted his head to one side as he looked at her. 'You don't look fine. You look stiff as a rod.'

'I'm beginning to think what they are all saying is right about you.'

'Me?'

'No, not just you. All American soldiers.'

'Well that's a relief I'm not being singled out.' He didn't look relieved.

'They say you are all over sexed, overpaid and over here.'

Joe considered the slur. To her surprise, he nodded in acceptance. 'Well I guess they're right. It's what happens when thousands of young men are massed together. And, if you believe their bravado, then I guess most of them *are* getting laid. Although I'm not sure I do. Their bravado, I mean.' He reached for his cigarettes. 'Do you mind?'

She shook her head and watched him light up. 'And I suppose today it's your turn to get laid too.'

He glanced up sharply, as he finished lighting his cigarette. 'You suggested we went upstairs.'

Anne's mouth dropped open. 'I wanted to see the bedspreads.'

Joe's mouth lifted at the corner. 'Well I've not heard it called that before!'

'I didn't mean I wanted to have … you know …' She mouthed the word, 'sex.'

Joe attempted to suppress his smile. 'Pity. I thought you did.'

Despite Anne's shock at the blatant way he was talking about a subject she had always been taught nice girls never acknowledge, she grudgingly had to admire him for it. Although talking about it was embarrassing, it appeared strangely liberating to see it didn't have to be that way. He was being truthful; perhaps it was time she was.

'It's not that I don't want to, Joe. It's just that …' She searched for the right word, 'I'm scared.'

His expression turned to concern. 'Hey, I'll be gentle. You know I wouldn't want to cause you any pain.'

Anne swallowed. Pain? She hadn't even thought of that aspect.

Joe stepped forward; his arms open. 'I promise. I'll take it as slow as you want.'

Anne remained where she stood. 'Don't pressure me, Joe.'

Joe lowered his arms. 'I'm not. I guess what I'm trying to say is that I'm okay with it. I just misunderstood what you were saying. I'm sorry.'

She dared to look at him. He appeared genuine.

'Are you disappointed?'

'Yeah sure … who wouldn't be? But not with you.' He looked at his cigarette as if its appeal had suddenly faded. He opened the window, stubbed it out on the sill and flicked the butt outside. 'I bet half the guys back at camp have never even kissed a girl, let alone got laid anyway.'

Joe had told her he was willing to wait so why did she feel so miserable inside? He walked towards her and tilted her chin upwards, so she was forced to look into his eyes.

'I don't like the thought of you being scared. I hope you're not scared of me.'

'No, not you.' She fiddled with the button on his shirt. 'Someone I know is pregnant and she's not married to the father.'

'Betty?'

'I can't say.' He slid his arms around her as she stepped into his arms. She rested her head against his chest. 'What if I fall pregnant and you leave me?'

'I'd never do that.'

'You can't promise that. What if you get yourself killed?'

'I don't plan on doing that either.'

'No one does. But it could happen.'

'Well this is a cheerful conversation.'

'I'm serious. I don't want to be a single mother and I certainly don't want to have to give up my child.'

'Look, Anne, it's okay. I get it. I really do. You want to wait until you've a ring on your finger. Look, we've only been together for a few months. We are still getting to know each other, so I get it. It's too early for you. But you know what? That's okay because we have plenty of time. There's no rush.'

He wrapped his arms about her a little more tightly and rested his chin on her head. She nestled against him and watched her fingers rise and fall with each of his breaths. She could almost feel his heart beating, as it gently slowed to a calm, steady beat. She felt safe and comforted, yet felt she was missing out on something she would come to regret.

'Are you okay?' asked Joe after several minutes of silence.

She nodded. 'I think so.'

Joe wasn't convinced. 'Are you sure?'

'Well, we could just lie on the bed … and talk.'

'That sounds good to me. And I promise I won't ravage you.' He looked down at her and found her smiling.

'Now you're teasing me.'

'Maybe.' He stroked a loose strand of her hair into place. 'To be honest, training *was* tough, and it'll be nice to put the old feet up.'

They climbed on the bed and lay down, Joe ensuring he was on the far side of the mattress with his arms firmly by his sides. Anne laughed at his virtuous position.

'Hey!' he protested. 'I'm trying to be the good guy here!' She laughed again at his mock indignation. It had been a long time since she'd laughed so much. It felt good. Joe had been away far too long. He welcomed her closer and she snuggled into his arms.

'Thank you for understanding.'

'You want a ring on your finger first and that's okay. If I had a sister, I'd want her to want the same.'

They lay in silence, both watching Joe's hand trace the fine hairs on her arm.

'Anne.'

'Yes?'

'If I stop visiting you, it will be because I've been sent away again. I want you to know that.'

'What do you mean?'

'Orders can come without warning sometimes. One day I'll be sent somewhere at short notice and have no time to tell you. If I stand you up, it will be because I couldn't let you know. Things change so quickly.'

Anne nodded. She understood how things were, but it was still reassuring for Joe to confirm he would never end things without letting her know.

Eventually she asked, 'What was it like?'

'What?'

'The training.'

She felt Joe sigh against her cheek as she threaded her fingers through his. Joe began to talk, relating his experience as if he was telling someone else's story. A story of a far-off land, where tent cities were a man's home, strict rules were followed and high expectations asked. She suspected he gave her an edited version, one filled with newfound camaraderie, increasing motivation, and a growing self-belief inside each soldier. Anne didn't voice her fears. It was a good thing Joe felt the training was of some benefit, but unlike many, her stepfather had shared his experiences of war and how training could only help so much; the rest was down to luck.

Eventually, Joe draped the crochet bedspread over them for added warmth and they fell into a companionable silence. The winter breeze had grown to a late November gale, yet the harshness unfolding outside only heightened their feelings of contentment, cocooned together inside, as they were.

Joe's fingers slipped from her hand. Anne realised his breathing had deepened. Something had changed. She dared to look up at his face. He was sleeping, his handsome face, absent of the worries of the day, almost two years younger. She raised herself onto one elbow and looked down upon him. She'd never had the opportunity to look at him like this, without his knowledge, without someone seeing her feelings in her eyes. The opportunity was too enticing to miss.

Her gaze followed his hairline of tousled, dark hair. It was boyish, army neat, yet with the tendency of relaxed unkemptness. This man did not preen in front of the mirror. There was no need. She dropped her gaze to search for those teasing brown eyes. She knew they were there, hiding behind fragile lids edged with dark, tapered, silk lashes. His dark stubble fascinated her, each bristle just emerging from an early morning shave. She was tempted to experience this uniquely male side to him, by stroking his jaw with a light touch of her fingers. Now his lips. She had experienced his lips often, from chaste kisses to lingering, deep passion, but had not really appreciated how perfect they were. Nature was truly skilled, able to carve unique symmetry and fullness yet retain masculinity in each refined curve.

Anne continued to watch him sleep, as time ticked away in some distant room of the house. Joe's masculinity intrigued her, casting its magic so she could not look away. Gone was his veil of sleeping innocence, in his place was a man with more power over her than he would ever know. She could feel the change happening now, swirling liquid fire, pooling deep within her. She hadn't experienced such magic before, for that is how it felt, a spell, caused by his body, moving through her in the most intimate way. Was this how Joe had felt when he thought she was willing? Had he felt the same burning desire, with its insatiable hunger that demanded fulfilment? It felt natural, yet rebellious. Good, but dangerous. And despite being a virgin, she felt, in that moment, she could become a temptress equal to him … should she dare wake him. She was surely tempted, but Betty's final goodbye would not allow her. And Joe needed to sleep. He had spent three weeks in crowded tents, with noisy flapping canvases and snoring men. His days had been spent rising early and undertaking gruelling exercises, where those who were not up to standards disappeared overnight. The strain, stress and physical fatigue had finally overwhelmed him in the absence of such scrutiny, and it had only finally happened in the safety of her company. She would let her Cornish Yank sleep for he needed the rest far more than he knew himself.

Chapter Eighteen

Joe tilted his head to listen for sounds of movement behind the front door. No one had answered his knock, but there was an earnest conversation, between a man and a woman, taking place somewhere and it wasn't coming from inside the house. He looked around at the empty front garden and lane stretching off into the distance. Anne had invited him to have tea with her family and although it wasn't something he was looking forward to, it was an indicator of how she viewed their relationship. She now considered him one step up from a man she dated. It felt good, although eating with her family felt more of a trial than a pleasant experience. Calling it tea, was kind of strange to start with. He followed the sound, hoping to find Anne. Best get the experience over with as soon as he could.

The trail took him around her house to their backyard. He recognised Anne's parents' voices and realised their conversation was more heated than he'd first thought. He paused behind a water tank, which collected water for the garden.

'She said she wouldn't be late. He's due to arrive any minute. What am I going to talk to him about? Henry! I said put that fork down and come inside.'

'It's just a meal.'

'It's more than a meal and you know it!'

Joe smiled. It appeared he wasn't the only one wanting to make a good impression. He slid off his cap in readiness to introduce himself.

'What are you so upset about? I think it's good to meet him properly.'

'I don't want to meet him properly.'

Joe retreated a step. Perhaps now was not the right time to do it.

'Why?'

'Because I don't want Anne to be dating an American. I wish she would just end it.'

'She's young. She's just having fun.'

'Anne isn't that sort of girl. She thinks she's in love. She's not. She just thinks she is.'

'Does it matter?'

'Of course it does! He's going to be sent away. It could be any day. Anne will spend the rest of the war waiting for him. He might not even come back.'

'But he could.'

'And then what? He might just go back to America and she will be left brokenhearted.'

'They might marry.'

'I hope they don't. Mrs Friar understood. He will take Anne back to America and we will never see her again. We won't see our grandchildren grow up.'

Anne's stepfather remained silent. Joe imagined him leaning on his garden fork considering his wife's words.

'The *Royal Cornwall Gazette* have had notices warning women not to marry American soldiers.'

'Really? Why?'

'Let me get it.' A bustle of footsteps and a rustle of paper and she was back. 'I'll read it to you.'

'There's no need to do that, Martha.'

'The headline says "Warning About Marriage" and it goes on to say that American soldiers need permission to marry from their commanding officer or they could be court martialled. It also says that if an English woman marries an American, she doesn't automatically become an American and could be kept on Ellis Island as an alien. Dear Lord! An *alien!* You see, Henry, things are more complicated. Anne will have to move to a new country to be with him. It's easy for a woman to fall in love with a man wearing a uniform. A smart uniform turns him into a hero, but the reality is that the very same man, who seemed so handsome and brave, still wears smelly socks and snores when he's had too much to drink.'

'Is that a dig at me? I only have a tipple at the weekends.'

'Don't be silly.' Anne's mother took on a pleading tone. 'I'm serious. If he was to do the honest thing, which I very much doubt he will, Anne's troubles will only just begin. She knows nothing about America. She will be far away from everything she has ever known. War changes a man. She will be so lonely. And she'll be called an *alien*!'

'And you will miss her.'

'Won't you? I want her to meet a nice English boy and live nearby. But her head is in the clouds and she'll pine for him for the rest of the war.'

'Then you need to tell her.'

'She won't listen to me.'

'What makes you so sure?'

'Because she thinks she's in love. She knows little about Joe. She's never met his family or his friends back home. She only knows what he tells her. She hasn't even seen him out of uniform … or at least I hope to heaven she hasn't. This type of love is based on fairy tales when the handsome prince comes riding in to rescue her. But it's not reality. It won't last. Real love is different. It's when you know all about them, their faults and all, but still accept them for who they are. It may not be so romantic or make your heart beat so fast, but it has more chance of lasting the rest of your life.'

'Is that the sort of love we have?'

'Well, you snore so we must.'

Henry chuckled. It was Joe's cue to leave. He returned to the front of the house, uncertain whether to leave or go through with the charade of having tea with them. He should be angry at her mother's judgemental concerns, but he wasn't. Her concerns were real and had an element of truth. He couldn't guarantee he would return from the war. No one could. Anne would feel his loss greater the longer they were together. He believed he loved Anne, yet something always held him back from telling her so. Was it because of his uncertain future or could he see no future with her? Despite what he told Anne, he found it hard to envisage a future together, as if by doing so he'd be tempting fate. Anne's mother was right; despite their conversations Anne didn't really know him at all. She'd fallen in love with the uniform and the novelty of a foreigner not necessarily the man inside. He looked at the presents he was carrying and felt like a fraud.

Anne appeared on her bicycle, bumping down the lane with her coat and scarf flying. 'Sorry I'm late.' She dismounted, leant it against the wall and pulled off her mitts. 'We had some trouble at work.' She opened the door without elaborating and called to her parents. 'Joe's here!' Joe slipped his cap under his jacket's lapel and quickly ran his hand through his hair.

Her parents appeared in the doorway on the other side of the room.

'Hello. I'm Anne's stepfather. I hear you've been teaching my boy baseball?'

Joe transferred his presents to one side and shook his offered hand. 'Pleased to meet you, sir. I have. Billy's a fast learner.' He turned to the woman who had yet to meet his eyes. 'Thank you for the invitation, ma'am.' His gaze swept the table, neatly laid with a small selection of cakes and sandwiches. A dish of pears took pride of place in the centre and he wondered briefly if they were from his homeland. 'This looks a mighty fine spread, ma'am.'

Her mother inclined her head at the compliment. 'Thank you, Mr Mallory. I try my best.'

Joe remembered his gifts.

'I have something for you, just to show my appreciation.' He handed Henry a pack of cigars.

'Look, Martha, cigars! These will make me look like a right gentleman.'

Joe smiled. 'I don't know about that.' He saw Anne's expression and realised his blunder. 'I'm sorry, I didn't mean how it came out. The officers in the army have a liking for cigars and I was thinking of them rather than the gentry.'

Henry examined one in his hand. 'Yes, I believe you are right, American officers do.' He placed one in the corner of his mouth to imitate how they smoked them. 'How do I look?'

'Like a man in charge of an army, sir.' The compliment appeared to please him. 'And what else have you got there?'

'Henry!' scolded his wife.

Joe gave Anne's mother a box of chocolates. Hidden underneath was a packet of stockings. She thanked him for the chocolates, but when she discovered the stockings, her face turned crimson. She hurried to the pine dresser, placed them in the drawer and shut it firmly, leaving Joe unsure if she was pleased at the luxury or insulted. Maybe stockings hadn't been a good idea. The collar of his shirt suddenly felt unbearably warm.

'Well, I think it's time we sat down,' said Henry. He swept a hand towards a chair, indicating where Joe should sit. They took their seats, Henry settling in his favourite chair at the head of the table.

'I have something for Billy too.' He lifted the remaining gift in his hands, a poorly wrapped baseball bat.

Anne's mother only saw a potentially destructive weapon in his hand and instantly confiscated it. 'Billy will be here soon. I will give it to him later when the best china has been put away.' Joe watched her hide it in the corner of the room and return to the table as if it had never existed. She pasted on a smile and poured him a cup of tea. Joe watched the steam rise from the swirling, tanned liquid.

'What do you think of England, Joe?' asked Henry.

He looked up. 'I like it very much. The people have been very friendly.' Martha's arm cut across him as she handed Anne a cup. 'But I'm still trying to get used to the rain.'

'This winter has been unusually dry,' said Martha. 'We've nothing to complain about.'

Anne came to his defence as she offered her stepfather a sandwich. 'Joe wasn't complaining, Mother.'

Martha settled herself into the seat opposite him.

'I most certainly wasn't, ma'am. I like the changing seasons here. It's simply different to what I'm used to.'

Martha's eyes softened. 'I expect there's a lot of things you have to get used to and, Lord knows, I'm the first to admit that we don't appreciate that as much as we should.' She offered him the plate of sandwiches and he obediently took one. 'Thank you, Joe, for helping us fight Hitler. Sometimes it feels like Cornwall is being invaded by America and I sometimes forget that American troops are also someone's son. Your mother must worry about you.'

Joe carefully placed his sandwich on his plate. It was difficult to know how to respond when you didn't understand the rules of the game. Anne answered for him.

'His mother died when he was young. Remember?'

'Oh! I'm sorry. I forgot.' He looked up to find her embarrassed apology was real. In a way he had hoped it wouldn't be, so he could label her a vicious woman who cared only about herself. However, if the last few months had taught him little, one thing it had taught him was that life was more complicated than he once thought. People could not be put into boxes and Anne's mother was yet another fine example of this. She wanted his relationship to end with Anne. She didn't want him here and she wanted him gone. However, she was not a bad person who didn't understand love and grief, in fact, he suspected, she knew it too well and it was the driving force behind her stance now. He wondered what had happened in her past which meant that she didn't want Anne to date him now?

Henry saved the conversation dying an awkward death. 'What is the American army doing to keep you young lads under control?'

Joe was thankful for the change in conversation. 'Since our return they've increased our physical training.'

'It sounds exhausting,' chipped in Anne.

'But necessary. I think after our last trip away, we came home rather full of ourselves.' He exchanged a knowing glance with Anne, who blushed and hid her smile behind her teacup. Her mother's eyes darted between them.

'Sounds like the British army. Although in my day we were a scrawny lot.' They spoke a little more about life in the army, the only thing, apart from Anne, that was a common bond, but it soon dried up, both aware that detailed discussions were not permitted, no matter how friendly the other man was.

To everyone's relief, Billy finally arrived home, untidying the house within minutes of his arrival with his body, cap, coats and discarded bag. He sat at the table and was immediately told to wash his hands. The chaos of scraping chairs, ill co-ordinated limbs and enthusiasm at seeing his American buddy again, was a welcome distraction to those that remained at the table. Conversation flowed more easily, thanks to Billy's incessant questions about America. Finally, their talk turned to something much closer to home.

'Christmas is next week. Perhaps Joe could come over?' suggested Billy enthusiastically.

Anne had already hinted at it, and although Joe wanted to experience a family Christmas with Anne, something he'd not had since his mother's death, the official invitation from her parents had yet to be received. Joe realised her mother and stepfather's expression didn't change, which told a story in itself. Anne had already tried to persuade them and had failed so far. This casual invitation to tea was their way of mollifying her, whereas Anne saw it as a step towards a festive invitation.

He stared at the small slice of cake on his plate during the silence that followed. He realised silence had a sound of its own, pulsing, droning and strangely hollow. He moved it around needlessly, but it looked dry as if it was waiting to stick in his throat. The silence seemed to go on forever. Joe decided to end it.

'Thank you for the invitation, Billy, but I think it's best to decline. I could be called away for training at any time and I would hate it if your mother went to the trouble of setting a place for me and I was unable to turn up.'

His decline was readily accepted by her parents and although Billy voiced disappointment, he accepted it too. After all, he was young and took everything at face value. He had a lot of growing up to do, thought Joe sadly. Anne was the only one whose disappointment lingered. He wanted to reassure her that they would only be separated for this one Christmas, but he knew that he couldn't truthfully do that. His stomach began to churn. He didn't want to come between a family, but he had somehow found himself slap bang in the middle of two opposing sides – and he was the problem. The sadness on Anne's face was what her mother was trying to protect her from and, in that moment, he saw it too and finally understood. How much worse would Anne feel if they were together for longer? Separation was coming by either war, death or repatriation, and Joe had to admit, if only to himself, neither Anne nor himself could stop it coming.

Joe surveyed the temporary camp, set up to cater for another overnight training session. He could just make out the mud and tents, connected by slippery duckboards, in the dark. Male voices seeped from the interior of each tent, as silhouettes of soldiers navigated their footing carefully between them. Despite Anne's mother's opinion of it being a dry winter, it had rained. Maybe she hadn't realised, holed up in a house, but when you're living under canvas, you notice every change. The evenings were long and dark, the nights were cold and wet and he had every right to not like it.

He wondered in which tent he'd find Frank. Each tent shielded muted male voices conversing, giving the false impression of warmth and comfort.

He chose to return to his own tent and walked briskly towards it – retreating to his own bed and stewing in his own anger felt just the right thing to do. He had a lot of stewing to do. The evening before had been a disaster, from the moment of overhearing Anne's mother, to his cowardly goodbye. Where had it gone wrong? Only days before, he'd returned from the amphibious training feeling motivated, energised, and highly charged. And when Anne had suggested 'going up stairs' in Oak Cottage, it had felt so right. It was a huge hit to his ego when he realised he'd misunderstood her. No guy liked being shown a candy store then told it was closed. But he had soon got over it. He was an adult, even saw the funny side, and Anne was worth the wait. Yet somehow walls of expectation had closed in on him from all sides. Anne wanted a ring on her finger. Her mother wanted them to part. Her stepfather – Joe had no idea of what he really thought. Billy thought everything was just great. Joe? What did he think? Oh, and by the way, Joe, you have a war to fight first!

Joe hunched his shoulders against the next inevitable shower, which immediately seeped down the collar of his jacket and into his bones. He swore, as he almost bumped into another soldier coming the other way. The other soldier immediately returned the curse. Joe ignored him.

He should have ignored her mother too, but as he said a private goodbye to Anne, he had found himself telling her that he may not see her for a while. She asked why and he became evasive, as if he held some military secret he could not share, but he knew the truth. He was a coward and he was trying to say goodbye. When the moment came to be truthful and kind, he had flunked it.

Joe wiped the raindrops away from his face with his sleeve and pulled back the canvas flap of the tent. A small crowd of men were gathered in the centre, laughing at the cheap entertainment in front of them. Bolton stood in the middle, thrusting his hips as he licked the air with his tongue. Joe frowned. What was so funny? Bolton's eyes met his and he smiled. He casually held up a photo between two fingers and slowly turned it to face Joe. It was Anne.

Enraged, Joe dived at him. The men around scattered for cover as he knocked him to the floor. They rolled briefly before Joe managed to overpower and straddle him. He heard someone calling his name, but did not care. This was between him and Bolton, and all the other crap going on in his head right now. The punches came hard and fast, powered by an uncontrolled rage he didn't know he could possess. Bolton's face was barely visible, hidden behind his raised arms as he tried to protect himself. Yet still he punched, each one with a name. Bolton. His father. His brother for leaving him. Anne's mother. Hitler. The damn winter weather. He felt himself being dragged away, but still he fought, scrambling and shoving to get back to the man on the floor who was beginning to sit up. If it was not for the painful punch to his own jaw, which jerked his head suddenly and reset his mind, he would have continued striving to get back to the man on the floor and finish him off.

'Sorry, pal. I had to do it.'

Joe dabbed his bleeding mouth as he turned to his assailant. It was Frank.

‘Are you wanting to get court martialled, Joe? What happened to “waiting for the first punch”?’

Joe watched Bolton be reluctantly led away. ‘It slipped my mind. He had a photo of Anne. He has no right to it.’ He wasn’t sure he did any more, but that wasn’t the point. ‘She said there was a second photograph. Bolton’s got his grubby hands all over it and probably doing Christ knows what—’

‘Leave it to me. I’ll get it back for you.’ He draped his arm around Joe’s shoulders and guided him away. ‘But right now, pal, you need to calm the hell down and not let him get to you.’ He gave him a quick hug under the cover of a rough shake. ‘Let’s go have a beer and, maybe, you can tell me what’s eating you up inside.’

Chapter Nineteen

Late December, 1943

Christmas Day came and went. As soon as it was over, the 175th received orders to prepare to leave. Trucks lined up for them to climb aboard. In no time at all, the soldiers were tightly packed into the convoy and leaving their base. Joe thought of Anne, glad that he had warned her he could leave anytime, yet it was of little consolation. As he looked at the base growing smaller in the distance, he wondered if he would ever get the chance to see her again. The convoy snaked its way through the countryside. Inside the troops speculated, yet again, as to whether it was another training session or the real thing. Even now, after all their time in England, they remained in the dark regarding the date of the allied invasion, and what part they would play. Sometimes they wondered if the Major General even knew, as it seemed that everyone in the 29th Infantry Division was repeatedly being sent from one place to another. There was no point demanding to know more; it was far easier to just follow the rest. The army had turned them into obedient players, thought Joe as he looked at the other men around him, even if the rules of the game was yet to be learnt.

As the coastline came into view, it became more apparent that whatever was happening was one step up from their assault training in November. The trucks came to a halt and the troops jumped down to be immediately herded into temporary, tented marshalling areas. This was where they were to wait for further commands. It wasn't long before they were informed that this was to be their new temporary home and to make themselves comfortable. They were allotted tents and did their best to make the cold space their own. They could do little else but follow orders and hope for the best.

When the general briefing came it gave them new focus, something to think about other than being endlessly paraded, inspected, and constant checking and rechecking of equipment and weapons. The 175th was to take part in Exercise Duck 1 on the third of January. It would involve over five thousand troops. Landing crafts would be loaded in Falmouth and Dartmouth, using hard concrete ramps built for the purpose. Troops would be transferred from the marshalling base to the embarkation ports by truck. The ships and landing crafts would assemble off the coast of Slapton Sands in Devon. A simulated bombardment of the beach would take place prior to the troops disembarking. Once ashore, the goal was to secure the beach by advancing inshore, neutralise any enemy fire by blowing up the pillbox defences and secure a beachhead.

'You know what this means, don't you?' whispered Frank beside him.

Joe looked around. Hundreds of men sat in rows behind and in front of them on hard wooden benches with wisps of smoke spiralling up in the air. They were all listening intently, but realisation was dawning. Their role was far bigger than they had dreamt it would be.

'Yeah, sounds like we are training to be one of the first to land and face enemy resistance. It's going to be tough.'

The briefing came to an end as suddenly as it started. They stood up, eager to be moving again and began to filter out of the tent. There was a strange tension in the air – energised motivation, tinged with nervous excitement. The air hummed with male voices discussing what they'd been told. As their speed slowed in the inevitable bottleneck at the tent door, Frank reached into his jacket and withdrew a piece of paper. He thrust it at Joe.

'It's probably a good time to give you this. Here.'

Joe took the photograph Frank held in his hand and looked at it. Anne's face smiled back at him.

'When did you get it off Bolton?' he asked.

'Just before the briefing.'

'How?'

Frank shrugged. 'Slipped it from under his bedding when he wasn't looking.' Joe's eyes narrowed, unconvinced. They both knew it was not easy to do anything without someone watching. Privacy was a forgotten luxury, especially in this camp. 'I did! What can I say? I grew up sneaky. Had to. Had an alcoholic father.'

Joe smiled. 'Thanks, buddy.'

Frank waved his thanks away. 'Don't start turning soft on me. Let's get something to eat; I'm starving.'

Joe woke with a start. He looked around, every muscle on instant alert. It was still dark but something was wrong. Someone was shouting and they were mad as hell. He sat up in bed and realised other men were scrambling for their clothes. He recognised who was shouting; it was an officer, and he was ordering them to dress in full combat gear and line up outside. This was it! They were off!

Joe shook Frank awake. Despite their numerous drills, all were in panic, desperately trying to dress and fix their equipment in the semi-darkness. People were running and shouting. Everything was in confusion and all they could do was concentrate on what they needed to do. Finally, they ran outside and lined up, ready to climb aboard the trucks to be taken to the embarkation ports. Only there were no trucks waiting, only their officer. He inspected the line, before telling them to go back to bed. It was a false alert, designed to keep them on their toes and ready for action at any time.

Frank wasn't best pleased. He continued his complaining as they returned to their beds and began to undress. Despite being initially annoyed himself, he began to find Frank's anger amusing.

'What's upset you so much? Were you having a good dream?'

'I wish,' said Frank. 'I'm telling you, if they play that game again, my ticker's going to give out.' To Frank's surprise, Joe began to laugh. 'I'm serious. Look what they made me do!' He pointed to his feet. 'I was in such a panic I put them on the wrong feet!' Joe looked at Frank's feet, each boot curved outwards as if he was a clown. He began to laugh even louder and wondered if he was bordering on becoming hysterical. The world was mad, perhaps he was turning crazy too. But it felt good to laugh in the face of the looming battle … because it meant he was still alive to do it.

Finally, the orders came for the exercise to start and they were transported by trucks to the embarkation points, sited only a few minutes away. By now they were well-rehearsed and boarded their ship in an orderly fashion and waited to leave.

Initially their spirits were high, filled with mounting excitement for what lay ahead, but after enduring another false alert to leave, they were quickly reminded of the emotional roller-coaster ride they were on, where tension and excitement walked hand in hand with tedium and boredom

Dark humour remained the go-to remedy and their standard-issue life preservers became their target and, to their mind, a harmless release mechanism. Despite being no more complicated than rubber tubes, wrapped in canvas and inflated by gas canisters, the rudimentary belt could save a life in deep water … if only it was worn correctly.

However, their necessity and importance were quickly overlooked by many of the young men and it became a running joke for the man standing behind to inflate the life saver of the soldier in front. The butt of the joke, singled out by his inflated life preserver, could do little about it but endure the ear bashing from his sergeant and the laughter of his fellow soldiers. At first, Joe felt himself being carried along by the wave of adventure and comradeship yet as the surrounding troops settled down to another phase of waiting, he was reminded of Anne's photograph tucked into the pocket close to his heart. She was more sensible than those around him. These boys were not long out of senior high and had the world at their feet. She wouldn't see this as some elaborate game, which he suspected many on this ship did right now … even himself.

On the first of January, their company officer informed them that the date for Exercise Duck would be delayed from the third to the fourth of January. It was greeted with a murmur of discontent. The food and messing facilities were inadequate for the number of men on board and an extra day on the ship was not the news they'd been waiting for.

The command came. They arrived off the south coast of Devon. The simulated bombardment of the beach was the closest they'd been to how the final assault would be and although Joe knew there was no enemy within miles, and that dying was unlikely, it was a glimpse of what was to come. For the first time he imagined how Anne must have seen him when he returned from the amphibious assault training, feeling invincible and energised. Had she thought he was deluded? Hearing the noise in the distance, each explosion and fire a glimpse of how it might be, perhaps she was right to think that. He had been, at the very least, foolishly naive.

The order came, '29 Let's Go!' They climbed down the cargo net, slung over the side of the ship, to the landing craft below. Naval drivers welcomed them onboard the landing craft with a curt nod of their heads. The familiar seasickness was there to welcome them and slink into their bellies as they took their places. Joe looked about him. None of them knew the real name of the beach they were about to assault, a beach was a beach as far as they were concerned, but each man was determined to do their best. It was another chapter in this ludicrous adventure and a fine tale to tell their folks at home.

Although the landings were achieved, not all were accurate or timely, some landing craft being carried further afield to beaches along the coastline. They were told to assume machine guns, howitzers and anti-aircraft batteries were present and that the southern part of one beach was mined. Enemy defences along the beach and cliff lines would have to be overcome before the simulated pillboxes, containing machine guns, were to be assaulted and blown up. Once achieved, they must make their way inland to establish defences.

Weighed down with equipment, Joe entered the near freezing water and waded towards the three-mile shingle beach ahead. He looked along the coastline. Stretching as far as he could see were hundreds of men attempting to do the same, spilling from landing craft into the buffeting waves. At least he was not alone. Once ashore, Joe noticed the troops were tending to bunch together. If the simulated enemy fire had been real, he suspected none of them would have survived the hour.

As Joe advanced inland, the beaches were de-mined and cleared to establish three supply beaches for the arrival of further troops, equipment and military vehicles. Exercise Duck 1, carefully watched by observers taking notes, lasted two days. By the end, the troops were exhausted and lessons were learnt. Despite the mistakes, it was considered a success and the troops returned to Cornwall, a little wiser as to what was required of them. Joe had learnt a valuable lesson too. If the simulated fire were real, no amount of motivation or bravery could stop a bullet … especially if you didn't even see it coming. Life was too precious to waste and every moment of happiness should be grasped and treasured. Anne made him happy, more than happy and he believed he made Anne happy too. No one, not even Anne's mother, should rob them of it, and as soon as he could see her again, he would tell her so.

Chapter Twenty

'You can stare as hard as you like, it won't bring him back any sooner.'

Anne's stepfather's voice dragged her away from her sombre thoughts. A week ago, laden ships and landing craft had left the docks and gossip was rife regarding where they had gone.

'Do you think he will come back?' asked Anne, hopefully.

Henry squinted against the coastal wind. 'I don't know.'

'Mother would rather he didn't.'

Henry gave her a stern look. 'Now that's unfair, Anne. She likes Joe.' Anne rolled her eyes. 'She does! She thinks he's a polite young man. Your mother is just scared.'

Anne looked at him. 'Scared of what?'

'That he thinks it's all a game. That when he leaves – and he will one day – he will leave you brokenhearted.' Anne threw him a sceptical look. He nudged her shoulder with his own. 'He may not intend to but if he is killed he will.' He shrugged. 'What do I know about what really goes on in a woman's head?'

'I think you can make a good guess.'

Henry scuffed a stone with the toe of his shoe. 'I think your father was the love of your mother's life.'

Anne looked at Henry, surprised by the turn of conversation.

'She married him shortly after the war ended. Shame he died so young and missed out on you growing up. He would have been so proud of you, Anne. Just like I am.'

Anne smiled sadly at him. 'I think of you as my father now. I have few memories of him.'

Henry's chest rose with emotion at her words. He cleared his throat. 'I don't think your mother really got over Alfred. I think losing him broke her heart – she refuses to talk about him. I learnt to let sleeping dogs lie. It made for a happy marriage. You know your mother, she likes to …'

'To what?'

'… keep her emotions to herself. I often think that when people put up a wall, it's usually to protect themselves because they are afraid of being hurt all over again.'

What Henry was telling her explained a lot. Her mother's fear that she may suffer the same pain, although she could not stop her falling in love forever. There were also other reasons to keep people apart and in her most uncharitable moments, jealousy and prejudice came to Anne's mind. They exchanged sad smiles before returning their attention to the harbour in front of them. The docks seemed oddly peaceful, despite the activity still going on.

'If it makes you feel any better, I don't think Joe has gone to war. They would need more than a couple of thousand men and it would be mad to cross the channel and launch an attack in winter.'

Anne's heart lifted. 'So, you think it was another training exercise?'

He nodded. 'Your mother had a letter from a friend the other day. She says there are troops building up everywhere, not just in Cornwall. And not just American. Her friend wasn't explicit … walls have ears and all that. But you know your mother, she can always read between the lines.' His brows knotted in deep thought as his gaze raked the large expanse of water speckled with rowing boats and naval craft. 'Whatever they are planning will probably happen soon. And when it does, Joe *will* go too.'

Anne nodded in acceptance. She suddenly smiled at him. 'Mum loves you very much. We all do. You do know that don't you?'

Her stepfather attempted to return her smile but failed. 'I do.'

'So what's wrong?' asked Anne. 'You look sad.'

'I was remembering the evacuation from Dunkirk.' He sucked in his breath at the memory. 'The last time I stood on this harbour wall, the water was crammed with ships and fishing boats bringing our lads home. But they had a good welcome, didn't they Anne? I think every larder for miles was emptied to feed them all.'

'And the harbour is filling up again … ' observed Anne, 'but this time with more battle-hardy ships.'

'One day soon, they'll be leaving to take back the land lost to the Nazis. And many will die doing it.' He looked down at her. 'Hark at me. I brought you into Falmouth to cheer you up and I've done nothing but talk of sad things. Why don't you have a wander around, do whatever you women like to do, while I drop off a few things for the Home Guard?'

Anne agreed. Although, she didn't feel like window-shopping in the town's centre, it might help take her mind off Joe. She thrust her hands in her coat pockets and headed towards the shops.

The biting cold weather and post-Christmas blues had kept many people at home. Anne wandered aimlessly up and down the quiet streets, gazing at tired window displays with little motivation to buy. She wondered what Joe was doing right now and why he hadn't been able to see her before he left – if he had left. He'd warned her he may not see her, but his absence and the uncertainty of what he was doing were still painful to bear.

A woman's reflection in the window, as she crossed the street, caught her attention. Anne turned to watch her. She walked as if she didn't have a care in the world, her handbag and gas mask firmly clutched in one hand, a basket hooked over the other arm. Their eyes met briefly and the woman smiled brightly, before she entered the small shop and disappeared from view.

The explosion was thunderous. Angry, voluminous flames blasted from the shop. The noise of the explosion moved through her body, like a wave, sapping her thoughts and leaving confusion and deafness in its wake. Neighbouring windows blew out, hurling splintered wooden window frames and brick into the air and knocking her off her feet. Anne lay among the shattered glass, her arms raised over her head as numerous Pathé newsreels had trained her to do. The falling debris followed, thundering down like missiles, pummelling her body time and time again. Anne crawled to a doorway for shelter and was pulled half inside by someone's frantic grasp before they gave up and left her to seek shelter themselves. Finally, the debris stopped falling and an eerie silence followed. Everything was black and she no longer hurt yet she felt unable to move. Then the shrill ringing in her ears began, growing louder and louder until she feared her head would explode. Was this death, she wondered, with an eternal shrill of nothingness all around?

She tasted dust and began to cough, the act wrenching her back to reality. She was alive! She lifted her head. Broken glass slid off her body and pooled around her, reminding her of wind chimes in autumn or childhood stories of sprinkled magic. Such silly thoughts, considering the carnage around her. She looked for the shop, but it had gone.

Clouds of dust hung around her and where the shop once stood, black billowing smoke stretched up into the sky. The ringing in her ears faded as quickly as it had begun and was replaced with frantic voices of people desperately searching for survivors. Two strangers approached and helped her to her feet, asking if she was alright and reassuring her they would take her to the first aid post. She looked at her hands and saw they were bloodied, but when asked where she had been hurt, she had no idea. Everything felt bruised and battered, every muscle, every joint. She began to shake. The kindly strangers reassured her and encouraged her to go with them. She felt like a child, being taught how to walk, but she needed their support and allowed them to lead her away. She looked over her shoulder to see what she was leaving behind, but the shop was just rubble with crowds standing around.

'Was anyone killed?' she asked. She thought of the young woman, with a bright smile curving her lips. Her eyes began to smart. No one could have survived that blast. The woman's last smile had been for her and Anne knew, with certainty, that she would remember it for the rest of her life.

Anne stared at the cold mug of tea in her hands. She had been given it upon her arrival at the first aid point, but the nausea churning in her stomach had prevented her from drinking it. She noticed that her hands were still trembling and wondered if they would ever stop.

She should be dead. If she had walked a little quicker and decided to enter that shop, or even chose to walk by it, she would be dead now. No one could survive a bomb like that. Not even Joe. She had told him about her fears, but had she really accepted them as reality herself? She thought she had, but it seemed she had not. Joe could die. He might even be dead now. She could be dead now. How fragile life was, one-minute smiling brightly, the next nothing but dust and dirt.

Her trembling increased so much that she put the mug down. She stared at the skim of cold milk forming on the surface. The thought of not seeing Joe again was unbearable. She would never have the chance to kiss him, hold him, make love with him. A wave of grief swept over her at all she might have lost. Precious moments, new treasured memories, intimate exploring touches she had yet to experience. And she wanted to experience them – with Joe. Yet she had been wasting their precious time together by wanting her family to love him as much as she did instead of being together and living for today. She had refused to be loved by him unless he put a ring on her finger! What a stupid, priggish fool to demand such a thing from a man who was about to face war.

She heard her name and looked up. Her eyes filled with tears. Henry's familiar face was at the door, his love and fear for her clearly etched in every crease of concern. He rushed to her side and hugged her silently for some minutes, both instinctively knowing that sometimes words failed to capture what one felt deep inside. Eventually, Henry pulled away and searched for a handkerchief before pressing it into her hands.

'Now, now,' he chided her with glistening eyes. 'Enough of that. You will have me blubbering too. Dry your tears and let me look at you.'

Anne sobbed some more, only this time they were happy tears. Although she was now a woman, it felt oddly comforting to hear a fatherly voice lovingly chastise her as if she was a little girl again.

'How badly hurt are you?'

Anne touched the back of her head. The hair, matted with blood, cushioned a tender spot. 'I have a cut on my head and a few bruises. I'm told it looks worse than it is. Apparently scalps bleed a lot.'

'I saw the building. I can't believe you survived it.'

'I wasn't inside, only nearby. I don't think anyone inside could have survived it.' She dried her tears. 'There was no time to run to the air shelter. I didn't hear a siren or any artillery fire.'

'It wasn't a bomb, although the damage looks like it was caused by one. They think it was a gas leak. I heard the explosion and immediately came to help. I saw your handbag in a broken doorway and thought you were dead.'

Anne hadn't realised it was missing until then and told him so.

She picked up her gas mask. 'I didn't forget this though. Funny what goes through your mind. Different things seem important and other things … not so much.'

'The sort of experience you have just been through will change your view on a lot of things, Anne.'

Anne nodded. She thought of Joe. 'I think it already has.'

Chapter Twenty-One

Joe hadn't planned to see Anne again, but what had seemed sensible before Christmas, no longer made sense. He parked his motorcycle at the top of the lane and rehearsed the speech he'd composed in his head to explain why he hadn't been in touch. He knew it wasn't going to be easy. Duck 1 training covered some of the time, but not all of it. How did he explain he loved her, but willingly accepted the pressure from her family and his pals, to simply walk away? He could blame it on being scared as hell of being in love, but what sort of yellow-livered man did that make him? He could blame it all on his eavesdropping, and that it was her family who made him walk. The more he thought about his behaviour, the less he wanted to explain it. The thought of facing her mother didn't help things either. Fortunately, Billy saved him from that fate by arriving right on cue.

'Hey, Joe!' he called out as he arrived on his bicycle. He came to a shuddering, bumpy stop, and stood up, tilting his bike at a jaunty angle, while he kept his right foot on the pedal. 'Where have you been?'

Joe tapped his nose. 'Now you know that's official business.' He came closer, looked about him for enemy spies and added, 'but as it's you, I'll tell you. I've been away training for the big day.'

Billy puffed out his chest, extraordinarily proud to be gifted with such military intelligence from his buddy – a real American soldier. It didn't matter that they'd all returned relatively unscathed and most people in the community had already guessed it was a training exercise. This news came from the horse's mouth.

'I came to see Anne. Is she around?'

'She's up at the cottage. Mother asked her to light the fire to stop the house getting damp.'

Joe felt the tension drain from his shoulders. 'That's great. I'd like to talk to her alone.' As an afterthought, he added, 'You won't tell anyone, will you Billy?'

'Is it top secret? Are you not meant to be here?'

Joe smiled at him. 'Something like that.'

'I won't tell anyone, Joe. You can rely on me.'

Joe handed him a Hershey chocolate bar as a reward. 'I knew I could, buddy. How's the pitching going?'

'Still working on it,' said Billy, unwrapping his new treasure and devouring it in record time. 'I've been practising with the bat too.' Joe was quietly impressed.

'Maybe we could have a few training sessions together now that I'm back?'

'That will be great!' Billy straightened his bike. 'I have to go. Meeting some friends. Davey has found some washed-up k-rations downstream from one of the hard slopes built last year.'

So that's why he ate it quickly, thought Joe, he didn't want to share it.

'See you again soon?'

Joe smiled at the boy's enthusiasm. It was nice to be wanted. 'Yeah, sure. You can count on it.'

Joe watched the boy pedal away, seemingly without a care in the world. Only a kid could find war exciting and adventurous and ignore the gravity behind it, he mused. His smile faded. Four more years and he would be old enough to fight too. The thought of Billy being shot at was another good reason to get this war won and over with.

Joe approached the back door of Oak Cottage and checked if the key had been removed from its hiding place. He could tell from the crescent-shaped earth mound on the ground that the plant pot had been moved. He looked up at the chimney and saw faint wisps of grey smoke seeping out. Anne was inside, just as Billy had promised.

He quietly opened the door; afraid his sudden appearance could frighten her. He found her crouched before the fire, slowly feeding the flames with kindling. Just the sight of her made his gut ache at how much he'd missed her. He savoured the moment, before quietly rapping his knuckles on the door frame, still unsure and nervous how she would receive him.

She looked over her shoulder. The words he'd rehearsed went straight out of his head. No explanation warranted him leaving it more than a month before he got in touch again. How did he almost walk away? He deserved everything she wanted to throw at him … and more.

Anne slowly stood; her eyes filled with hope.

'Joe.'

Her expression and gentle tone were all he needed to forget the past and enjoy the present. He crossed the room to be with her. They held each other, tightly, both apologising and forgiving all at the same time.

Eager to soothe the other's worries and build confidence in their future together.

'I'm sorry. I should have come sooner. I've missed you so much,' whispered Joe into the crook of her neck.

'It doesn't matter.'

'It should.'

'No. I realised the other day that I don't want to waste a second on recriminations. Not a second. I want to enjoy these moments with you.'

'So do I.'

They sought each other's lips to seal the promise. Their first kiss on his return, but never their last. He didn't want it to end so continued it, trailing down her neck as she broke away to speak.

'I was so afraid. I thought I'd never see you again.'

'I'm here,' he murmured between kisses.

She laughed through her tears. 'Yes, you are here. I worry—'

'Don't.' He wanted to silence any future concerns, as he was here now and it was only the present that mattered. So, he did, in the only way he knew how. This kiss was more passionate than he had dared do before. He had dreamt of this perfect moment. To his joy, she responded how he had hoped in his dreams, inviting and teasing him to linger for more. He savoured the taste of her and the senses it ignited, discovering and relearning all the things that made Anne – Anne. How had he forgotten the scent of her light floral fragrance, as much a part of her as was her soft honey-toned hair? Her photo was just a snapshot, but Anne was here and now – living, breathing, feeling soft beneath his touch. A mesmerising mixture of womanly comfort, yet incredibly sexy with a temptress shape. Heaven help him, she was even arching towards him for more. He stepped back, breathless, before he got carried away.

'I'm sorry,' he said, slipping off his cap and raking a hand through his hair. 'I'm getting carried away. Lots of crazy thoughts buzzing around in my head. I know you don't want—'

'Yes, I do.'

He stared at her, unsure if he had heard her right. She was smiling at him, confident – even a little bit sassy. He liked what he was seeing and perhaps it wasn't all in his head after all. Even so, last time he'd blown it and he didn't want to make that mistake again.

His eyes narrowed. 'I'm not sure if we're talking about the same thing here. I'm not good at this sort of thing. I got it wrong before. Remember?'

‘Things have changed. I’ve changed.’ She stepped towards him and eased his cap from his hand and placed it on a chair. She looked at him, her eyes smiling, as if waiting for him to make the next move.

He, the American saviour of the free world, couldn’t think of a thing to say and had no clue what to do.

She laughed. ‘You look like a rabbit caught in a hunting light. Do I have to spell it out for you?’

‘I think you might have to, because, like I said, what’s going on in my head is pretty crazy right now.’

She reached up and touched his face with the back of a single finger. He had the urge to turn his face into her hand and kiss her there, but he couldn’t move, trapped only by the new sultry look in her eyes. A man could drown in those eyes. He made a lazy attempt to reach firmer ground, by using humour as his lifeline.

‘Do you realise you have a “sexy look” thing going on there?’

‘Do I? Good, because I haven’t been practicing and I’m a little nervous right now.’

Her truth was more than he dared hoped to hear. She wanted him and he, sure as hell, wanted her. He reached around her waist, unable to drag his gaze away from her eyes as she slowly traced the line of his jaw, across his light stubble and up towards his lips. His heart hammered in his chest as she kissed him gently, before leaning into him further. Now he could feel the full, glorious, length of her body against his. He heard her sigh and felt the same exquisite feeling rising inside him like a wave. He sought her lips for another kiss, this time a little more needy, a little more feverish than before, but still unsure of the landscape ahead. Anne, breathless, braced against him, just enough to tease but not enough to part. They remained connected, body to body, soft curve to firm muscle, their lips together in a soft featherlike touch. Joe knew he was lost; Anne was in control now.

‘Tell me what you want, Anne. I’ll do anything you ask.’

He felt Anne smile beneath his lips. ‘I want to make love with you, Joe Mallory,’ she murmured breathlessly, ‘as if tomorrow will never come.’

Joe followed Anne up the stairs. Somehow, they made it to the bedroom, despite their eagerly taken journey willingly hampered by their frantic, excitable kissing and a reluctance to be parted. It felt, as they stumbled up the steps, they dare not let go now they had each other near, as if by breaking their connection, whether by touch or kiss, would somehow burst this magical moment exploding upon them.

They entered the bedroom laughing, high on the intoxicating mood that had taken them there. Their laughter died when the chill of the room enveloped them and they saw the large bed, owned by another, defying them to use it. They sobered, looked at one another and each reached for a curtain. They slowly drew their curtain across the pole until they met in the middle. They let the material fall and reached for each other's hands. Two people, standing alone, hidden from the world, fearful that the magic might already be fading. Yet the magic had not left them, but quickly grew again – feeding on the love they felt when they looked upon the other. It flourished as they stood in silence, seeping into their mind and soul, making everything right and good and giving them the gift to simply *be*.

Shallow breaths, filled with whispered promises and words of love, spilled from their lips as they eased each other's clothes from their bodies and left trails of kisses where the fabric had been. Each discarded garment revealed more of the other, stoking desire, fanning their passion, but not yet able to quench the hunger inside.

They slipped beneath the cold sheets to seek comfort in each other's warmth, and it was not long before their naked, heated skin burned a fire that could warm the room. Limbs, free of the cold, became soft and tender to the touch, heightening each caress, each stroke, each frantic grasp made from mounting desire. Yet still they needed more, demanded more, gave more, casting a sheen of passion on every twist, stretch and flex of a limb, hip or back.

Honey curls framed her face, her expression changing before him with satisfying ease. From sultry tease, even demanding temptress, to an equal match to quench a deep need. Yet it was only after he had explored every part of her, gave all of himself to her, did her vulnerability, sated and weak, return to her face. And as she lay in his arms, he felt as weak as a kitten, and wondered if she felt that too. As he watched her, she sensed his gaze, slowly opened her eyes and looked at him. His heart swelled and his throat grew thick, for he saw the depth of her love shine from the two blue windows into her soul and, when he was at his most vulnerable, he felt whole – as a man, as a person, as a human, in a way he had never felt before.

Fear of the future had been their shackles, but now they were free, severing the ties by not discussing it, thinking about it, or daring to plan further than when they could next meet. They sometimes met in the churchyard, under the old yew tree, unaware that its towering branches and thick gnarled bark was a symbol of immortality, as well as an omen of doom.

They laughed and kissed by the sweeping estuary waters of the River Fal, purposely ignoring the hard-standing slopes, built in secret by drafted-in civilians for loading military craft, as they played no part in their own unique world.

As winter made way for spring, they made love in Oak Cottage, in the light of the open fire or the warming rays of the sun shining through the window. Inside the cottage walls they were alone and indulgent in their make-belief life, where even making a studio appointment for a joint photograph to be taken as a keepsake seemed to be tempting bad luck.

As the days passed more ships, temporary tented camps, troops, weapons and equipment arrived. Ammunition was stored and protected in woods and along minor roads, barges were secured and camouflaged under secluded creeks and rivers, while military vehicles were camouflaged by netting and hidden under overhanging trees. *The day* was approaching, but no one knew when, looming on the horizon like a dark silent cloud. One could feel it in the air, see the diesel and oil in the water, observe the impatience of the soldiers, as well as their hosts. Whispered rumours relating to the various clandestine movements undertaken by the army and navy, circled the gossip vine by word of mouth. Around and around the gossip messages went, until new news turned out to be old news … or no news at all.

Despite carefully crafting their own world, where they loved and felt loved, Joe found himself keeping a secret from Anne that he would rather not keep. Not long after they'd reunited, he'd visited her stepfather for permission to ask Anne to be his wife. He told himself, it was the honourable thing to do. He had no wish to come between Anne and her family and he knew their acceptance of him was vital.

Henry had stopped digging the soil when he'd seen him approaching.

'Does Anne know about this?' her stepfather had asked him as he leaned on his fork.

'Not yet, sir. I wanted your permission first.'

The old man studied him with kindly, slate eyes.

Joe had felt the need to explain further. 'I don't want her to have to choose between her family and me.'

Henry had tilted his chin. 'What are you implying?'

'If I don't receive your permission to marry Anne, then I won't ask her.'

'But you will tell her that we said "no".'

Joe had braced his shoulders. 'No, sir. I would not.'

Henry had studied him, then, unsure of his motive had asked, 'To save your pride?'

'No, sir. To save something more worthy.'

Henry had nodded. 'You meant to save our relationship with Anne?' Joe didn't reply. 'And if I say yes, when do you plan to marry?'

'Soon. Before I go away.'

'Go away …' Henry had echoed, thoughtfully.

Joe had known, from his tone, what was running through the old man's head then – Anne alone, or perhaps worse with a child or widowed and grieving.

'I like you. You are a good man. In ordinary times …' Joe had felt himself stiffen as he waited for Henry to finish. '… but I can't give my permission, son. Ask again when you come home alive.'

Joe had tilted his chin in defiance and commitment. 'I will, sir. As soon as we've won the war, I will come back here and ask for your permission again. You can count on it.'

'I'm protecting Anne. You understand that don't you?' her stepfather had said.

Joe had nodded, although in truth he didn't understand then and he didn't now.

'You are a fine lad, Joe. Fearless. Confident. Go wherever you are ordered. Do whatever your officers want. You've been told you are the best of the best. Maybe you even feel untouchable by death.' Joe had felt his chest tighten at his words, for he was hearing the army's truth, which had been carefully constructed for him and was all he had to get him through the next few months. Henry had seen into his life and he felt resistant to him probing further. And to his surprise, Henry appeared to suddenly relent and withdraw. 'I wish you well, Joe. No hard feelings. I can see the army has done a good job on you … just like it did on me all those years ago.'

Chapter Twenty-Two

From the beginning of April, prohibited zones began to appear along the coast, to the inland depth of ten miles. Post boxes were taped up, beach visits and binoculars banned, while road signs erected at every access point forbade public entry. On command of the War Office, only civilians living within the zones were allowed access, on condition they were able to show their newly issued identity cards and answer questions satisfactorily. As the average breadth of Cornwall was only twenty-two miles, the prohibited zones greatly impaired civilian travel throughout the county resulting in Cornwall effectively becoming separated from the rest of England. Fields and woods, which ran alongside narrow roads, were requisitioned, cordoned off with barbed wire and guards put in place. To Anne, and all those who had grown up and lived their quiet lives in Cornwall, it felt that every mile had the American presence stamped upon it in some way. Yet, despite the clash of their cultures and rising tensions, their aim was the same – to defeat Hitler. Their presence continued to be viewed as a friendly invasion, while the Americans fondly nicknamed Cornwall their forty-ninth state.

Anne arrived home from work and closed the door, glad to shut the world out. Every military change was a reminder that Joe would soon be leaving and although she was able to ignore the war when they were together, when she was away from him it was hard to forget. She found her mother surrounded by neat piles of uniforms.

'What are you doing?' asked Anne, touching a line of buttons on the front of one of them. 'These look like American uniforms.'

Her mother snapped a thread with her teeth. 'The US army put out a call asking for the help of any women who could sew. They've had new uniforms delivered and need their badges sewn on.' She snipped another length of thread with her best needlework scissors, making Anne smile. Her mother's habit of cutting the thread with scissors at the start and using her teeth at the end made no sense. 'I've got a pie in the oven. It will be ready soon. Although, at this rate no one will be sitting at the table. Henry is on duty with the Home Guard tonight and I've all these uniform badges to sew on.'

'I'll help you.' She noticed Billy wasn't home. 'Where's Billy?'

'He's in his room sulking.'

'Why?'

'I told him off for fighting. I thought he'd have grown out of that by now. He'll be leaving school this year and has to grow up if he's going to keep a job.'

'Shall I tell him that tea is almost ready?'

Her mother nodded. 'Yes, you better had. Don't want the pie going to waste.'

Anne climbed the stairs and went to his door. She paused and tilted her head to listen for any evidence he was in there.

'Are you alright, Billy? Tea's ready.'

A muffled voice inside told her to go away. Anne smiled. Billy reminded her of her younger self, when you said the exact opposite of what you really felt inside. She opened the door to find her brother lying on his bed. He immediately turned towards the wall, dragging his knees up to his chest.

'You've still got your shoes on. You'll get the bedspread dirty.'

'Don't care.'

'You should care. You'll have to sleep under it tonight.' Anne closed the door quietly behind her and walked over to him. 'Here, let me take them off.' When Billy didn't resist, she untied his laces and eased each shoe off in turn, before nudging them away with her hip so she could sit down. 'Mother says you've been fighting. I thought you'd grown out of that.'

'Tell that to the army.'

'You are not in the army, Billy.'

'Wish I was. It would get me away from here.'

Anne playfully nudged his arm. 'It's not that bad here.' When he didn't answer she decided to try a different tack. 'What were you fighting about?'

'You don't want to know.'

'I wouldn't ask if I didn't.' Billy remained silent. 'Did you start it?'

'Yes. No.'

Anne sighed. Her little brother was being particularly difficult today. 'Who were you fighting with?'

'Four friends from school. *Ex*-friends.'

'Four! Oh, Billy, you should have walked away. Four against one? Nothing is that important.'

Billy sat up and looked at her. His face, thunderous, sported a swollen eye and cut lip. Anne's jaw dropped open in horror.

'They'd seen you out with Joe and were calling you names.'

'Names? What names?

'Well … it was just one name. The sort they give girls who date Yanks.'

'The sort *you* gave girls who date Yanks.'

'That was different. You're my sister and Joe … well he's my mate.'

Anne smiled at her brother as he fiddled with the edge of his sock.

'Thank you for sticking up for me.'

Billy looked up at her suspiciously.

'I mean it.' She neatened the creases in his sock. Although she dreaded the answer, she still had to ask. 'What did they call me?'

'Yankie Annie.'

Yankie Annie. *Yankie Annie.* Anne began to laugh.

'You don't mind?' asked Billy, surprised.

'It could have been a lot worse!' When her laughter died down, she tried to be more serious. 'Who won?'

Billy smiled, intrigued that his sister was finding it funny. 'I did. Two ran off, one started to cry and Terry lost a tooth.'

Laughter began to bubble up inside Anne again. This time she didn't attempt to control it but basked in its glowing wave of joy and fun. It felt good, the perfect release from all the doom and gloom around her. The feeling must have been contagious, for Billy joined in too, and as they retold the story together, elaborating and reimagining it, their laughter grew and grew.

Chapter Twenty-Three

21 May, 1944

They were on the move again, tightly packed into a snaking convoy of trucks. No one knew where or when they would stop, but that had been the way of it for some time now.

'I swear, I think the army are doing this on purpose,' complained Frank, beside him. 'This is some sick joke they've got going on here.'

Frank was not the only one to have such thoughts as many of the soldiers were fed up with being sent from pillar to post. They just wanted it to be over now, so they could all go home.

The truck convoy began to slow. It stopped and they were ordered to get out. They stood in groups, with rolls of bedding slung over their shoulders and weighted down with their equipment and uniform. An area surrounded by barbed wire, filled with rows of tents and guarded by soldiers, greeted them. This hive of pitched canvas was to be their new home for the time being. Joe looked around. The surrounding countryside, with its typically British undulating horizon, was familiar to him despite the overwhelming army presence scarring its beauty. Realisation struck him like a hammer … this new marshalling area was near Anne's house.

They were told to make themselves at home and a new daily routine was quickly formed. Equipment checking and rechecking, packing and repacking, sometimes Joe thought they were just ordering them to do it to keep them occupied. Routine drills and the familiar boredom filled their day, all carried out and confined to one of many sausage-shaped marshalling areas hugging the south coast. Several days passed with no further information, just rumours murmured and discussed amongst those who were forced to wait. The restrictions placed upon them was driving Joe crazy. This time things felt different from the training exercises that had gone before, despite many still not accepting it as so. To be so near to Anne, with leaving imminent yet no way of saying goodbye, was like enduring a silent torture. During the day it was hard to live with the real possibility that he might never see her again, but during the quiet hours of the night, when the mind raced and his body felt like a tiger pacing a cage, it felt especially tortuous.

'I've got to get out of here. I must see Anne. It might be my last chance.'

Frank pulled Joe aside and away from the food queue. 'Are you crazy? It may have escaped your notice, but we're surrounded by barbed wire and guards. No one is getting in or out of here, least of all a love-sick fool.'

Joe shrugged him off. 'I'm not asking for your help.'

'Good! 'Cos I'm not giving it to you! Do you want to be court martialled?'

'Have I been court martialled yet?' snapped Joe. He saw the concern on Frank's face and relented. 'Of course, I don't,' he reassured him.

'You will be if you're caught.'

Joe turned away. He didn't want to hear Frank's concerns, despite knowing he meant well.

Frank grabbed his arm and jerked him back. 'Look, buddy, we could get our marching orders any day now. This isn't the time to play house.'

Joe felt his energy drain from his body. 'I know. I've got eyes. I can see what's going on here and I know what it could mean.'

The corner of Frank's mouth lifted in a smile. 'Hey. It's time to take your mind off her. I have a craps game set up. Wanna join me?'

'Haven't you had enough of betting?'

Frank feigned hurt feelings. 'What else am I going to do in this lousy place? It's not as if there's anywhere to spend my wages around here.'

They both looked around at the temporary camp in the fading light. The tension and anticipation were almost palpable.

'You go and enjoy yourself. I feel like going for a walk.'

Frank looked at him suspiciously, before lifting his hands in surrender. 'I don't want to know. Just do your thing and join in when you're ready. The less I know about what you're up to the better.'

Joe watched his friend walk away. If he had been in his shoes, he would have said exactly the same. Attempting to break out of a fortified camp to see a girl, when any moment you could be sent to war, was a mad thing to consider, but these were mad times and he had to say goodbye.

Joe walked around the perimeter, surreptitiously assessing the hastily erected rolls of barbed wire which stretched the entire outer limit of the camp. He could use wire cutters and cut through the layers. It would take several minutes and leave a hole. They would be waiting for him when he got back. Or he could dig a shallow gully under it and fill it in. That would take longer and he would have to repeat it when he returned. He scrutinised the surrounding area. The entire wall of wire was in full view, he had no cover, even now as night fell. It would take too long to dig a gully and crawl out. He was bound to be seen. Nausea churned his stomach as he saw his chances of seeing Anne again blowing up, one by one, in his face.

His attention was snared by a flurry of activity around a truck near the entrance. It was being unloaded and, from the military labelling, it appeared to be food. From the amount being delivered, Joe concluded their departure to God knows where, was not going to be for a few more days yet. He watched a truck leave and another arrive. It gave him an idea which was ludicrous, but suddenly seemed more feasible when he saw the driver get out. He immediately walked over to him.

'Rivers? Is that you?'

The man unloading the back of the truck turned around. 'Joe! Hey, it's good to see you again!'

Joe glanced over the packages. 'What are you dropping off?'

'New uniforms and they smell like hell.'

'Why?'

'It's the anti-gas ones.'

Joe frowned. It was another sign that this was different to any other training exercise they had been on before. *He had to see Anne.* Rivers continued unloading the back of the truck.

'Some think it's another training exercise. What do you think?' asked Joe. Even now, with all the mounting evidence, he still hoped time was on his side.

Rivers paused and looked at him sympathetically. 'Not this time. This isn't the only camp, Joe. They're all along the south coast. Ammunition and military equipment are on the move everywhere. The roads are full of convoys. Something big is coming and there's no stopping this train.' He continued unloading the back of the truck. 'I've asked for a transfer. I didn't sign up to fetch and carry for the army. I signed up to fight. They don't want us to show we can fight … but we can … and we will.'

'Where are you hoping to be transferred to?'

'The 761st Tank Battalion. They won't keep the Black Panthers out of France.' He paused and looked at Joe. 'I'm telling you; the allies are gonna need all the help they can get and I reckon there'll come a time when the colour of a man's skin ain't going to be such a barrier any more.'

'Rivers … I have to get out of here.'

Rivers frowned, pausing in his unloading. 'Are you crazy?' he whispered.

Joe didn't reply.

'Damn! Are you deserting?' Joe reached out his hand to calm him, but Rivers shook him off in disgust. 'I thought better of you than that. Here is me wanting to fight for our country and you are wanting to skip the hell out.'

Joe stood in his way. 'I'm not deserting my country!' he argued under his breath. 'I just want a couple of hours. I have to say goodbye to Anne.'

Rivers shook his head. 'I'm not helping you, Joe. You'll get us all court martialled.'

'If we are caught, I will tell them I ordered you to do it.' Joe grasped the package Rivers was holding. The two men stared at each other in militant silence.

'I'm going to get out of this camp one way or another, with or without your help,' warned Joe quietly.

'And if you're seen crawling out under the wire you may just get shot in the back for being a spy.'

'It's a risk I'm willing to take. But not by wire … rather by hiding under the truck.'

'Now I know you're crazy!'

Joe grabbed his sleeve as he turned away. 'I *said* I'm going to do it, with or without your help. But don't worry, I'll choose another truck.'

'Must be some girl to risk falling under the wheels of a military vehicle.'

'She is. She lives near Feock, not far from here.'

'Far enough.' Rivers' eyes narrowed. 'Is she the one who made you come and talk to us?'

Joe smiled. 'Yeah. She's *the smart one*.'

Silence fell between them as Rivers considered the request. He thrust the package into Joe's arms. 'I must be as crazy as you are. Finish unloading this one and climb into the back to collect another … only don't come back out.'

'And what about him?' he asked, referring to Rivers' colleague.

'Buck is okay. He's a sucker for a pretty woman too.'

Joe smiled his thanks and took the package from Rivers. He carefully laid it where Rivers indicated, quickly glanced around him and climbed into the back of the truck. The depth of the truck provided the perfect hiding place, its shadowed corner allowing him to quietly observe the camp he was leaving behind. Soldiers walked between dimly lit tents, filled with shadows. Soon they would be preparing to settle for the night and the noise would quieten, no one knowing what tomorrow would bring. Rivers' outline suddenly appeared at the open rear. He gave a curt nod of his head, before noisily pulling the canvas closed and plunging him into solitary darkness. He was at the mercy of Rivers and his friend now, for if they were stopped, he had no reasonable excuse to be hiding in the back of a truck, other than desertion or betrayal.

The journey seemed to go on forever as Rivers was asked to stop at several military checkpoints. Each time, Joe froze, fearing the plan would fail. He had promised to take the blame, but he knew Rivers was still risking a lot. Each time he listened intently to the murmur of voices on the other side of the panel, not allowing himself to breathe until the truck was on the move again.

The final stop remained silent of voices. He heard someone get out of the truck and walk around to the back. The canvas was roughly pulled aside. It was Rivers.

'You have two hours. I won't be able to wait for you so make sure you are here.'

Crouching, Joe walked to the entrance and jumped down. 'Thanks. I really mean it. I won't be late.'

Their eyes locked as they shook hands in farewell. 'You better not be, or we'll all be in deep shit,' warned Rivers. Joe knew, in that moment, Rivers had taken the risk for him as a *friend* and not because Joe had promised to take responsibility. Rivers knew he wouldn't be able to walk away unscathed because of Joe's testimony. They would both suffer the consequences.

Joe's throat felt thick with emotion. He attempted to swallow it down. 'Thank you. A brother could not have done more.'

Rivers' throat moved too as he nodded curtly. 'You better get going and see that lady of yours.'

Joe remained in the shadow of the hedge, as the dimly lit beam from the truck's shielded headlights, disappeared into the distance. He looked about him to take stock of where he was and began to make his way to Anne's house. On several occasions, the sound of a vehicle's engine forced him to hide in a ditch or behind a hedge, until they had passed, but eventually he found himself outside Anne's bedroom window. He selected a couple of small stones and threw them at the glass. He was about to throw a third when the sash window was pushed up. Her face appeared; her hair tousled as if he had just made love to her.

'Joe? Is that you? What are you doing here?' she whispered urgently.

'I have to see you. Meet me at Oak Cottage?'

She nodded and disappeared to dress. Joe breathed in deeply. She had not wasted time questioning him. It was as if she already knew he had come to say goodbye.

Chapter Twenty-Four

Anne pushed open the door of Oak Cottage to find Joe waiting for her. She ran towards him and wrapped her arms around him, as he did with her. She knew, from his tight embrace, that the day of his departure was imminent.

'Don't tell me you're leaving.'

'We can't ignore it any more.'

'I don't want to hear it.'

'I've come to say goodbye.'

Tears gathered in her eyes, wetting her lashes and blurring her vision. 'No!'

'Yes.'

They began to fall, unhindered, a salty sign of her pain. 'I don't want you to go.'

'I don't want to either. We have less than two hours.' He held her away from him, so he could look earnestly into her eyes. 'I had to see you. I've wanted to tell you so many times but couldn't find the right words.'

'What? Tell me what?'

'I was afraid to—'

'Joe! You are scaring me. Tell me what?'

He cupped her face, his eyes searching deep into her soul. 'That I love you.'

The warmth of his words swept through her, leaving her heady with joy.

'And I love you,' whispered Anne, earnestly, 'and will always … until the day I die.'

Their kiss was fevered, a gentle mix of salt and trembling lips, that sealed their words into minds and hearts.

He wrapped his arms about her again and held her tight, rubbing his cheek into the soft waves of her hair. 'Everyone I've ever loved has left me and, I guess, I was afraid to say it. But what have I got to lose now? I love you, Anne. I love you. I love you. I love you.' He sighed. 'Damn, that feels good to say and knowing you feel the same way …'

Another kiss, more fevered than before, both wanting to grab the magic between them and lock it away forever. An unspoken pact was made between them and Anne welcomed the look of lust in his eyes. Joe lifted her up in his arms and kissed her, before cradling her against his body as he climbed the stairs.

For one last time, they chose to ignore the world outside and what was in store in the days and months ahead. For the next hour none of that mattered, only their own private sanctuary made just for the two of them. Here one could love and be loved, both attempting to quench an overwhelming desire – one to keep a part of the other and the other to leave something behind. Making love was now a fevered compulsion, as beyond the cottage walls, and across the channel, waited battlegrounds that would ensure their inevitable separation. That moment loomed sombrely outside and waited for Joe, and like a vast, dark fog, Anne knew it would swallow him whole.

They lay in each other's arms – exhausted, sated, but their lust finally spent. A single candle cast a flickering warm light on their naked limbs, reflecting the sheen of their passion. Somewhere in the house, their time together methodically ticked away on a small, uncaring clock.

Anne lifted the pendent Joe always wore around his neck. 'What is this for?'

'It's my dog tags. It has my name, serial number and immunisation status on it.'

'Who is William Mallory, Baltimore?'

'He's my father. He's my next of kin.'

Anne rested her head on his chest and watched it rise and fall as she traced her fingers along the ridges of his chest muscles.

'I won't know if you die, will I?'

'I won't die.'

'But you could.'

'I won't. Why would I get myself killed when I have you waiting for me?'

Anne lifted her head to look at him. 'Promise me you'll come back to me.'

The corner of his mouth lifted in a wry smile. 'Try keeping me away.'

'Don't do anything heroic. I want you to stay safe.'

'I can't promise that.' He kissed her head 'Don't look so sad. As soon as it's over, I'll be back.'

She gave him a shaky smile. 'You better or I will search you out.'

Joe pulled her towards him and held her tight. 'I'll write to you.'

'I'd like that. Lots of letters. And I'll write to you,' said Anne, somewhat comforted.

'Lots. And often.'

'Every minute of every day?'

'Every second of every minute of every day.'

They both laughed, somehow it felt comforting to make such ridiculous vows.

They lay in silence for some minutes before Joe spoke again. 'I have loved it here. You have a beautiful country. The kids are just swell. Everyone has been so friendly … well not everyone. You have a few strange ways, and I've grown a taste for your lousy warm beer. We've been here for almost a year now. Kind of feels like home to me.'

Anne lifted her head to look at him and raised an eyebrow. 'Have we turned you into a Cornishman?'

Joe laughed. 'I don't think my accent will ever pass as an English one.'

Anne rested her head on his solid, muscled shoulder. The clock continued to snatch their time together away. Tick, tick, tick …

'We should have had our photograph taken together. You have one of me but I have nothing to remind me of you while you are away.' Her chin trembled with regret.

Joe moved beneath her as he withdrew a cigarette packet and pencil from his pocket. He placed the only remaining cigarette between his lips then returned it to the box, before writing a short message on the packet.

He gave it to her. 'Something to remind you of me.'

Anne carefully took the crumpled packet, with the solitary cigarette that had touched his lips, and held it against her heart. 'I'll keep it safe until you return to smoke it.'

His sombre voice, barely a whisper, warmed the top of her head as he held her close. 'Anne, whatever happens to me—'

'Hush … don't talk of dying now. You were right. You're not going to die.'

'Whatever happens to me, I want you to know that I have never loved anyone as much as I love you now.'

Anne lifted her head to look into his eyes. His face began to blur as she attempted to blink away her tears.

'I love you too, Joe.' Her voice, soft and broken, didn't sound like her own. She lifted his dog tags and stared at them in the soft light. If he died, they would be ripped from his torn body to identify him, proving he had existed and had died for his country. She pressed a heartfelt kiss on their cold metal surface. ‘A kiss from me to you to hang around your neck and keep you safe. Please take care, my Cornish Yank, and come home to me. I’ll be waiting for you.’

Chapter Twenty-Five

Last week in May, 1944

The 29th Infantry Division were to land on the beaches of Normandy. Fifty miles of coastline had been divided into five sections and given a name – Utah, Omaha, Gold, Juno and Sword. Securing Utah and Omaha was the American's aim. The British were responsible for securing Gold, Sword and Juno, with help from the Canadians for the latter. Securing Omaha from German control was the goal of the 29th and 1st Infantry Divisions. This section of the beach had been divided again into sections – Charlie, Dog Green, Dog White, Dog Red, Easy Green, Easy Red and Fox Green. The 29th Infantry Division would be responsible for assaulting and securing the stretch from Charlie to Easy Green. Support would be provided by the air force and navy, with the aim of diminishing the German defences prior to troops landing. The first assault wave of the 29th would be undertaken by the 116th Regimental Combat team. The 175th Infantry Regiment would follow later. It had taken years to plan, every detail and scenario raked over and discussed, not that the troops who would carry it out knew the details. For now, they were told to wait for their orders to leave, until then they were back to packing and repacking their equipment – and waiting.

Joe stared at the equipment he was expected to carry. He had laid it out neatly in front of him, a routine done so many times now that he'd lost count. He knew every item off by heart – an assault jacket, nine grenades, combat rations, half-pound TNT, rifle ammunition, bayonet, gas mask, poncho, weapon, shovel and newly-arrived field jackets that stank as bad as their uniforms. In total, the equipment felt between sixty and ninety pounds in weight. If they didn't get to shore soon after landing, they would surely drown in the surf. The most important thing was Anne's photograph, lying amongst the newly issued French money and phrase book. He picked it up, kissed it for good luck and slipped it between the pages of the book and into his pocket.

The forces network wireless and the grey flickering films shown in the temporary movie theatre, helped keep them occupied, but inevitably the uncertainty and waiting began to gnaw away at the nerves. When the call finally came to board their crafts on the third of June, a new wave of energy swept through the camp. Finally, something was happening.

‘Do you think this is it?’ asked Frank as a convoy of trucks lined up to take them to their embarkation points.

Joe watched the troops lined up ahead as they jumped into the back of the trucks in turn. They appeared full of energy, focused and keen to be gone.

‘I hope it is,’ continued Frank, as they stepped forward in their line together. ‘I want it over with so I can go home.’ He shivered. ‘The British summer is too chilly for me. When I get home the first thing I’m going to do is take myself off to the nearest baseball game and buy myself a hotdog … maybe even two … with lashings of mustard. Mmm … mmm.’

As Joe listened to Frank’s musings, an uneasy feeling shifted in his stomach. He remembered the last time he’d spoken to Anne’s stepfather, and the expression on his face as he looked at him. Standing here, watching these men, he finally understood what he had seen. These men were brave, but it was a bravery based on ignorance and naivety, for most had never been near a battlefield. They all looked so young. Many, he suspected, would be under the legal age to drink back home and at least half had probably never shaved.

‘Hey, Joe. I’m talking to you,’ said Frank. ‘Do you think this is another dry run?’

‘Let’s hope not,’ muttered Joe, under his breath, as their line moved forward to climb aboard. ‘It’s time we did what we came to do.’

The convoy of trucks took them to their designated embarkation points. Ships and landing craft waited for them to board, as hundreds of soldiers spilled from the transport and lined up to embark. They had rehearsed this before, they were the human cargo of a well-oiled logistic operating machine, where every sea craft had a purpose and every man had a set of skills. Individually they were weak and vulnerable, but together they were unstoppable. A wave of military might, congregating on the waters of the normally tranquil Cornish coast, before they assaulted occupied Normandy.

Once on board their ship, they had expected a speedy get away. They were soon disappointed. News came that the weather had turned bad, making any planned channel crossing, and subsequent landings, too treacherous to attempt. They were to remain on board and departure would be delayed until the weather improved. A frustrated groan echoed around the ship. Conditions below deck were already cramped, the food unappetising and there were only so many craps games a guy had the motivation to play. The men were ready to fight, not wait.

Chapter Twenty-Six

5 June, 1944

Anne stood in her garden looking across to Carrick Roads and the English Channel beyond. Ships, tugs and landing craft were moored everywhere, ready to be manoeuvred out into the channel by harbour craft. Yet nothing seemed to be happening. It had been several days since Joe's visit. He had given her the news that she didn't want to hear and left her passion-filled memories she would never forget. Was he on one of those ships? Was he scared? Was he thinking of her? How was she going to endure the next few months until he was returned to her? At least she had his letters to look forward to, and they would come, she knew they would. The alternative was unthinkable.

'Anne?'

Anne turned at the sound of the familiar voice. Betty stood no more than ten feet away, a little paler, her hair a little less curled, and with a deep sadness in her eyes. A sadness that Anne feared would never truly go away. Anne ran to her and they hugged, glad to be together again, but unable to find the words to voice it. It was some minutes before either felt brave enough to face the other and talk about what had been taken away from them.

'Are they leaving soon?' asked Betty eventually, as she looked at the ships and hooked her arm through Anne's.

'Yes.'

'Is Joe on one of them?'

'I think so, but I don't know for sure.' Anne looked at her friend. 'How are you?'

Betty smiled sadly. 'Surviving, although I don't know if I deserve to.'

'Please don't say that. I wish you'd let me write to you.'

'And be reminded of home? No, I couldn't have coped.'

'Do you want to talk about it?'

Betty hugged her cardigan around her. 'Yes. Desperately, but my parents don't want to know.'

'I do. You can talk to me.'

Betty smiled her thanks.

'What did you have?'

'A boy.' Betty's face almost crumpled at the word. Anne hugged her again. Eventually Betty broke away, wiping her tears with her trembling hand. 'He had the most beautiful blue eyes. 7lb 10 oz. I called him David. I was allowed to nurse him for six weeks, before he was taken away.'

'I'm so sorry.'

Betty sniffed loudly as she composed herself. 'Don't be. I should have been more careful. He's gone to a good family. The husband is a vicar. Can you believe my son having a vicar for a father? Much more respectable than having a single mother bringing him up.' She began to laugh, but it was forced and stilted. 'I'm sure I will learn to live with what I have done. Or at least hide how much pain I feel.' Her eyes filled with tears which sparkled in the sun. 'I hope it becomes easier, because when I think about him, the pain of guilt is unbearable.'

Anne put her arm around her and kissed her head. 'You can talk to me anytime. And maybe one day, David will come looking for you.'

'I hope so, because although I only washed him, fed him and clothed him for six weeks, he was my miracle. But he deserves a proper family, with a mum and dad and all he could want. He wouldn't have had all that from me, just my love.'

Anne wanted to tell her that her love was the only thing that mattered, but she knew it wasn't what Betty needed to hear.

'I know what you're thinking, Anne … a mother's love is all a child needs. I've thought about that every day since I found I was carrying him. There will always be part of me feeling that I have failed him, but my greatest fear is that he will never forgive me … because I know I will probably never forgive myself until he does.'

They stood in silence, Betty's head resting on Anne's shoulder, watching the ships and landing craft probably crammed with American soldiers.

'What a grand time we had with our American friends,' mused Betty, sadly.

'Do you wish you could have told David's father about him?'

'It was best he didn't know, whichever one he was. It's bad enough going to war, without knowing you're leaving a child behind. I wonder if they are scared.'

'It doesn't matter if they are. To me every one of them is a brave soldier,' said Anne.

They shared a smile, before Betty added, ‘And nearly every one of them claiming to be a cousin of Bob Hope.’

Chapter Twenty-Seven

Finally, the weather cleared and the order to leave filtered down from the top. The news was greeted with a cheer from the troops. Joe cheered too, caught up in the surge of patriotic determination sweeping through the men. They were fed up with waiting for the unknown. The battle ahead was the perfect diversion from the waiting, as waiting only allowed a man time to think of all he could lose. Joe pushed the memories of his time with Anne to the back of his mind, wanting to keep them safe and as perfect as could be.

Under darkness, their ship moved away from the coastline and out to sea. The engines rumbled quietly beneath, if it were not for the riverbanks and the port of Falmouth receding into the distance, it would be easy to think they weren't moving at all. In Joe's mind, it felt like Cornwall was waving them goodbye, despite not seeing a single civilian in the darkness.

Seasickness tablets and sick bags were issued with instructions to take one tablet immediately and another in four hours' time. Neither lasted long. A religious service was performed on deck, and although Joe bowed his head in prayer, along with hundreds of other troops, he wondered if anything or anyone could help them now. Yet despite all the signs that this time it was real, many men still clung to the belief that it was another training exercise, because to believe it was happening meant there would be no turning back.

The choppy waters of the English Channel greeted them. After a while, the number of ships and craft increased as the allied force gathered in the deep waters south to the Isle of White. Each American soldier was issued a letter from General Eisenhower, his carefully chosen words hoping to encourage the young men heading for Normandy.

Soldiers, Sailors and Airmen of the Allied Expeditionary Force!

You are about to embark upon the Great Crusade, toward which we have striven these many months. The eyes of the world are upon you. The hopes and prayers of liberty-loving people everywhere march with you. In company with our brave Allies and brothers-in-arms on other Fronts, you will bring about the destruction of the German war machine, the elimination of Nazi tyranny over the oppressed peoples of Europe, and security to yourselves in a free world.

Your task will not be an easy one. Your enemy is well trained, well equipped and battle-hardened. He will fight savagely.

But this is the year 1944! Much has happened since the Nazi triumphs of 1940-41. The United Nations have in-flicted upon the Germans great defeats, in open battle, man-to-man. Our air offensive has seriously reduced their strength in the air and their capacity to wage war on the ground. Our Home Fronts have given us an overwhelming superiority in weapons and munitions of war, and placed at our disposal great reserves of trained fighting men. The tide has turned! The free men of the world are marching together to Victory!

I have full confidence in your courage, devotion to duty and skill in battle. We will accept nothing less than full Victory!

Good Luck! And let us all beseech the blessing of Almighty God upon this great and noble undertaking.

Gen Dwight D. Eisenhower

'I guess this is the real thing this time,' said Frank, solemnly as he roughly folded the letter and slipped it in his pocket. They looked out to the vast expanse of sea. Despite the cloud, patches of clear sky and bright moonlight offered them a view that would ingrain itself in Joe's mind forever. The shadowy outlines of hundreds of battleships, destroyers, cruisers, mine sweepers, transport ships, patrol boats and more, stretched as far as the eye could see. On board each craft were hundreds or even thousands of men, from different parts of the world, all heading for the beaches of the north coast of France. They came from different cultures, different races and different lands, but together they were stronger and had the same aim – to defeat Hitler and fight for freedom.

'Joe?'

Frank's voice dragged him from his thoughts. He offered his friend some gum. 'Yes. I think you're right. This is the real thing this time.' He took one himself and popped it into his mouth, hoping it would somehow keep the seasickness at bay. They fell into a sombre silence, watching the fleet. It was a strange sight to see, so many people but not a single face. One lone person wasn't strong enough to defeat evil, but together so much could be achieved. 'So many ships,' he marvelled. 'There must be thousands. I could almost walk back to England just using their decks.' *I could walk back to Anne.* The thought of not doing so wrenched his heart.

As the journey progressed into the dark depths of the channel, the mood of the men on board darkened too. Was this an omen? Soldiers began to pray again, while others quietly swallowed down their unshed tears. The ship's chaplain walked the length of the ship several times, speaking to those who needed comfort in this uncertain time. Joe knew that the chaplain would be in even more demand, should the casualties be high.

The sound of a low rumble approached from above. Frank and Joe looked up at the birdless sky. Hundreds of bombers were moving across the vast expanse of space, filling it with their dark, ominous silhouettes like a migrating flock of man-made birds. Their flight was steady and rigid, the pilots' expert skill clearly on display in the unity of their tightly controlled flight; they were heading towards the German defences to prepare the way. The sight gave Joe more comfort than the chaplain's few well-chosen words. They went below deck in the hope of getting some sleep, but it was fitful and didn't last long. In the early hours of June sixth, the naval bombardment to blow up the German defences had begun. D-Day had finally arrived.

Joe's ship had come to a halt about ten miles out to sea. Despite the number of troops on board, the men were quiet as a grave. The weather was grey, with low cloud and short showers, yet somewhere in the far distance amphibious tanks and the first wave of allied troops were attempting to land under a constant bombardment of German machine, field guns and mortars. Speculation swept the troops that the plan to destroy the German defences had not been wholly successful. Flashes of artillery fire lit up the clouded sky, with remnants of the smoke screen previously used to hide the fleet, long faded away. Landing craft ferried soldiers towards the beach, returning emptied and bloodied or not returning at all. A haze of battle smoke filtered into the air, blurring the horizon in a blanket of carnage and despair.

'Are you scared?' a man asked beside him. Joe turned and saw it was Bolton, yet somehow, he looked different to the man he knew before. Gone was the arrogant swagger and thrust of his chin; he looked approachable, sincere, even gentle somehow.

'Are you?' asked Joe. Even now he couldn't help but question his motives for asking.

Bolton half-smiled. 'Yeah.' He jerked his head towards the battle in the distance. 'Knowing that men are being killed and blown up just a few miles away kind of puts things in perspective, doesn't it?'

Joe frowned. Was this his way of calling a truce? If so, he would take it. This was no time to continue meaningless fights.

'Yeah, it sure does,' he replied.

Bolton turned and walked away, soon swallowed up in the crowd of men. Joe had the strange sense that whatever happened next, he wouldn't see his nemesis again.

By 9 a.m. the tide was turning. A new short-lived naval bombardment tried to destroy the remaining beach defences before more troops landed in the rising waters.

Frank's humour had finally deserted him. 'Will you visit my mother, Joe? Whatever happens, tell her I didn't suffer.'

'I'll visit her, Frank,' he promised, despite knowing he may not be able to keep it. 'You don't have to worry about that.' It seemed to give his friend some mental comfort and that was all he could offer right now as the ship deck was crowded, with little room to lie down, let alone rest. Sleep had become a luxury they seemed to no longer need, for their bodies had been running for several hours now, on nerves and fear for what was to come.

The waiting continued until noon the following day. Although the other beaches had been secured, news reached them that landing on Omaha beach had been particularly brutal. Despite the confusion, it was apparent that although great gains had been made, it was still not fully secured. Although some advancement inland had been made, spasmodic machine-gun fire and underwater mines remained a threat to incoming troops.

The order to leave was finally given. Joe and Frank lined up at their points in readiness to climb down into the arriving landing craft below. Joe wondered how, or if, he would be returning.

'29, Let's Go!'

It was their call, the one they'd been trained to respect and obey. Their minds focused on the job ahead; they didn't bid farewell to the troops who would follow, but climbed over the side and down the cargo-net ropes. Their boots slipped on the wet ropes but they eventually reached the craft. The naval men on board, their faces haunted and sombre, would not meet their eyes. Their avoidance was a message of foreboding for the horrors ahead. The flat floor of the craft was slippery, but soon they were so tightly packed Joe could no longer see it. The motor propelled them forward towards the beach, but the choppy waters and rising tide soon hampered their progress, tossing the craft, so it rose and fell at stomach lurching gradients. A few began to vomit, adding to the slippery floor beneath their combat boots. The short journey became so bad that despite rubbing shoulder to shoulder with their army brothers, each one willing to risk their life for you, any place would be preferable to this one, where engulfing nausea gripped at stomachs and made you feel like death. Any place – even if it were the bloodied sands of a battlefield.

The motor eased and the craft slowed, stopping short on a sand bar as the tide reached the beach. Frank and Joe exchanged glances and for a fleeting moment, Joe glimpsed the old Frank. His smile was shaky, even forced, but it was there, nonetheless. He was his best buddy and they would have each other's backs, no matter what, no matter when, no matter how.

A nearby landing craft exploded nearby, bombarding them with shrapnel as they huddled together for protection. One man cried out in pain, his back badly torn by the twisted flying metal. All was confusion. Joe wanted to help him but the front ramp was already beginning to lower. A round of spasmodic machine shots peppered the air before the ramp was fully down, hitting Frank in his face and blowing half of it away. He fell where he stood, the boots he had once worn on the wrong feet, not yet wet.

Joe froze, attempting to register the horror he'd just witnessed. *Frank's dead. Frank's dead.* His friend's lifeless body was hastily dragged aside by someone else's desperate hands to clear the route for the men to leave. Joe had frozen for mere seconds, but war waited for no man to register their grief. The pressure of bodies behind him was too much to hold back, forcing Joe to step forward and leave his dear friend behind.

Frank's dead. Frank's dead. The water rose instantly around him to his chest, forcing him to raise his rifle high above his head. His heavy equipment weighed him down as his feet desperately tried to maintain the touch of firm ground. *Frank's dead.* The water rose to his neck, but no further. He was still able to breathe! *Frank's dead.* It took all his strength to force each leg through the never-ending wall of water, each step a battle carried forward and dragged back by each tidal wave. Yet, he felt Frank by his side, willing him forward, chiding him, bullying him to get to dry land. *Do it! Keep going!* Joe fought every step as he knew others had struggled, possibly failed, if they were given a chance at all. The evidence was all around him as he waded through the deep water: floating bodies still waiting to be collected from the previous day's intense fighting. Finally, the level of the water receded down his thighs and he was able to rise out of the sea and onto the sandy beach in front of him. He had made dry land.

Bloated bodies, dragged from the sea, lay in the sun to greet him, along with the dead who lay where they fell. As far as the eye could see, the debris of war scarred the coast. Thousands of incoming troops continued to spill from the landing crafts driven close to shore, quickly advancing through the discarded tanks, demolished sea defences … bodies. *Keep moving! Keep moving!* Joe reached near the top of the beach, his boots stepping on the high tidal line, discoloured pink, hinting at a sea stained red from blood. Here the lucky dead had been reclaimed by the army and were lined up in rows for burial, yet still some wounded were being tended to, while squads attempted to neutralise spasmodic bouts of fire. *Keep moving!*

Minor battles still raged in isolated spots, but the main ones were further inland. The deadly gunfire sounded ferocious, but it was where his platoon was heading. It was his turn to kill or be killed.

Joe knew he would never forget what greeted him on the beaches of Normandy, or the sweet smell and taste of human decay that contaminated the salty sea breeze, or that pungent smell of damp, anti-gas impregnated uniforms that clothed young men no older than boys. And somewhere out in the heaving waves, was Frank who'd become just one more of many he'd been forced to leave behind. Next time it could be him – and, strangely, he no longer cared.

Chapter Twenty-Eight

Anne stared out of the bus window at the passing scenery. The green, ever changing hedges blurred before her. She lifted her gaze to the countryside beyond; some fields lush and green where cows grazed at leisure, others intensively cultivated to produce the food so desperately needed. It had been a week since she'd woken to find the ships gone. She could only guess that Joe was on board and they had taken him with them. Later she heard on the wireless that the initial invasion had been a success, but it had not reassured her that he was still alive.

'What are you thinking?' asked Betty beside her.

'I was thinking of Joe.'

Betty patted her hand in comfort. Anne looked down at Betty's hand protecting hers. She was such a dear friend, knowing instinctively that waiting for Joe's first letter would be unbearable for her and supporting her all she could.

'Thank you for coming with me. I had to see it before it's gone.'

Betty gave her hand a brisk squeeze. 'I understand. I would want to see it too.'

This morning Billy had come home with the news that the American camps were being dismantled. Anne felt a desperate need to see Joe's camp before it was removed. She couldn't explain why; it wasn't as if he was there now, yet somehow seeing it would give her comfort that the young handsome American had existed at all.

'Will you know which one was his?'

Anne nodded. 'Yes. He told me. I think we will be arriving soon.' A few minutes later Anne recognised the area. 'Here! It was here! We must stop the bus!' She rose quickly, dragging Betty with her, but the bus wouldn't stop. Betty immediately took charge and ordered the driver to let them off. After some toing and froing, the driver reluctantly stopped and they scrambled out before he changed his mind. The bus drove away. In front of them was what had once been one of the marshalling camps. Large coils of barbed wire surrounded rows of tired, wind-beaten tents, flapping in the breeze. Children's laughter snared their attention. A small group of excited girls and boys ran from tent to tent, their arms filled with all the treasures they'd found. Their presence gave Anne and Betty the courage to go in and explore for themselves.

They wandered around the large tents first as Anne hoped these would give a glimpse of Joe's day-to-day life. Each tent had a story, told vividly by what was left behind. A projection screen and benches. Anne imagined Joe sitting on one of the seats and the air thick with cigarette smoke, as Hollywood films played out on the screen in front. They entered another. Anne ran her fingers along the medical equipment and trays, now dusty from dirt blown in by the wind, and she wondered if this had been a rudimentary medical centre once. The next big tent was just as basic, with pipework and showers; easier to guess and sadder to imagine as to its use. She had seen Joe's naked body many times by now and the ache to see him like that again pained her more than she could bear.

'Let's go somewhere else,' she said, turning away and stepping outside.

Anne looked about her. The camp felt like a ghost town. A magazine, caught up in the wind, tumbled across their path until it fell into a waterlogged rut of a military wheel track. There it flapped its remaining dry pages helplessly, as the sodden print and images of American models, with perfect smiles, darkened and turned to mush.

Anne and Betty continued to solemnly explore. Sometimes they discovered things that seemed to make no sense, such as the vast amounts of unopened boot dubbing, which suddenly had no purpose and wasn't required at all. Abandoned crates, filled with food, and army issue pots and pans, hinted at a mess hall marquee. Once again, Anne allowed herself to imagine it full of hungry, noisy young men, and Joe amongst them eating heartily and without fear. Anne smiled to herself. How provincial and polite her mother's neatly laid table and plates of sandwiches must have seemed to him when he came to visit.

They left the communal areas, connected with dirt-covered duckboards, to explore the smaller tents. These would have been where the soldiers slept, played card games and, perhaps, where Joe remembered her, thought Anne.

As they entered the first, even Betty, who'd been talking throughout, fell silent. Personal items were scattered on every bed, as if they'd left in a hurry, but expected to return. Bed linen lay crumpled and tossed aside, haphazardly scattered with American sweets, magazines and photos of home. Anne's gaze wandered over the pictures – proud parents, smiling girlfriends and loving wives with their children who always seemed to be laughing at the camera's eye. Each area had a locker, with doors left tantalisingly ajar. Anne watched as Betty dared to look inside. Carefully stuck on the interior with gum was the Hollywood elite. Rita Hayworth, in a sultry blue dress, stared out of languid liquid eyes. Betty Grable, wearing only her bathing costume, teased a man to hold her. Jane Russell, lying against a cushion of hay with her shoulder strap falling lose, inviting a man to dare touch her, with a haughty lift of a brow.

'Sometimes I wonder why Joe loved me.'

It was only when Betty slipped her arm around her waist, did she realise she had spoken her thoughts aloud.

'I don't wonder and nor must you.' She steered Anne away. 'Anyway, I bet Joe's locker is empty. Which tent do you think it is?'

Anne shrugged. 'I don't know. There are so many and I wouldn't know what to look for to find it.'

They continued to roam, feeling more sombre with every minute that passed. They found musical instruments, cameras and many letters and parcels from home, left behind for safekeeping, just in case they returned. Most tents were the same, scattered remnants of their previous life, but one tousled bed caught her eye. Lying on the blanket was a postcard of a large urban city. Beneath was the word "Baltimore" and although the message was addressed to someone else, it was the closest Anne had found to being near Joe. Suddenly drained of her stamina, she climbed on the bed, wrapped the coarse blanket about her as she hugged it to her chest and finally allowed her tears to flow.

They stayed for several hours, although most of the time was spent watching from afar, as members of the US army had arrived. They came with one aim – to clear the area and it was done with the callous efficiency required. Tents and army equipment were loaded into waiting lorries and quickly driven away. No sooner had they gone, then new unyielding machines came to bulldoze away the rest. Photographs of smiling loved ones, the letters and parcels from home, met the same fate as their Hollywood stars. Everything the soldiers left behind was bulldozed into high piles or deep pits and set alight or buried.

Anne and Betty watched in silence, their thoughts full of the soldiers' families and what they would say if they could witness this scene. Their eyes filled with tears as they remembered them too – proud, loud, even arrogant at times, but always polite and fun to know. Yet soon there would be no trace of them, even their treasures that they once held so dear would be no more than black smoke dancing in the sky.

Chapter Twenty-Nine

1955

Anne read the final words on the gravestone, a poignant reminder of the war and how things used to be. *We'll meet again*. The simple phrase was a favourite among many who had lived through the war. For Anne it conjured up her own unique memories, some intimate and loving, some so vivid and emotive that she could almost smell the camp bonfire, the new uniforms of the 29th as she sewed on their badges and the diesel and oil slicks washed up on the shore. And, of course, there were the sounds and flashes of bombings in the distance, the haunting voice of Vera Lynn on the wireless or the sound of Joe's motorcycle coming over the hill. She swallowed down the tears threatening to fall. The war had been terrible, yet even in the darkest times there was some good to find amongst the hardships, the worry and the grief. There was the fighting spirit and camaraderie of the community. The ability to seek out pleasures when none appeared to exist. The loves found and the loves lost. It was a unique time, when Britain hosted Americans and cultures clashed, yet minor resentments were far outweighed by gratitude, respect, curiosity and friendship from both sides.

'I think she will be pleased with how it looks.'

Henry's voice woke her from her memories and forced her back to reality. She blinked, almost surprised to find herself in her village churchyard again.

'Yes, I think she would be. I'm glad they've finally put it up. Six months seems so long. Mother hated the thought of being in an unmarked grave.'

Anne thought of Joe and wondered where his body was laid to rest; if it was ever found at all.

'They have to let the ground settle first. If it's put in too early, it will lean in time.'

Anne placed the bouquet of flowers on her mother's grave. 'At least she's free of pain now.'

'She hid it well,' said Henry. 'Too embarrassed to see a doctor. Too stoic to share it with us. She didn't want us to worry. Everything she ever did was for her family.'

'I let her down. She wanted me to marry and have children.'

'You didn't let her down. She wanted you to be happy and thought that if you married a nice local chap, you would find happiness.'

'Her attempts at matchmaking were rather desperate.'

They both laughed at the memory. It became a running joke that her mother always invited someone new for Sunday roast; usually single and of marrying age.

Henry closed the remaining button of his coat. 'She worried for you. She said she felt responsible for your future.'

'I don't see why.'

'Because of the American.'

Anne frowned. 'I don't know what you mean.'

Henry took her arm and led her away from the grave. 'You know what I mean – she didn't exactly encourage it. She was afraid you would either marry him and go off to America or be left a widow with a child to rear.'

'Well, neither happened because he was killed.'

'Which is why I asked him to wait until he came home alive.'

Anne paused, forcing Henry to stop walking too. 'Wait for what?'

'To ask you to marry him. He came to see me and asked for my permission to ask for your hand.'

'He didn't tell me.'

'He said he wouldn't. He didn't want to come between you and us. He said he would ask you when he returned.'

Anne's heart heaved with pain. Every remaining day of the war she'd rushed home from work, hoping and praying there would be at least one reply to her many letters, reassuring her he was well; none ever arrived. After a while she stopped writing as there was only one conclusion to be drawn: he had been killed shortly after landing. Henry's confession gave her comfort. Over the years her memories of Joe had grown in perfection, so much so that she had even come to fear that she'd embellished their love. However, Henry's words proved that Joe had loved her as much as she had loved him and his protection of her was both honourable and self-sacrificing. She had known perfect love and it was hard to forget it or settle for anything less.

Anne's alarm clock rattled her awake, its bell having been damaged long ago in a mysterious incident involving Billy and his baseball bat. She got up, washed, dressed and went downstairs to lay the breakfast. Billy was now a man and had the appetite of one. Her stepfather and half-brother entered the kitchen just as she was serving up the porridge. Thirty minutes later, they had left for work. She cleared the table, washed the dishes, grabbed her hat and coat and ran for the bus.

The bus that would take her to work was five minutes late. The driver greeted her with the cause of the delay before she had a chance to ask.

'Cows.'

'Ah, of course,' said Anne as she paid the fare. 'It's that time of year.' Anne settled into her usual seat and stared out the window. She had lost count how many times the neighbouring farmer had herded his cows to fresh grass when his lower field had been eaten bare. He always chose the same month and time of day to do it. He was a creature of habit, much like she had become. After years of uncertainty caused by the war, habit and normality was a comfort … yet Anne still yearned for more.

Despite the delay, she was the first to arrive at the office. She unlocked the door and, for a moment, stared at the keys in her hand, remembering when they were first placed there.

'As senior secretary, with few home responsibilities, we felt you were the best person to hold the keys.' Mr Sullivan senior, the fourth generation of Sullivan and Sullivan, had patted her hand believing what he said was a compliment. Anne had translated it differently. She was a spinster, without a young family to make demands on her time. She would be glad of something extra to do. Despite this she has remained silent and accepted them with a smile.

She stepped inside and carefully hung her hat and coat on the hook. She surveyed the line of desks and began allocating the office jobs according to the secretaries' skill set. Next, she checked the shorthand accuracy of the letters that required typing. The final task, before Mr Sullivan, his son and the other office staff arrived, was to prepare a tray of tea and biscuits for her boss's arrival. She looked at her reflection in the mirror before the steam from the kettle obliterated it. Had she aged much overnight? She tucked a strand of hair behind her ear and attempted a smile. It made little difference. Thankfully the steam began to settle on the mirror before she could look any closer. The door opened and the rest of the staff arrived. The workday had officially begun.

She filled the teapot and carried the tray into Mr Sullivan senior's office, just as Miss Truscott used to do before her cataracts forced her to retire. As she poured the tea she glanced up and saw, through the open office door, one of the younger, prettier secretaries watching her. The girl reminded her of herself, when she used to watch the elderly spinster all those years ago. Was she pitying her too?

I repaired spitfires once. I helped win the war, she screamed inside.

The day was busy but nothing Anne could not cope with. At the end, when everyone had left, she locked up and popped into the butchers who had kept back some brisket, her stepfather's favourite cut of meat. Meat rationing had finally ended the previous year and it had become their Friday treat, one she no longer had to remind the butcher about. She held the wrapped package protectively on her lap as she sat in the same grubby seat on the bus that had taken her to work in the morning. She stared out the window and saw the cows grazing in their new field. She had known them since they were calves and had watched them grow day by day whenever she travelled on the bus. At least tomorrow was Saturday and there would be a break from her humble weekday routine, not that she was looking forward to what she had planned.

It was time to clear her mother's things. Henry couldn't face the task, but Anne felt stronger. Perhaps she was more like her mother than she would have accepted before. Her clothes were the hardest, not because they smelt of her, but because they no longer did. The woman she knew had slipped away, but had left her mark in each repaired tear, each substitute button and each reinforced seam; a vivid reminder of her mother's fast-working hands and her habit of cutting the thread with scissors yet finishing the task with her teeth.

Her personal items didn't take long. She wasn't a woman who liked cosmetics or an array of perfumes, just a touch of lavender on her wrists and a modest stroke of lipstick for special occasions.

Anne saw her mother's hairbrush, already coated with dust. She picked it up and turned it in her hands. It was an inanimate object, but had always played a part in her life. As a child she would lie on her mother's bed and watch her brush her hair, as an adult she would borrow it if she couldn't find her own. How could she throw it away now? She carefully teased the last strands of her mother's hair away from its tired bristles. It had too much of her mother imprinted on it to discard forever.

The drawers of the dressing table were next. Here, Anne discovered, her mother was a bit of a hoarder, as each was filled with trinkets, shells, broken brooches, necklaces and clip-on earrings that no longer held tight. Pins, nets, strange broken bits with no home, old worn purses, threadbare scarves, it seemed to go on. Amongst the clutter lay three neatly penned envelopes, with a different name on each – Henry, Billy and Anne. Anne's heart began to race. Her mother had written them each a letter and she was about to talk to them from beyond the grave.

My dearest Anne,

This is the hardest letter to write as I'm finding it difficult to say the right words when I know by the time you read this I will have died. I won't be there to explain myself more clearly or answer the questions I know you will have. Perhaps the first thing I must say is that I love you and always will.

The second thing is that I am proud of the woman you have become as there is no woman kinder and more caring than you. I would like to take some credit for those virtues, but I know you far exceed mine and I have reconciled that your good looks always came from your father's side. I hope what I am about to write will, in some way, help you understand my actions.

When I was young, I fell in love with your father. He was handsome, impeccably mannered and a very gentle and loving man. I was in love for the first time in my life and it felt wonderful. When the war started, he was sent to fight. We wrote to each other frequently. He promised me a glorious future and we soon became engaged. I had no interest in any other man. I was overjoyed when the war ended. We immediately married upon his return. It wasn't long before I realised he had come home a changed man. He had mood swings, violent outbursts and such terrible nightmares. He was no longer capable of loving or receiving love. I didn't recognise him any more. I had wasted my courting years waiting for him to come home and when he did, the man I fell in love with had gone. At least I had you. When he died, I am ashamed to say I was relieved as I was finding it increasingly difficult to shield you from his violent outbursts. If it was not for my parents' love and support, I don't know how I would have survived our short marriage.

When you started dating the American soldier during the war, I worried that history would repeat itself. War is brutal and changes a man. There was also the added fear that if you married and moved to another country you would be out of our reach to support and love you. The change in your father frightened me. I did not want the same for you.

I felt it was the right thing to not encourage your romance. However, over the years I have begun to doubt my decision. Now my time is near, I question what right did I have to interfere at all ... for interfere I did.

Private Joe Mallory did write to you, my dearest Anne. He wrote often and frequently and, to my shame, I burnt every one. At first, I felt resolute in intercepting and burning both your letters but as his letters continued to come, despite never having received any from you, I grew more and more ashamed. He must have been a good man to keep writing when there seemed so little hope.

How was I to tell you what I had done? I consoled myself that you appeared to be getting over him and making a life of your own and, perhaps, it would be better if I didn't open old wounds. This is the route I took and hoped you would find someone else. You didn't, despite my best efforts and now I know I will no longer be around, I have finally faced what I had refused to before ... that I was wrong and cowardly to not tell you while I was alive and to beg for your forgiveness face to face.

Please remember, my dearest Anne, that although what I did was wrong, it was done with the best intentions and love. All I can do now is try to rectify my wrongdoing in the hope you will, in my absence, find it in your heart to forgive me.

On the back of his last letter was a Baltimore address. I can only guess that he would soon be going home and was leaving a trail for you to find him. I hope you do and that you both find the happiness you deserve.

All my love, always and forever,

Mum.

Anne stared at the Baltimore address at the bottom of the page. It was written in neat capitals as if her mother had made a concerted effort to print the address clearly. Had her mother remembered it all these years, or had she made a note of it in a moment of self-doubt? Anne would never know for sure, but she had learnt one thing – Joe had survived the war and this foreign address, written in blue ink, offered her a bridge across the sea.

Anne watched Betty's eyes race across the page as she poured her a cup of tea. Once or twice Betty gasped and threw her a surprised glance, before returning to the letter in her hand. She placed it carefully on the table between them and sat back in her chair.

'Joe did write to you!'

Anne nodded as she fiddled with her teaspoon and stared at the open letter in front of her. All those times her mother had offered to post her letters and she, like a fool and eager to get to work, had believed she had finally accepted their relationship and handed them to her.

'What an awful thing for your mother to do!'

'Mother was scared for me.' Betty raised her eyebrows at her. 'Honestly, I don't blame her. I feel sorry for her. I had no idea my father was a violent man. She protected me so well.'

Betty rolled her eyes. 'You seem to be taking this bombshell very well. I would be livid if my mother had burnt my love letters.'

'We don't know if they were love letters.'

'Now you're just being silly. She burnt yours too.' Betty frowned, angry on behalf of her friend. She picked up her cup and noisily sipped the contents. It seemed to calm her resentment a little. Anne gave her some time to brood over the subject; heaven knew Anne had needed some time herself before she could face the rest of the day.

'Mother thought I was naive about life and how war changes people. She was also afraid she would lose me. She found herself in the position of having been deceitful and not knowing if or when to come clean.'

Betty looked at her through the rising steam of her tea as she sipped again. 'I suppose if I thought Cathy or Jennifer were heading for heartache, I might be tempted to do something similar in order to protect them.' Betty placed her cup in her saucer and stared at it for a moment. 'You were young. Joe was your first real boyfriend. It was a strange time. The country was jam-packed with eligible, handsome men and I think many, including me, threw caution to the wind.'

Anne smiled as memories of dance halls filled with boisterous American soldiers came flooding back. The silent memory felt like a scene from a film. A film she'd fleetingly played a part in, but was now archived and best forgotten.

Betty smiled too. 'I think your mother would be very relieved to know how you've forgiven her.' She placed her hand on the letter and slid it across the table towards Anne. 'The question is – what are you going to do about it now?'

Anne stared at the letter. 'That question has been on my mind. For a long time I blamed Hitler and the army's postal service for his lack of letters. Then I worried he no longer cared for me. It took me a long time to put those doubts aside and finally accept he must be dead.'

Betty nodded. 'I remember.'

Anne touched the letter, but did not pick it up. 'But I eventually came to terms with it. And now I find none of those reasons were true and he is still out there.' She looked up at Betty. 'And it scares me.'

'Scares you?'

'Now I can write to him, but what if he doesn't want to hear from me?'

Betty understood, as she knew her friend would. 'He may be married.'

'Yes, with children.'

They fell silent, pondering on all the various scenarios.

'If I did write I think it would be best to be polite, but formal. I would hate to cause him problems.'

Betty nodded with conviction. 'He may have changed. He might not have aged well.'

'Joe may think I've not aged well!'

'He could never say that. I swear you improve with age, whereas I've had three children and they've taken a toll.' Betty winced as she realised what she'd said. Even now, after all these years, Anne knew she still thought of her little boy – and felt the physical ache his absence left.

Anne squeezed her hand in sympathy. 'Cathy and Jennifer are so sweet. They look just like you.'

Betty laughed. 'Poor them. I think they look more like their father.' She tapped the letter. 'So?'

Anne released her hand and sat back in her chair. 'I don't know.'

'I suppose the war may have changed him for the worse. Perhaps your mother knew what she was talking about and was right to do what she did. You don't have to write to him, Anne. He doesn't know what your mother did.'

'I did consider letting sleeping dogs lie,' said Anne echoing her stepfather's stance when confronted with a difficult situation, 'but I hate the thought that he believes I never bothered to write back. I'd like to explain. I don't want him to think badly of me.'

'But you won't tell him the rest.'

'The rest?'

'That you missed him. That you took a long time to accept he was not coming back. That even after the war you never seriously dated anyone again. That sometimes I worried about you so much that I thought you would never recover.'

'Did you?'

Betty nodded. 'You loved him so much, Anne. I know that because I saw the pain it caused you when he was taken away. You were grieving for so long. I recognised it because it was how I felt too. We grieved together for those we'd lost.' She covered Anne's hand with hers. 'Only this time you have a chance to explain what happened. Maybe, one day, I will be lucky enough to get that chance to explain to my son too.'

Chapter Thirty

Joe paused at the door of his office, taking a moment before his arrival became known. His law firm was small, but he could not fault the dedication of those who worked with him, and today's success was down to them just as much as it was him.

Someone roughly patted him on the back. 'Hey! He's back!'

A flurry of warm greetings enveloped him as one by one his secretary, junior clerk, cleaner, friendly neighbour and, finally, his friend and colleague, Mitch, came to congratulate him.

'Knew you'd do it.'

'Taught them a thing or two.'

'Well deserved, Joe.'

Someone produced a bottle of cheap champagne. Soon they were exclaiming in delight as the released cork hit the ceiling and a fountain of bubbles were eagerly captured in a circle of cheap glasses and mugs.

As he watched them, he couldn't help but recall the first day this present career path had started. He'd been walking along the sidewalk outside his place of work when a woman stopped him. 'My son is Chick Isiah Marshall,' she had said, 'and I need your help.'

The name had sounded familiar. His interest was piqued so he walked with her and listened to what she had to say. The woman told him that her son, accused of robbing a woman, was innocent. Joe realised that only that morning he'd been reading about the case in the paper and thought the boy didn't stand a chance.

His mother had other ideas and although she told him she had little money, she was willing to sell everything to avoid having the defence attorney appointed by the judge. The man had failed to successfully defend a man of African descent for the last two years, she argued, and she didn't trust him now. Joe didn't disagree; he had the same reservations.

He attempted to explain he'd only recently qualified as a defence attorney, but she still wanted him anyway. 'Why?' he questioned.

'Because,' she said, 'my nephew met you during the war and recommended you to me'.

'Who is your nephew?' he asked.

'Homer Marshall.'

Joe had realised, there and then, he could no longer refuse even if he'd wanted to. How could he say no to his harmonica-playing friend?

He took the case on the spot for a nominal fee. He did the work in his spare time as he knew the firm employing him wouldn't take it on. Against all expectations, except for the confidence placed in him by the Marshall family, he'd won.

The Chick Marshall case was the first of many referrals. Soon, he was setting up his own firm near the area where his clients made their homes. It was the run-down part of the city, and the money he earned was at stark odds to the wealth generated from his father's office, sat high on the skyline of Baltimore City, but the job satisfaction was greater than anything he had felt before.

'We did it!' said Mitch, smiling broadly. They shook hands, which ended in a brief, back-thumping, celebratory hug. 'You turned the jury around. I swear I even saw one of them weep.'

'They all should have wept,' said Joe, waving away a slice of celebratory cake which had miraculously appeared in the path to his office. 'The charge was a travesty.' He threaded his way past the happy throng of people to his cluttered sanctuary, closely followed by Mitch, who closed the door.

'Look at them smiling,' mused Mitch, as he watched them through the glass in the door. He threw Joe a glance. 'And that's down to you.'

Joe sat at his desk and surveyed the chaos. His desk was littered with files and notes; it would feel good to tidy it away now the case had come to an end.

'I couldn't have done it without you.' He searched for a cigarette and offered one to Mitch. 'How do you feel about becoming an equal partner?'

Mitch frowned as he took one. 'An equal partner? With you?'

Joe inhaled his cigarette and pretended to be interested in the fresh plume of smoke. 'Are you trying to tell me that you didn't go to Howard University School of Law?'

'Of course I'm not.'

'Which makes you a lawyer.'

'You know I am.'

'So why are you finding the suggestion so hard to believe?'

'Well, for one, I've only just qualified.'

'You've been qualified for a year and I wouldn't have won this case without you.'

‘I can’t be equal. I haven’t any money to put into this place.’

‘Not yet you don’t, but I see you as an investment.’ Joe leaned forward in his chair. ‘Look Mitch, if we want to play our part in the civil rights movement, you know, as well as I do, that people who represent that fight have to be in more leadership roles. That’s why you went to law school, isn’t it?’

‘Sure it is.’

‘Then just see this as another step along the way. Look, Mitch, I need you as much as you need me. We work well together and I trust you … like a brother … and that’s saying something coming from me.’ He stood up. ‘So what will it be? Are you on board? On equal terms?’

‘Sure as hell, I am!’

The door opened, causing them both to turn round. Joe’s smile faded as he recognised the man standing in the doorway. He hadn’t seen him in more than two years, yet here he was, a little greyer, a little weightier, but with the same steely blue eyes he remembered as a child.

‘Who are you?’ asked Mitch, smiling, but a little confused.

‘It’s alright, Mitch. He’s my father.’

Mitch frowned. Joe couldn’t blame him for his surprise; he had never mentioned his family before. Mitch offered to shake hands with his father. The offer was ignored. Joe felt the hairs raise on the back of his neck. His father hadn’t changed and probably never would.

‘I could do with a coffee, boy.’

‘Mitch is not an errand boy,’ cut in Joe. ‘He’s my law partner.’

Mitch looked from one to the other. ‘Look, I can see you’ve a lot to catch up on. I’ll start working on the next case.’ He collected a file from the shelf and looked at Joe. ‘Let me know when you’re done.’

Joe gave a curt nod of his head, although he doubted his father’s visit would take long. He braced himself for the onslaught of criticism he knew would soon come.

‘I had a hard job finding you. Every building looks the same in this part of town.’ Joe tightened his jaw as his father’s gaze examined his desk. ‘Your standards have slipped since I last saw you. You could do with an office manager. How do you work in this chaos?’

‘I’ve been busy.’

‘I know. You’ve made quite a mark in the city. No one thought you would win this last one.’

‘He was innocent.’

His father looked at him through his bushy eyebrows. 'Now you know as well as I do, that doesn't mean anything without the right defence.'

'Is that a compliment?'

'You're wasting your time defending these types of people.'

'These types?'

'Now don't come all innocent, you know exactly what I mean.'

Joe slowly nodded. 'I do … and that is the saddest thing of all.' Joe studied the man he'd spent half his life idolising and missing, and the other half despising. Now he felt little except a deep sadness that the chasm between them only grew bigger each year.

'How is Milly?' asked his father.

'We divorced a year ago. I did let you know.'

His father walked to the window and gazed out onto the street down below. 'Not much of a view. How many offices are in here? Two? Three?'

'Two. The other is a—'

'How would you like to work for me? You'll have a big office, fine views over Baltimore and a better wage than you earn from your current client base.' He laughed without humour. 'You have grown a reputation. I think we can both agree that it's best to put yourself on the right side of history.'

'I am on the right side of history. I'm staying right here.'

'Well I'm not going to beg. The offer's on the table. I will leave you to think about it.'

'I have thought about it.'

'These things require some time.' He walked to the door. 'Let me know what you decide. Oh, nearly forgot …' He turned abruptly, patting his pockets until he found what he was searching for. 'This came for you about two weeks ago.' He dropped a battered envelope onto the desk. 'It has an English postmark. It seems your growing reputation has reached as far as Europe.' He laughed at his own joke.

Joe stared at the envelope bearing his old home address, written carefully in a familiar feminine hand, which made his heart thud in the cage of his chest.

'You do realise I don't ask just anyone to join my firm. I only ask the best.'

Joe looked up in surprise. His father's praise of his legal skill was no minor accolade. Not only was this man a seasoned lawyer and considered one of the best and most expensive in Maryland, he was also his father who found uttering words of praise almost impossible. Joe waited for the compliment to be snatched back, by way of a well delivered sarcastic comment, but none came. He had meant what he said.

'I know,' replied Joe quietly. His father nodded in acknowledgement, braced his shoulders and walked out the door.

Joe looked at the letter again. Several minutes passed, but the letter remained where it was left, untouched and unread.

'Is it clear to come in?'

Joe looked up to see Mitch's head peeping around the door frame. It was a relief to see a familiar face.

'I'm sorry for my father's behaviour. When I was younger, I didn't see his attitude as wrong. I've grown up a lot since then.'

'What made you see the light?'

His gaze dropped to the letter lying between them. 'The war. Seeing the world for the first time. Making new friends. Meeting a woman called Anne.'

Mitch jerked his head towards the letter. 'Is that why he came? To give you that?'

'It was an excuse to come here, but the real reason was to ask me to work for him.'

'And are you?'

Joe shook his head. 'No, and his visit today has just confirmed that I want no part of his world any more.'

'Are you okay? You look a bit—'

Joe brushed off his concern. 'I'm fine. Just give me a minute, will you?'

Although Mitch still looked concerned, he had come to know him well enough that he knew he needed some time alone.

'Yeah, sure. See you later.' He quietly closed the door. Joe listened to Mitch's gentle tones as he warned the others not to disturb him. Joe smiled at his thoughtfulness. He stared at the letter. A mixture of feelings swirled around inside him. Excitement, nervousness, even fear that his rising hopes might be dashed within minutes of opening it.

Yet what did he hope to gain by reading it? Did he even want to meet her again? Time had not stood still. They were both more than ten years older, jaded with wisdom gained by life's experiences. Although he fundamentally still felt the same inside, he knew that he was not.

How could he be after witnessing his best friend die at Omaha, before he even set foot on the beach? Even now, sitting in his dark, cluttered office, he could still remember, as if it was yesterday, the hundreds of dead soldiers, lined up on the pink-tinged shoreline of France. The lucky dead, as at least those soldiers had died with their bodies intact. There had been so much more to come.

The 175th fought, village by village, town by town, through Normandy and Brittany, each soldier starting the day with the gnawing feeling that it could be their last. The only two things that kept him sane, in a surreal landscape where skirmishes and battle destruction sat side by side with the local French population going about their daily lives, was the ground they gained and writing to Anne. Only she never replied. At first, he'd excused it. Life in the army was a strange mix of strategic planning and chaos, where plans changed on a dime and unexpected skirmishes felt like all hell had broken loose. What chance was there for a letter from Cornwall to reach the right man? Correspondence was of minor importance when accompanying supplies took priority. Joe accepted her silence at first, as he had other things on his mind – like trying to survive. The Netherlands came next, then Germany and although ground was gained and occupied countries regained their freedom, the price paid was high. Many of his friends were injured or died and that experience alone could change a man – and it had changed him. He had landed on Omaha, inexperienced and brave, never having shot a gun in real combat before. He returned home a cynical, battle-hardened soldier, with the inability to feel anything much at all. Perhaps that's why he hadn't visited her after the war to demand answers. He couldn't take any more pain by facing the truth.

Yet, the last time he had felt anything was when he was with Anne. He had searched for it by rushing into marriage with a woman as damaged as he was, having lost her fiancé in the Pacific war. They barely knew one another, but they tried their best, until one day they agreed amicably that they had made a mistake and it was best to end it before children came along. They separated and eventually divorced. The legal process was cheap and quick, which suited them both.

Since the ending of his marriage, his personal life had found an even keel. He'd already earned a solid reputation for winning lost causes that nobody wanted but now his employees filled the gap where a family should have been. They were an assortment of characters, from a range of backgrounds, but all with determination and goodness in their hearts.

After-work drinks and family get-togethers were the norm, where an invitation to celebrate Thanksgiving didn't rest on the colour of one's skin. The fight for equal civil rights was gaining momentum and he wanted to play his part. It felt good to fight for the freedom of others, without having to shoot a gun.

His mind wandered to Anne. He could see her now, riding her bicycle as the sun set behind her, floating in his arms as he taught her to swim, caressing her naked thigh on their last night together. He opened his desk drawer, reached towards the back and located a small tin. Surprisingly, his hands began to tremble as he withdrew it and fumbled like a child to open the lid. Inside was Anne's crumpled photograph. Its travels, initially from soldier to soldier who never understood its worth and then later across Europe as his constant companion, was evident in each watermark, crease and frayed edge. It had been years since he had last dared look at her face. And despite its state, she was still as beautiful as he remembered.

He rubbed his brows to try and block out the memories. Was Anne even the same woman as the one he knew before? Did he want to have his memories spoilt by seeing her again, without the threat of war driving them as much together as it did apart? If he ignored it, he could keep his memories of her perfect, wrapped and kept safe in the recess of his mind.

Yet there was always the question that nagged him. Why had she cut him off so ruthlessly? Perhaps the letter would provide an answer and bring resolution to something that could still evoke feelings that he long thought had died. There was only one way to find out. He took a deep, shuddering breath and reached for the letter that had crossed the Atlantic to find him.

Chapter Thirty-One

Anne breathed in deeply to savour her peaceful surroundings. The day before had been Billy's wedding. It was simple and small, tinged with sadness that their mother wasn't there to see it, yet still filled with warmth, joy and appreciation for all that they had. Yes, she had received a few well-meaning consolatory comments that it would be "her turn next time", but overall, it had been a wonderful day. It had also been hectic. As Anne was too old to play and too young to sit back and rest, most of the last-minute preparations and tidying up had fallen to her. She didn't mind. The extra responsibilities kept her busy and stopped her thinking about herself.

Anne smiled as the warm summer sun glistened on the surface of the deep blue waters of Carrick Roads. She was quite alone. Her stepfather had gone fishing, Betty had just left, and her brother and his wife were away for a few days on their honeymoon. She couldn't remember the last time she was truly alone in the middle of the day. She should enjoy the moment. In a few days, Billy and his wife, Joan, would be returning to live in their home and Anne wouldn't be the only woman in the house. Two women running a home was never a good combination, perhaps it was finally time she moved out.

Joe hadn't replied. It had been heartbreaking to wait for a letter from him again. It evoked the same raw feelings that she'd felt waiting all those years ago. It was also unsettling as it confirmed that no matter how much she reassured Betty that she was emotionally over Joe, it wasn't true. But the waiting couldn't go on forever. Yesterday she'd watched her younger brother kiss his bride and realised that loving someone should not be this hard. His silence could only mean that those exciting and romantic days, with the love of her life, were now firmly in the past.

At least she'd taken the opportunity to explain to Joe why she didn't reply to his letters. She hoped he was happy; she certainly didn't hold any ill feeling towards him for his present silence. Why should she? He had left her with a trove of precious memories that could never be spoilt.

Anne smiled at the memory of their first conversation and how he followed scanty clues to find her again. He'd arrived unannounced, sending her in a thrilling panic as she attempted to make herself look presentable for him. The feeling, based on nervous excitement and romance, never really left her whenever they met.

A distant engine's rumble marred the birdsong, a quiet reminder that life went on elsewhere even if you couldn't witness it for yourself. She wondered what the driver was doing. Was it a tractor turning hay? A lorry delivering coal? Or a family out for a Sunday drive on this fine summer's day?

The noise grew louder and more distinct, reminding her of Joe's motorcycle. This one sounded newer than the one he'd used, bought at an overinflated price with his excellent army wage. Heapojunk; although it never failed to get them where they wanted to go.

The noise grew too loud to ignore any longer and she turned to see who was coming down their lane. She briefly wondered if Billy had bought a motorcycle, until she remembered he was still away on his much-anticipated honeymoon.

She recognised Joe as he came to a halt and flicked the stand down with that all too familiar way of his. For a moment she forgot to breathe, unsure if he'd stepped out of her imagination to play a joke on her. He climbed off the motorcycle and walked towards her as if it was something he did every day. He was wearing casual trousers, a plain T-shirt and a short jacket. She realised this was the first time she'd seen him like this. She gasped in a shaky breath.

'Hi.' He smiled at her as he frowned into the sun, withdrawing something from his pocket. 'I'm looking for the lady who wrote me this letter?' He lifted the battered envelope, torn at one end and now bearing the postmark stamp of its journey across the sea. She recognised it instantly.

Anne found her voice. 'Are you returning it?'

'Hell no,' he said, returning it to his pocket. 'This one's a keeper. A man doesn't get a woman's written apology too many times in his life.' He stopped to look at her and his smile faded. 'Sorry to hear about your mother. I know she didn't like me, but I could still tell that she was a good woman and I know, from experience, how painful it is to lose your mother.'

'She didn't not like you, Joe. She was just scared.'

'And she had every right to be. She didn't know me or my family …' He winced. 'And if she did … an alcoholic suicidal brother who took part in a lynching and a cold and racist father—'

'Don't talk yourself down, Joe. You are not like them. I've learnt that some men make better fathers than others.'

Joe considered her words for a moment before deciding to change the subject. 'How's Billy? Has his catching improved?'

'He's caught himself a wife.'

Joe laughed. 'Billy? Old enough to be married? That does make me feel old!'

Anne smiled. It was good to hear Joe's laughter again. 'He's on his honeymoon now. They've gone to Bournemouth.' Anne could tell the town meant nothing to Joe. On his last visit to England there were no road signs and they went where they were told. If they didn't get sent there, it didn't exist in their world. They had an invasion to train for.

'How is your stepfather?'

'Well. He's glad Mother didn't suffer too long. Knowing that helps him … or at least that's what he tells me.'

'And what about you? You didn't say much … other than you weren't married.'

'I'm a senior secretary to a firm of solicitors.'

'Sounds good.'

'It's okay. Not as exciting as mending spitfires with your friends. That felt more satisfying … helping the war effort and showing we could do the same jobs as men. It felt good.' Joe's brown eyes studied her silently. Anne felt a rush of heat rising to her cheeks. 'When did you arrive?'

He blinked at her question and searched his memory for the answer. 'Eh … a couple of days ago. Bought myself a bike and decided to take my time travelling through England to Cornwall. Kind of missed the scenery first time round.'

'Did you like what you saw?'

A slight curve appeared on his lips. 'Yeah,' he replied softly. 'Still do.'

His words, intimately spoken, turned the conversation around to the subject they had both been avoiding, but would inevitably come. Her heart felt too vulnerable to cope with the rising beat it was thumping out. She breathed in deeply to calm herself down.

'I tried writing a reply. Must have tried a hundred times.' He lifted his chin. 'Thought maybe it was best to just come over and talk to you instead.'

'That sounds ominous,' Anne joked. 'America to England is a long journey for just a conversation.'

'I've travelled this far before … and some conversations are best done face to face.'

They looked at each other as Anne noted the changes and found comfort in the things that had not. She was under no illusion that he was not doing the same.

Anne touched her hair self-consciously. 'I hope you're not too disappointed. Ten years can distinguish a man, but a woman finds it harder to wear.'

Joe laughed. 'Are you suggesting I look distinguished? I've not been called that before. And for your information, I don't agree that women can't wear the years well.'

'American women seem glamorous … at least the film stars are.'

'I mean from where I'm standing, you look just fine to me.'

'I do?' He was being polite, she told herself, but it was still nice to hear.

Joe nodded, seriously. 'More than fine.' He glanced at the estuary, inhaled deeply then looked at her again. 'I still have your photograph somewhere.'

'You do?'

'Yeah. Did you keep the cigarette packet?'

Yes, wrapped in tissue paper in my jewellery box.

'I think I have it somewhere.'

They quoted his written message in unison, 'We'll meet again.'

'Not very original, I'm afraid.'

'It meant the world to me,' she replied softly.

Silence fell as her words were absorbed.

He suddenly stepped towards her and opened his arms. She hadn't seen anyone do that for some time, unless they were courting or married. Friends and acquaintances didn't hug in England.

'What's a man got to do around here to get a hug from an old friend?'

She relented, quietly pleased for the casual excuse and walked into his arms. She had wondered if it would feel strange to be held by him again. To her surprise, it didn't. She rested her head against his shoulder, enjoying the warmth of his arms wrapped about her. It felt just the same, as if she'd just stepped back in time. She sighed with relief.

'I'm glad you wrote … but your letter kind of scared me,' said Joe, his quiet confession for her alone. 'I was scared to tamper with something that had been perfect.'

'I know. I felt the same too.'

They remained embraced, their comforting arms forming a space for just the two of them to speak what was in their hearts, free of judgement from those who would never really understand. It also prevented seeing the disappointment or joy in each other's eyes.

'I wanted to say the right thing. I didn't want it to be misconstrued.' His gentle voice carried all his worries within its quiet tone.

'Me too.'

'Wasn't sure if I wanted my life turned upside down.'

Anne felt her heart sink inside. She dared not look up. 'I didn't write to cause you trouble, Joe.'

'Wasn't sure what I had to offer.'

Compelled to reassure him, she pressed herself away from his chest to look at him. 'I don't need you to offer me anything.'

'I don't?'

She shook her head. 'No.'

'But what if I want to?'

Anne frowned. 'I don't understand.'

'I married—'

'Oh!'

'But I'm divorced now. No children. I'm a lawyer. In fact, I have my own firm.'

'Congratulations.'

'Thanks. It's small but doing well and the client base is taking me in a certain direction. The work means a lot to me so I can't leave America right now.'

'I don't expect you to, Joe. I didn't write to—'

'I still don't get on with my father, and my friends are a mixed bunch, but they're all really good people.'

'Why are you telling me all this?'

'Because, all in all, I have a good life now.'

'And you're not sure if you want your life turned upside down. I understand.' Anne smiled sadly as she freed herself from his arms. 'I'm glad things are going well for you and I didn't mean to upset things.'

'Well you have.'

Anne turned away, feeling foolish that she'd written at all. He reached for her arm and turned her to face him.

'You made me realise that success means nothing unless you can share it with someone you love. Sure, I have friends, but there's only one woman I have ever really loved.'

'What are you saying?' She hoped she understood, but they had miscommunicated before.

Joe framed her face with his hands. 'Do I have to spell it out for you?'

'You might have to.'

His soft lips kissed hers. 'It's been a long time and I don't want to scare you. I'm scaring myself enough as it is. I know what I want, but I want to make sure you know what you might be getting into.' His lips made a trail of kisses down her neck, as he spoke. 'I've missed this, but I don't want to rush things. Your mother was concerned about you leaving your country. I get that and want to honour her by allowing you the time to decide. Of course, that is if you *want* to have a future with me.'

Anne reached for him and kissed him in reply.

'I think we'll be fine, though,' Joe whispered, smiling into her hair. He found her lips again. Her body awoke in a familiar, reassuring way, telling her that little had changed, no matter how much she feared it might. She knew, from Joe's shuddering breath and warming skin, he was feeling the same too.

'Come back to America with me, Anne. We can take our time … get to know one another again … see if you like living in America. Once *you* are happy …'

'Once we are *both* happy.'

'We'll get married and find ourselves a home of our own together. That's if you want to.'

'I want to.' They kissed to seal the promise to live the dream that had been lurking in their hearts for the past ten dormant years. 'Will our house have a white picket fence and a porch?'

'Yes … and a swing for our children to play on.'

They were smiling now, his cheerful eyes reflecting the overwhelming joy she felt herself. Suddenly the future looked exciting and fulfilling, and it would be theirs as they had just promised to make it so.

'But we won't rush into it,' she teasingly cautioned.

He laughed. 'No, definitely no rushing into it for us.'

She grew serious. 'And do you think we'll make it, Joe?'

‘We survived the war, didn’t we? I think we have a pretty good chance.’

Anne slid her arms around his neck and looked up into his smiling brown eyes. She had missed him so much, but now he’d come for her, just like he had done in her dreams.

‘Yes,’ she whispered as she kissed his lips. ‘My love. My darling. My Cornish Yank.’

* Ends *

Author's Note

On 2 February 2004, the 29th Infantry Division of the United States of America was awarded The Honorary Freedom of the town of Falmouth.

Thank you

Dear Reader,

Thank you for choosing to read *Waiting For Our Rainbow*. I hope you enjoyed watching Joe and Anne's romance blossom during his training for the largest amphibious military assault in history.

The story was initially inspired by the childhood memories of an elderly Cornishman. He recalled African American soldiers arriving in Cornwall and throwing sweets to him as they passed by in their trucks. Their sudden appearance, kindness and generosity was indelibly imprinted on his mind for the rest of his life.

I began to research this period in Cornwall's history and learnt how young and inexperienced many of the soldiers who took part in D-Day were. What did their training entail while they were in Cornwall? What cultural differences did they face? How did they spend their time off? Many romances developed during this uncertain period, and although there were many incidences (both comical and serious) that would linger in both the American and British memories, ultimately they knew their time in Cornwall would end. This period in Cornwall's history made a perfect backdrop for a romantic fiction writer.

I hope this work of fiction, inspired by memories, newsreels, photographs and advice from historians, shows my admiration for the American soldiers and their resilient British hosts during this period. If you enjoyed this novel as much as I did when researching and writing it, I would be so grateful if you could take the time to write a review on the online retail site where you purchased it. It needn't be long, just a few words will do, so others will feel it worthy of reading too.

Love

Victoria

About the Author

Victoria Cornwall grew up on a dairy farm in Cornwall. She can trace her Cornish roots as far back as the 18th century and it is this background and heritage which is the inspiration for her Cornish based novels.

Victoria is married and has two grown up children. She likes to read and write historical fiction with a strong background story, but at its heart is the unmistakable emotion, even pain, of loving someone.

Following a fulfilling twenty-five year career as a nurse, a change in profession finally allowed her the time to write. She is a member of the Romantic Novelists' Association.

For more information on Victoria visit:

Twitter: www.twitter.com/VickieCornwall
Facebook: www.facebook.com/victoria.cornwall.75
Website: www.victoriacornwall.com

More Choc Lit
from
Victoria Cornwall

The Thief's Daughter

Hide from the thief-taker, for if he finds you, he will take you away …

Eighteenth-century Cornwall is crippled by debt and poverty, while the gibbet casts a shadow of fear over the land. Yet, when night falls, free traders swarm onto the beaches and smuggling prospers.

Terrified by a thief-taker's warning as a child, Jenna has resolved to be good. When her brother, Silas, asks for her help to pay his creditors, Jenna feels unable to refuse and finds herself entering the dangerous world of the smuggling trade.

Jack Penhale hunts down the smuggling gangs in revenge for his father's death. Drawn to Jenna at a hiring fayre, they discover their lives are entangled. But as Jenna struggles to decide where her allegiances lie, the worlds of justice and crime collide, leading to danger and heartache for all concerned …

Visit: www.choc-lit.com for more details.

The Captain's Daughter

Sometimes you need to discover your own strength in order to survive ...

After a family tragedy, Janey Carhart was forced from her comfortable life as a captain's daughter into domestic service. Determined to make something of herself, Janey eventually finds work as a lady's maid at the imposing Bosvenna Manor on the edge of Bodmin Moor, but is soon caught between the two worlds of upstairs and downstairs, and accepted by neither, as she cares for her mistress.

Desperately lonely, Janey catches the attention of two men – James Brockenshaw and Daniel Kellow. James is heir to the Bosvenna estate, a man whose eloquent letters to his mother warm Janey's heart. Daniel Kellow is a neighbouring farmer with a dark past and a brooding nature, yet with a magnetism that disturbs Janey. Two men. Who should she choose? Or will fate decide.

Visit: www.choc-lit.com for more details.

The Daughter of River Valley

Can you trust a man with no name?

Cornwall, 1861

Beth Jago appears to have the idyllic life, she has a trade to earn a living and a cottage of her own in Cornwall's beautiful River Valley. Yet appearances can be deceptive …

Beth has a secret. Since inheriting her isolated cottage she's been receiving threats, so when she finds a man in her home she acts on her instincts. One frying pan to the head and she has robbed the handsome stranger of his memory and almost killed him.

Fearful he may die, she reluctantly nurses the intruder back to health. Yet can she trust the man with no name who has entered her life, or is he as dangerous as his nightmares suggest? As they learn to trust one another, the outside threats worsen. Are they linked to the man with no past? Or is the real danger still outside waiting … and watching them both?

Visit: www.choc-lit.com for more details.

A Daughter's Christmas Wish

A Cornish Christmas wish sent across the ocean ...

Christmas, Cornwall 1919

A promise to a fellow soldier leads Nicholas to Cornwall for Christmas, and to the teashop managed by Rose; the youngest daughter of a family whose festive spirit has been blighted by their wartime experiences. But as Nicholas strives to give Rose the best Christmas she could wish for, he begins to question whether his efforts are to honour his friend, or whether there is another reason ...

Visit: www.choc-lit.com for more details.

Daughter of the House

The daughter of the house is often overlooked ...
Evelyn Pendragon is spirited but lonely, and largely ignored by her parents whose attentions are taken up with her brother, Nicholas: the expected heir to the family's Cornish estate and the one who will carry on the Pendragon name.

Stifled by her aristocratic existence, Evelyn finds companionship in an unlikely place when she befriends Drake Vennor, an apprentice gardener on the estate.

But When Evelyn's life is thrown into turmoil by a tragedy, she realises just how much she has come to rely on Drake. Will family expectations and the burden of the Pendragon name mean she must turn her back on him when she needs him the most?

Visit: www.choc-lit.com for more details.

Daniel's Daughter

Sometimes the truth is not easy to say and even harder to hear …

Cornwall, 1895

Grace Kellow is a young woman with a strong sense of who she is and where she comes from. As the daughter of a well-respected Cornish dairy owner Daniel Kellow, her existence in the village of Trehale is comfortable and peaceful.

But then handsome Talek Danning comes striding over Hel Tor, and soon after his arrival Grace is hit with a revelation that leaves her questioning her identity and her place in the Trehale community. In her hour of need, Talek and his sister Amelia offer Grace sanctuary – but wherever Grace runs, her secret will follow …

Visit: www.choc-lit.com for more details.

Introducing Choc Lit

We are a British independent publisher creating a delicious selection of fiction.
Where heroes are like chocolate – irresistible!
Quality stories with a romance at the heart.

See our selection here:
www.choc-lit.com

We would love to hear how you enjoyed *Waiting for Our Rainbow.* Please leave a review where you purchased this novel or **visit www.choc-lit.com** and give your feedback.

Choc Lit novels are selected by genuine readers like yourself. We only publish stories our Tasting Panel want to see in print. Our reviews and awards speak for themselves.

Could you be a Star Selector and join our Choc Lit Tasting Panel?
Would you like to play a role in choosing which novels we decide to publish? Do you enjoy reading women's fiction? Then you could be perfect for our Tasting Panel.
Visit *www.choc-lit.com/join-the-choc-lit-tasting-panel* for more details...

Keep in touch:
Sign up for our newsletter for all the latest news and offers: www.spread.choc-lit.com.

Follow us on:
Twitter: @ChocLituk
Facebook: @Choc Lit
Instagram: @ChocLitUK

Printed in Great Britain
by Amazon

46208349R00133

untr[illegible]

mary frances

published by penteract press, 2021
penteractpress.com
penteractpress@gmail.com
twitter.com/penteractpress

cover image by mary frances

designed by anthony etherin

typeset in minion

second edition
(first paperback edition)

isbn 978-1-913421-12-0

untravelling

departure

early light daybreak of emptiness a constant low hum
compasses spinning fast a geometry of dreams slowly solidifying
vast directionless unfamiliar as a moon the imperative now is movement
anything is possible nothing is clear there are many miles to go and no map to follow

morning star storm clouds one of these things may be good augury
the idea of a journey already fading something more like a test perhaps a task
the air has the feel and smell of dawn a distant shiver of lost magic
we are on unknown land anything is something to aim for we sharpen our eyes

air cools rapidly becoming granular between mountain and cloud a confusion
unstable ground crumbles under our climbing on boundaries of fray and unravel
possibilities appear then disappear cast adrift and floating out of reach
we move cautiously through unguessable weather and other kinds of unsettledness

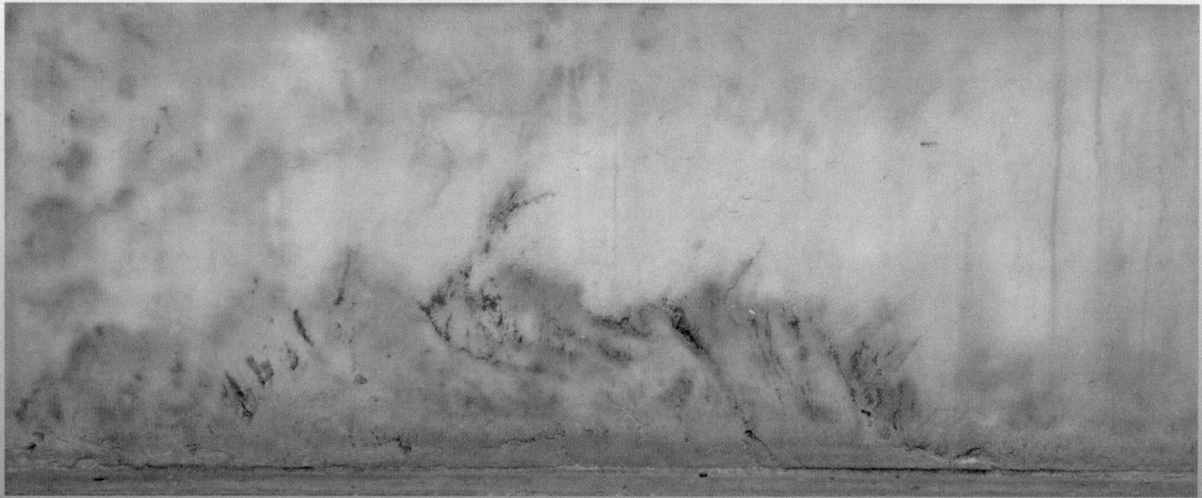

slow descent into fog low cloud turmoil the ambiguity of smoke and mirrors
anxious uneasy the instability of perception and the contamination of dreams
nothing here seems real just barely there and yet we are here we are here
at the same time perhaps barely here and possibly transparent

sudden swift wind of fallen branches breathing cinder dust and char
this is flatter land flattened land where many souls have gone missing
broken headstones under a gallows-tree slow scattered ashes of lost futures
the wind here has a texture and a voice and a harsh scent of waste and sadness

luminous skies submerge emerge in the disruption and whirl of things
white smoke caught in the crush and flow of wave to particle to wave
of end to beginning to end makeshift patterns hang in the air too long then not at all
far below us silent footsteps the memory of a cello faint eruptions and the falling ash

closer to the river the wreckage of a too-late harvest under weighted clouds
a place of myths and gods in ancient light the atmosphere here is gravity and rain
this may be how wars look before we have understood what is happening
this may be magnetism or alchemy and whatever this is it is not weather

caught in the aftermath of something we do not recognise everything stands still
a lesson in patience searching for footholds in dark recesses of water not water
calmer breathing eyes clearing at the edge of quiet this is an oasis of a kind
the land closed into a folded map leaving us to question the meaning of a tree

waiting now for a sign we catch the tang of ice-cold sea but the air is dry as bone
sensing the nearness of other lives how time passes slowly on a vacant set
they say the gravel train stopped here once hovering a while soundless before moving on
we scratch messages in pale sand with found sticks we listen to the sound of nothing

a sense of hardly moving of dry drowning and the disorientation of rise and fall
the landscape in flux liquifying as we weave across softened ground
as if lightning is melting the sky we walk through the flicker of ruined film
caught in a slow dissolve the fade to grey no credits left to roll

clearing to unclearness overshadowings contesting the return of light
hushed sounds of mourning a place of pilgrimage of wreckage of relics
tiredness overcomes us as a charm as if all lostness might be cured by sleep
patchy rainfall the reappearance of colour somewhere at the clay edge of green

the ghost lands

traces of the city we left fading now in drained colour and the dimming of things
calm shelter and balm of the incoming tide approaching moving our way
that might be an evening star or a satellite this might be an escape route
there are many ways to be lost and always some pull to turn around to turn back

bewildered nightmares hold the drop and contagion of burnt-out nights in the mountains
our eyes roll back from scabs of fire-damaged darkness blistered clouds hanging in singed air
the world of ceremony and dream-shift turned now to something more troubled
something we forgot to see when it was safer something we forgot to bring as a gift to our gods

maybe no-one saw the change coming maybe everyone did
caught in the wolf eye looking hopelessly for ways to make amends to appease
we would not choose to stay but already it has become impossible to leave
strangers to ourselves now on a road to nowhere darkness returns

mirror

puzzled now without a viable language turning our eyes from a raining sun
a weather-light that does not belong to any season we have known or any story
pulled by a misremembered past and the strangeness of things moving backwards in time
we take our bearings and lose them if you asked us now we would not even know our names

quiet scuffles of small-toothed creatures a bell ringing somewhere far below
this is the hiding place of past sorrows ghost-sounds in the first light
we walk on the deep underground imagining signs in the mud signals in the fall of branches
we tread with caution measuring the blue in the grey

time fades to a foxed mirror we dream of passing through soft as moths
in our pocket a rough-edged stone to keep as talisman or some kind of proof
a sudden restlessness is this the place we were seeking without knowing
we hover out of focus adrift in a floating world

apparition over the water some forgotten history the scent of blossom and wine
things now lost forever sharp breath of herbs on a river breeze soft music in warm air
we stand still curious cautious of the allure of forsaken places and the rising death-shadow
inhaling a long ago and a somewhere else and a never known and a dream of

everything we see now is further away everything we approach is already behind us
we recognise these outlines but not their meaning more than the day is dying here
and we no longer understand what is meant by direction what is meant by distance
what is meant by purpose what is meant by destination what is meant by speed

passing settlements abandoned to ruin ripped flags torn books split timbers
wild dogs running through rubble swift visions faint voices the thread of an argument
all written and unwritten laws buried with the long-lost chronicles
each breath and each footstep echoing for miles untranslatable

the path clearing only to a river stench of rot and wreckage under a twisted moon
slippery unstable underfoot we trespass and unguarded we leave traces
our bootprints in mud-tide our smell and sweat and night-fears hanging in heavy air
the intermittent flicker of spirit wraith and spectre the darkness here is audible

night wanderers in spectral space caught in the hiss and rush of rising foam
condensation evaporation delirium drowned-out voices submerged limbs
harsh and urgent whispering a daze of white river drizzle tumbling to the forest edge
left desperately counting how many things must have ended here in these wild shadows

land returning from a night at sea the melancholy of a window vigil the watch and the wait of it
drawn by birdcall in wild spray what is left of our sight reduced now to blur and shimmer
bitter water churning somewhere between threat and calm like the dregs of a life story
caught in a confusion of random dreams the captain's wife and the curve of a fish

later in grey silence cloud and wave rewinding in streams and spools
day to night to day a drowned bell tolling the hours time passing time reversing
a rolling back and a rolling away and a quiet softly broken by low songs
something like madrigal something like counterpoint something like lament

nightfall lights stream past us windward away from the realm of the fisher king
beyond watery moon-grief storm and prophecy an anthem or a curse
darklight over land and loch the capacity to redeem everything in a sudden shower of silver
sometimes in light like this we can feel the earth turn on its axis

the fading

awakening under the dark cliff at the dirt edge of the sea
the shift and restlessness of fallen stars falling stones this is the endland
the magnification of all our mistakes looks back at us here in this abject emptiness
still we are unfrozen unbitten unfollowed or so it seems

the stone is abrasive like sandpaper to the touch or cold electricity
traces of remembrance and forgiveness perhaps less an arrival and more a return
how untravelling takes us away to arrive back with our voices changed
when the ice thaws at last there will be nothing here and no-one will believe us

all midnight crossings are met by the happening of drowned ghosts
the many the old the unseen twisting in the rise and pull and drag
loss and forfeit apparition and return endless repetition of the improbable dance
at the rim of the sea in foam-mist and salt-spray theatre of unwritten memory

for years we heard tales of high windows though there had never been a crossing
a library a prison a monastery a glass palace lost bombed deserted destroyed by fire
appearing in dim light for brief moments the sounds of blue songbirds and winter voices
an illusion ruined by vandals claimed by lightning soon even the stories will disappear

past the storm fields everything changes the shortest way is through flood plains
we trudge over sodden bogland here where the old woman prayed and the holly tree died
small things bite and flicker and trip us the rustle of insects a ripple of cloud
our breath shallow our steps cautious approaching something like an ending

dynamic forces shifting contraction compaction expulsion grinding tectonic plates
shattering the lost balance of inverted luna inexplicable as an underground sky
cloud moon mountain moon white moon nickel moon milk moon unmoon
moon of beneath moon of mixed fortune moon of fragile harmony

a sheen of cool calm or some mirage or trickery a certain illusion dishonesty of depth
planetary regressions redrawn in the skies we step out between searchlight and splinter
our steps sharp and hollow our eyes level steady we walk we just walk straight ahead
every portent every omen shattering at last and all of them behind us now

we see it then in the wake of the last swift shadow a breath of light and a portal
through cloud and stone and monster and memory change comes to us as a nightgift
in moments like this lies a kind of hope perhaps a break in the timeline
the sequence reversing in the sound of held breath time itself weaves a circle

on the other side of somewhere else a quietness simplicity
something unwilled and obvious and as ordinary as an angel or an egg
the riverbed not quite dry the air just cool enough the singing imaginary
through neutral space a long drift of forgottenness tracing its silent path

silvered brightness tests our eyes erasing shapes as if there were nothing left to find
horizons become indefinite vague and meaning little to us now
the earth holds us in silence in stunned and sudden silence
fading light running water stillness pale stars

the shock of change comes out of nowhere and in the end it carries no message
this is another nowhere but we wait here quietly for the next thing to happen
not a plan not an intention but we are awake and we are listening
somewhere perhaps inside ourselves the faint sounds of promises being made

finis

found images by mary frances

text cut-up and rearranged by mary frances
from collected responses to the images

with warm thanks to all the friends and strangers
who have looked at my work with so much curiosity and imagination